RELATIVE DANGER

CHARLOTTE DOUGLAS

**ZEBRA BOOKS
KENSINGTON PUBLISHING CORP.**

ZEBRA BOOKS are published by

Kensington Publishing Corp.
850 Third Avenue
New York, NY 10022

Copyright © 1995 by Charlotte H. Douglas

All rights reserved. No part of this book may be reproduced in any form or by any means without the prior written consent of the Publisher, excepting brief quotes used in reviews.

If you purchased this book without a cover, you should be aware that this book is stolen property. It was reported as "unsold and destroyed" to the Publisher and neither the Author nor the Publisher has received any payment for this "stripped book."

Zebra and the Z logo Reg. U.S. Pat. & TM Off.

First Printing: December, 1995

Printed in the United States of America

For Christopher Wilson

One

The blast shook the building at 2:47 P.M.

It rocked the walls of the teaching auditorium and rattled maps in their brackets above the chalkboards. Class was almost over, and the explosion, louder than the sonic booms of fighter planes passing overhead from McDill in Tampa, diverted everyone's attention from my lecture on Civil War Reconstruction.

In the front row Gina Ortega squirmed, her dark eyes wide with fright. "It sounded like a bomb."

"Yeah," Clyde Staley joked with a nervous laugh, "unless a train hit the building."

"Maybe lightning struck close by," I said, but the sharp, concussive noise, louder than Florida thunder, had sounded like a bomb.

The windowless classroom, deep inside the Arts and Letters Building, buzzed with anxious questions. Students fidgeted, some openly curious, others nervous and afraid, as they discussed the possible source of the blast.

"Class dismissed." I shouted to be heard above the clamor of voices.

While students surged out the doorways, impatient to discover the blast's source, I gathered my lecture notes. Above the shouts and chatter, the wail of sirens and the alternating pitches of ambulance horns approached. Squeezing through the throngs in the hallway, I fought my way upstairs against a tide of curious students, rushing toward the explosion's point of origin.

When I reached the second floor hall where my office was

located, the sight before me banished any thoughts of returning to work. The force of the blast had cracked the hallway's glass outer wall from top to bottom, fracturing my view of the roaring blaze in the parking lot beyond the building.

Huge clouds of black smoke billowed skyward in thick, choking plumes from a mass of twisted metal that had once been a vehicle. Bodies lay among the wreckage, some writhing in pain, others ominously still. Flames engulfed several other cars. Firefighters had arrived to battle the blaze, and the first wave of paramedics attended the wounded and shuttled sheeted forms away on stretchers.

From the strangely quiet and deserted hallway, I watched police erect a barricade around the parking lot and campus security officers hold back crowds of gaping onlookers. Directly below on a grassy quadrangle between the building where I stood and the parking lot, another group of officers secured an open area.

The thwacking beat of helicopter rotors sounded overhead, and a med-evac chopper landed on the wind-flattened grass. Rescuers rushed two sheeted stretchers, bristling with tubes and wires, into the helicopter, which took off again almost as quickly as it had landed.

Hypnotized by the horror, I attempted to turn away, but the disaster riveted me in gruesome fascination. Although no other sounds but the noises of rescue vehicles penetrated the fissured glass, I recognized too clearly the agony on the faces of students behind the police cordon. Some clung to one another and sobbed. Firefighters, their faces sooty and grim, worked to extinguish the blazing cars before the gas tanks of others ignited.

The med-evac chopper had disappeared when another helicopter, carrying a local news crew, soared through the columns of smoke and hovered like a blue and white vulture over the scene. Patrol cars with flashing lights ringed the area, and uniformed officers struggled to direct the evacuation of vehicles away from the perimeter of the lot, whose core still blazed like an inferno.

I turned at the clattering of high-heeled shoes on the hallway's tiled floor. Carol Donahue, breathless from exertion, hurried toward me.

Her plump face glowed pink with alarm. "Alexandra! Thank God, you're okay."

Carol, professor of English and my best friend since childhood, hugged me as if she hadn't seen me in a year, rather than an hour before.

"I was at the Administration Building when I heard the blast, and I ran all the way back." Her words came in short puffs as she gasped for air.

She linked her arm with mine, and we watched silently until the blaze had been extinguished and only smoking heaps of rubble remained where cars had once been.

"Come." She tugged at my arm. "Maybe there's news in the faculty lounge."

I tore my attention from the war zone in the parking lot and followed Carol to the lounge, where other faculty members had assembled. All wore expressions of shock and disbelief as they gathered around the worktable and drank coffee in eerie quiet.

Gilbert Trenwith announced that Matthew Koenig, dean of the arts and letters college, had promised to bring news as soon as he could, so for now we simply waited. Gilbert, classics professor, sat with Reginald Hartwick, who taught art history, and Emmett Nyagwa, head of African-American studies. The three faced Carol and me across the wide oak table, but no one spoke.

I searched for Moira Rafferty, but the sultry professor of British history had made herself scarce since her dramatic scene at Saturday night's faculty party. I shuddered at the memory of that social disaster, which seemed insignificant compared to what had happened in the parking lot.

Everything about the morning seemed unreal. Had it been only two weeks since I had sat at a meeting in this same room, unaware that my brother Nick was dead?

I rose and poured myself another cup of coffee I didn't want, driven by the need to do something. I stood at the window that overlooked the bay, trying not to think of the chaos on the opposite side of the building.

The tension in the silent room grew unbearable as we waited for an explanation of the morning's disaster and identification of the casualties.

Behind me, Reginald pushed away from the table and paced in the narrow confines of the room, clutching his long arms across his chest, while one scraggly eyebrow twitched. He stopped and tugged at his nervous brow. "Doesn't anyone know who was injured?"

No one answered. Whoever had been hurt would be known to all of us. The students who used that parking lot attended classes in the Arts and Letters Building.

"God knows," Reginald's voice rose with a pitch of hysteria, "anyone of us could have been right there when it happened, whatever it was."

"Maybe a car fire got out of control," I suggested.

"A car bomb, more likely, from the sound of it." Gilbert Trenwith laced his long fingers together and pushed outward, cracking his knuckles.

Carol winced, but whether at the crackling or his suggestion I couldn't tell.

"Not a car bomb," she said. "That's not rational."

Gilbert cracked his knuckles again. "Nothing rational about terrorism. Remember Oklahoma City?"

"But why set off a bomb here?" Carol asked.

Again, no one answered. I couldn't stand the quiet and wanted to scream to break its lock on the room. First Nick and now this. My superstitious mother had always insisted that events occurred in threes. Dear God, I begged, no more, please no more.

Gilbert finally broke the silence. "If it was terrorism, the terrorists will let us know exactly why they've done this. Media attention for their latest cause most likely."

Emmett Nyagwa was the only one who hadn't spoken. He

hunched unmoving at the table, his dark eyes glowing like fire, his grim face set, emotionless.

Shirley Clarke, Dean Koenig's secretary, hurried in, carrying a slip of paper. She held up her hands as everyone turned to her. "Don't ask. I haven't heard anything except that classes are canceled for the rest of the day."

Her usually cheerful face was ashen and somber, and her hands trembled as she tacked the cancellation notice to the corkboard. She rushed from the room without a backward glance.

The door closed behind her, then opened again abruptly as Moira Rafferty shuffled in.

"God, I need a drink," she muttered and slumped against the wall just inside the door. "According to the radio in my office, one student is dead, two others critically burned, another six injured. What the hell happened out there, a war?"

Carol placed an arm around Moira's shoulders and led her to the sofa beneath the windows. She sat beside her, holding Moira's elegantly manicured hands in her own tiny, plump ones.

"Did the radio say what caused it?" Gilbert asked.

Moira shook her head, and her thick red hair spilled across her face like blood. The image chilled me.

"No more than we already know," Moira said. "Just that a car exploded and several others nearby . . ."

She fell silent as Dean Koenig entered the room. His gray hair, always neatly trimmed and combed, was matted to his forehead, and streaks of soot smeared the square contours of his face. His white dress shirt, soaked from the spray of the fire hoses, clung to his body, and blood stained one rolled cuff. He sank onto a chair at the table, his head sagging on his chest and his arms hanging limply at his sides.

When he looked up, fatigue glazed his eyes. "I have to get over to the hospital to identify some of the casualties, but I wanted to fill you in before I go."

His voice was hoarse from smoke. I thrust a cup of coffee into his hands, and he smiled his gratitude. Then his face crumpled, and tears streaked the grime on his cheeks as he spoke.

"Kristin Montgomery is dead—they think. It was her car that exploded," he drew a ragged breath, "but they can't find enough of her to identify yet."

"God in heaven!" Carol jammed a fist against trembling lips.

The dean continued the gruesome account. "Chad Devereux, her boyfriend, walked her to her car after class and had headed back toward his dorm. He turned around to wave, and that's when the car blew."

"Was he hurt?" Emmett asked. "He's one of my best students."

Koenig nodded. "Poor kid tried to get her out. He's been airlifted to the burn unit in Tampa. They don't know if he's going to make it."

He sat for a moment as if in a stupor, then gulped down his coffee and struggled to regain his composure.

Tears streamed down Carol's cheeks.

"One student in the car next to Kristin's was also taken to Tampa," he said. "Six others, less seriously injured, were taken to the hospital here. I need to get over there now to make certain of their names before contacting any parents."

"What caused the car to explode?" Reginald asked the question we all wanted to ask.

Dean Koenig shrugged. "The medical examiner and a forensics team are going over the scene now. We know Kristin was a smoker. If there were gas fumes in the car and she lit a cigarette, that might have caused it. Right now, they just don't know."

He stood and glanced around. "I'll let you know more as soon as I know." He started toward the door, then turned back. "If there's any good in all this, it's that Kristin's class was dismissed five minutes early. If she had left class at the regular time, there would have been hundreds in that lot when her car went up, instead of those unfortunate few."

"I have to get back to work," I said as soon as Dean Koenig left, unable to stand the strained atmosphere any longer. "I'll be in my office if anybody needs me."

I fled the lounge and hurried along the corridor, averting my eyes from the cracked window across the hall as I entered my office door. I locked it behind me with shaking hands and leaned my head against its cool, smooth surface.

Kristin Montgomery. Chad Devereux.

I jerked open the top drawer of my desk and reached into its depths. My hand closed on thick sheets of folded notebook paper, clipped together, and I withdrew them, removed the paper clip, and spread them on my desk. In the weeks before Nick died, I had collected the notes from beneath the windshield wiper of my car in the campus parking lot.

Smoothing the top note open, I read the message written on lined notebook paper in a large, looping scrawl:

Kristin, babe—
    I have to go into town after my next class. Wait for me and give me a lift, okay, doll?

                                  Love ya! Chad

The other notes were variations on the same theme. Kristin, a day student who lived in town, drove her chocolate-colored Toyota Camry, just like mine, to her classes at the university. When she had started dating Chad, his notes began to appear on my windshield by mistake. I had meant to return them with the admonition to check the license plate before leaving any more messages, but Nick's death had driven the notes from my mind—until Dean Koenig had announced the names of Kristin and Chad as casualties.

I leaned back in my chair, massaging my aching temples in a futile effort to relax and think calmly. Was the explosion the result of a senseless accident, a combination of a cigarette lighter and errant gas fumes? Or had someone intentionally blown up Kristin's car?

And if it had been intentional, had it been a mistake, a mistake that killed Kristin Montgomery instead of me?

With shaking fingers, I punched a number into my desk

phone and waited for Mitch Lawton to answer. Two weeks ago Mitch had been only a handsome stranger. Now I trusted him with my life.

"Alex, I heard on the radio. Are you all right?"

The calm tones of his deep voice soothed my frazzled nerves. "Yes. No!"

My words spilled out in a torrent as I described what had happened, ending with the story of the misplaced notes on Kristin's car, the car like mine.

"Whoa, hold on a minute," Mitch said. "You're jumping to some pretty wild conclusions."

My temper flared at his response. "Some pretty wild things have happened to me the past two weeks."

"That's true," his voice retained its composure, "but you can't let them distort your judgment."

"I haven't lost my good judgment. I'm just trying to make sense of things." My jaw tightened as I spoke through clenched teeth and became more defensive. I'd called for help, not a lecture.

"Some things in life never make sense," he said with irritating calm. "Why don't you have dinner with me tonight, and we'll talk about it then."

For a moment, I yielded, longing for the comfort of his company. But I didn't want to spend an evening hearing more about my lack of good judgment. I needed someone who took me seriously, who didn't think of me as an advanced case of paranoia.

"I wouldn't be very good company tonight."

"But, Alex—"

"I'm sorry I bothered you." I hung up.

I felt guilty as soon as I broke the connection. Mitch had been trying to be helpful, and my fears had probably sounded irrational. But the feeling deep in the pit of my stomach that I'd had ever since Nick died screamed at me that something was drastically wrong. I just couldn't seem to figure out what that something was.

I folded my arms on my desk and lay my head on them, closed my eyes, and began practicing the relaxation techniques I had learned for easing the migraine headaches that had plagued me since early adolescence.

As my breathing slowed and tension drained from my muscles, I was able to think more clearly. Maybe the feeling I associated with danger was simply a part of my grief. Maybe Mitch had been right. Maybe—

The buzz of the telephone jolted me from my thoughts.

"American Studies. Dr. Garrison speaking."

A silence resonated at the other end of the open line.

"Hello?" I was ready to hang up when the caller spoke my name.

"You're the only one who can stop this," the distorted voice whispered. "I've been very patient, but if you continue to refuse to cooperate, someone else is going to get hurt."

Images of the burning parking lot flooded my mind. "It *was* you—"

"Bring it tonight," the voice snarled. "Same time, same place as I told you before."

"Bring what? How can I bring it if I don't know what you want?"

I waited for an answer, but my caller was no longer on the line.

I felt panic rise within me, and I struggled against it. Hysterics would get me nowhere. I had to think. I closed my eyes and leaned back in my chair, willing myself to relax once more.

Somewhere in the events of the last two weeks was the key to the identity of my threatening caller and what he wanted from me. I ransacked my memory for a hint or a clue, anything to dissipate the waking nightmare that surrounded me.

Two

It had all started two weeks ago.

That morning, I left the faculty meeting, glad to escape the bickering and backbiting of the curriculum debate. All I wanted was to take medication to alleviate my blinding headache, brought on by the tense discussion, and rest for an hour before my next class.

The glass that formed the outer wall of the Arts and Letters Building reflected my passage down the hallway, and I viewed my mirrored image objectively: a slender woman in her mid-thirties, dressed in a well-cut suit with a silk blouse. Dark hair and eyes. The image projected the competence and assurance expected of Alexandra Garrison, head of the American Studies Department.

Self-assured? I smiled at the deception.

Beyond my reflection, the palm-lined campus of Suncoast University stretched to the bay, and across its sparkling waters the skyline of hotels on the beach rose against the vast backdrop of the Gulf of Mexico. Each glass-sheathed building of the university reflected the vivid blue of the cloudless Florida sky. Tranquility covered the campus, giving no indication of the chaos to come.

I slipped inside my office, closed the door and mini-blinds, and sank gratefully into an overstuffed chair usually occupied by one of my students. Shrugging out of my jacket, I kicked off my bone-colored pumps and wiggled my stockinged toes.

With an hour before my next class, I had time for a short nap, which I hoped would knock out my headache.

The throbbing in my left temple persisted, so I took a pill from the bottle I carried in my jacket pocket, swallowed it, and lay back in the chair's cushioned embrace. Closing my eyes, I propped my feet on the lower shelf of my bookcase and hoped the medicine would work quickly.

I had just fallen asleep when two light raps on my door awakened me. Before I could struggle from the depths of my comfortable chair, the door opened and Carol Donahue stepped inside.

"Don't get up, Alex."

She opened the mini-blinds slightly, allowing light to filter into the room, then eased her plump frame onto my desk chair. She studied me, her hazel eyes bright beneath her wispy bangs of reddish-blonde hair. "Another migraine?"

"How'd you know?" I growled, wanting to be alone.

"Closed blinds, shoes off, deep vertical line between your eyes. Doesn't take a rocket scientist to spot the evidence."

"I didn't know I was so transparent." I abandoned my nap reluctantly. "What's up?"

Carol sighed dramatically. "I had to get away from the freshman essays I was grading before I lost my sanity altogether."

Her facial expression was deadly serious. I knew that meant mischief.

She continued, straight-faced. "The ability to use language may be what separates humans from animals, but what separates this group from the lower vertebrates is that they're not afraid of vacuum cleaners."

I laughed at her analogy.

"Why do I put myself through this torture?" she asked.

"Because there's nothing else you'd rather do, that's why."

Her eyes sparkled. "I can think of one thing I'd like better. Making mad, passionate love to your gorgeous twin brother."

Carol, the epitome of propriety, loved to pretend she was a wild woman.

"Don't you ever think of anything but sex?" I asked.

"I don't know," she said. "Do you think I should be more like St. Benedict and throw myself into thorn bushes to drive away impure thoughts? But then I'd spend the rest of my life covered with fresh lacerations."

"You're utterly hopeless."

She grinned wickedly at me. "Speaking of impure thoughts, when is Nick coming home?"

I pulled myself upright and began searching for my shoes. "He's due back tonight. Why don't you and Sam have dinner with Nick and me tomorrow?"

"Only if you promise to make your special manicotti, removing all the calories, of course. And if I can get Sam away from his tax deadlines."

"Tax deadlines? Carol, this is October, not April."

"That makes it deadline time for all those on their second extensions." She headed toward the door. "You know how much those headaches do you in. Go home and get some rest."

"Right after my next class."

"I'll call you tonight after I check with Sam." With a waggle of her plump fingers, Carol was gone.

I experienced no sense of foreboding. I was unaware that when I saw her again, my nightmare would be only beginning.

I pulled into the driveway and sat for a moment, studying with appreciation the house I'd lived in all my life. I'd considered moving five years ago when my mother died but liked the location on the bluff above the bay just a few miles from the university. I did major renovating instead.

The once nondescript Cape Cod cottage now had tiered decks, bricked walkways, and patios that blended with the tropical landscaping in a grove of ancient oaks.

I had redecorated the inside, too, stripped away fusty carpets and draperies, disposed of the heavy, overstuffed furniture, and added windows that faced the water. I had bleached the hardwood floors, added minimal furnishings with spare, clean lines, and installed French doors onto the decks. The results were simple, uncluttered, the way I wished my life to be.

Inside, I shed my suit and blouse and pulled on denim shorts and a soft cotton T-shirt, then padded barefoot into the kitchen. As I poured a glass of tea, the simple kind made with teabags in the refrigerator, I absorbed the atmosphere of my home and wondered briefly if my calm came from the decor or the fact that every trace of my mother had been erased.

Out on the deck above the bay, I settled on a comfortable chaise longue to enjoy the dry and pleasant October afternoon. It was one of those rare Florida days, one of the few days in the year that didn't need air-conditioning.

As I watched a catamaran tack lazily across the channel, I thought of Nick's return. I had been more lonely than usual during his recent absence, missing our daily talks on the phone and our twice-weekly dinners together. Maybe I felt his absence more sharply because I needed his objective reporter's viewpoint on the curriculum dispute that had our usually congenial faculty at each other's throats.

I nodded off, lulled into slumber by the soft sea breeze, the hypnotic surge and retreat of waves at the foot of the bluff, and the sedative effects of my medication. I was jolted awake by knocking at the front door.

"Coming!"

I opened the door to find Carol, her eyes red-rimmed, tears streaking her plump cheeks. "He came looking for you at school."

Behind her stood a uniformed officer of the Florida Highway Patrol.

In that instant, I knew Nick was dead. Something deep inside snapped, and a great chasm opened within me, as time slowed to a crawl and stood still.

Carol reached out, enfolded me in her arms, then drew me inside to the living room. I felt like I was moving under water, pushing against an unseen weight and afraid to draw breath. She pulled me down onto the sofa.

I was only vaguely aware of Carol holding onto me tightly as the officer made his report. I tried to force myself to concentrate, but the patrolman was only noise, like a television left on in another room. All I heard was that Nick was dead, a fact my mind rejected while my heart screamed in pain at the truth.

One moment the officer was there, speaking to me in hushed, compassionate tones, the next he was gone. I hadn't seen or heard him leave. Carol dragged me to my feet and led me to my bedroom at the back of the house. Moving automatically, I removed my clothes, pulled on the nightgown she handed me, and obediently swallowed the sedative she offered.

The next morning I discovered Carol sprawled among the pillows on the living room sofa, snoring softly, tear tracks smearing the makeup on her round, pretty face.

Quietly I made coffee and went out to the deck beneath the oaks to watch the burgeoning light of the rising sun move across the bay, bathing the crests of its silver-blue ripples in shimmering pink and gold. Sunlight reflected off a sailboat at anchor off one of the spoil islands. Its bare, white masts stood stark against the colors.

Nick would never see another sunrise. I wished I could cry or scream, anything to dislodge the lump in my throat, but the hollowness deep inside held no emotions.

Carol moved about in the house behind me, and soon she joined me, sitting silently as we sipped coffee and watched the light gathering on the bay, turning the clouds on the western horizon from leaden gray to rose and lavender before bleaching them white.

"I don't remember much of what happened yesterday," I said, "except that the trooper said Nick died instantly and felt no pain."

Carol began to cry again. She went inside for a box of tissues, then returned to blow her nose and wipe her eyes.

"You were in shock, Alex. From the look of you, you may still be. Are you up to hearing what he said?"

Protected by an encompassing numbness, I nodded.

Carol took a deep breath, like a diver entering deep water. "Nick was driving west on Interstate Four outside Orlando when his car was forced off the road. The car rolled, and Nick was thrown clear—he wasn't wearing his seat belt. His neck was broken when he landed, and he died instantly."

A trio of brown pelicans skimmed low along the shoreline, and I studied them carefully, pushing the image of Nick's broken body from my mind. Something, perhaps that communal consciousness Nick and I shared as twins, insisted Nick's death was no accident.

"He always wore his seat belt," I said. "And why would anyone try to run him off the road?"

Carol shook her head. Her clothes were rumpled from her night spent on the sofa and her eyes puffy from crying. She had known Nick since we were children, had dated him in high school, and for a short time after graduation had even hoped to marry him, until she'd conceded his career as an investigative reporter and his insatiable wanderlust would never allow for a wife and family. In her own way, in spite of her long marriage to Sam, whom she adored, Carol loved Nick, too.

"Alex." Carol interrupted my reminiscences. "You have to make arrangements today. What are you going to do?"

"Do? About what?" I concentrated all my attention on a great blue heron, standing like a statue in the sand flats exposed by the receding tide at the foot of the bluff.

She knelt before me, thrust her face into mine, and, grasping me by the shoulders, shook me.

"Nick is dead, Alex. You have to decide what to do about a funeral, about his body, about notifying his friends and coworkers."

I could think of nothing to say. My mind refused to function.

"You have to deal with this!" She shook me again, trying to break through the numbness that gripped me.

Her efforts worked. The protective dike I'd built around my emotions crumbled, and wave after wave of pain poured through me, causing me to gasp for breath.

"Nick is never coming home, is he?" I began to cry in hoarse, choking sobs.

We wept in each other's arms as the morning light broke through the branches of the oak and flooded the deck, where we sat with our grief.

Later that morning, feeling strangely detached, almost disembodied, I called the funeral home and made arrangements for Nick's cremation, a request he had been adamant about when our mother had died.

The painful irony of his death pierced my numbness. He had survived wars in Panama, Kuwait, Somalia, and Bosnia and dozens of natural disasters in his reporting career, only to be thrown from a car on a highway. My uncommon brother had been lost to a common end. What good was his Pulitzer Prize now?

Carol's voice intruded on my memories. "Major Lowery from the highway patrol is here. Do you feel up to answering a few questions?"

I went into the living room to meet him, wondering if I would ever be able to look at the familiar uniform again without feeling a devastating sense of loss.

"I'm Alexandra Garrison." I'd had no experience with interviews of this type and didn't know what to say. I fell back on social graces. "Would you care for coffee, Major?"

The major's uniform and size were intimidating, but his eyes were kind as he accepted the coffee Carol brought. While I waited for him to sugar his coffee and state his business, I wondered how often his job involved the unpleasant task of dealing with relatives of those who died in accidents.

"These are just routine questions, Dr. Garrison, so don't be alarmed or attach too much significance to them."

I nodded, anxious to get on with it.

"Did your brother have any enemies, anyone who might wish to harm him?"

Despite his disclaimer, his question startled me.

"Not that I know of, but my brother was a newspaper reporter, and much of his work was syndicated. There's no way to know if something he wrote set someone off. The world is full of crazy people. Do you think someone forced Nick off the road on purpose?"

The major looked uncomfortable. "We can't be sure. Your brother's car left the road, and either those who forced him off rifled his belongings or, once he'd had his accident, someone else came along and checked to see if he had anything worth stealing."

I sat with my arms wrapped tightly around me, trying to blot out the picture of Nick's body, crumpled lifelessly alongside the road, with thieves pawing greedily through his pockets, but the image wouldn't go away. I drew a long, shuddering breath, trying not to cry.

"Was anything stolen?" I asked.

"We'll need your help in determining that. He still had his wallet, watch, and gun—"

"Gun? I didn't know he owned one."

The major looked even more uneasy than before, or perhaps what I sensed as uneasiness was merely the discomfort of his large, beefy neck in his tight uniform collar. He eased its constriction with his index finger.

"What most likely happened was someone accidentally clipped the front left fender of his car—we found the collision marks and embedded paint chips—forced him off the road, and his car flipped. Then when someone stopped to help and saw that he was . . . gone, they decided to rob him. Someone else came along then and scared them off. That's what the evidence seems to suggest."

"Of course." I didn't know how much more I could take.

Carol must have sensed my distress, and she stepped in to end the ordeal. "If that's all, Major, Alex has a great deal to take care of this morning."

The hefty officer set his coffee cup aside and stood, rotating his Stetson awkwardly in his hands. "Just one more question. Do you know what your brother was working on? Was he investigating something or someone in particular for his newspaper?"

"No, nothing. He was on leave for a month after returning stateside from Bosnia and had only been back at work two weeks. I don't know if he'd been given a definite assignment. Sometimes he follows—followed leads that might turn into a story, but others led nowhere."

I walked the major to the door, where he turned and offered his hand. "I'm sorry about your brother, ma'am, and sorry to have troubled you further."

I managed to close the door before the tears started.

That afternoon, with my emotions under control again, I called Tom Stanislaus, Nick's editor at the *Courier,* to ask him to speak at Nick's memorial service Saturday afternoon at my house. My garden on the bay was a place Nick had loved, where he had gathered often with his friends. I would bring them together there one last time.

While talking with Tom, I remembered the major's last question. "Tom, was Nick on any special assignment?"

"Nothing special. He had filed a few small features, but nothing like the major investigative work he'd done in the past. He was hoping to turn up a big story but, as far as I know, hadn't found any leads of any consequence. He was keeping at it, though. He turned up some of his best stuff that way."

He paused, and I prayed he wouldn't say anything consoling for fear I'd cry again. When he spoke, his tone was gruff and businesslike. "If you want, I'll have Joyce write the obituary.

With Nick's reputation, the wire services will pick it up, and Joyce will make sure it's done right."

"Thanks. And if you could tell Nick's friends in the newsroom about the service? They're all invited."

"Sure. Chin up, kid. I'll see you Saturday."

Everything seemed so ordinary, so normal. My mind still couldn't grasp the fact that Nick was dead, much less grapple with the why of his death. Had it really been just a senseless accident caused by a split second of careless driving? Or was my instinct right, that Nick had been forced off the road on purpose? And if so, by whom?

Over the many years of his career, he had uncovered mafia bosses, corrupt labor leaders, Colombian drug lords, petty crooks, and the attendant illegal activities in which they all had been involved. Was Nick's death the result of a festering vendetta? Would I ever know for sure?

I was still sitting by the phone when it rang. "Hello?"

The line was quiet, and at first I thought no one was there. Just as I started to hang up, the caller spoke. "Bring me the Gideon file tonight at 10:45. Leave it at the west entrance of Seaview Mall, or you could end up just like your brother," a muffled voice said.

The phone clicked and went dead before I could reply. The call, intensifying the atmosphere of unreality that had enveloped me since I'd learned of Nick's death, made no sense.

"Alex, are you okay?" Carol stood before me, staring in horror at my hands.

I glanced at my fists, clenched so tightly my nails had broken the skin of my palms and blood oozed in a rash of scarlet crescents.

"What is it?" Carol grasped my hands and forced my fists open.

"He said he wanted a file, and if I didn't bring it, I'd end up dead, like Nick."

"Who said that?"

"I don't know. I couldn't recognize the voice. I'm only guessing it was a man."

"What file?" Carol looked as confused as I felt.

"Some biblical name . . . Gideon, that was it. None of it made any sense, and the voice sounded distorted, like someone trying not to be recognized."

Carol snorted in disgust. "The world is full of sickos, crazy people who get their jollies from unfunny jokes. Forget it. You have too much else to deal with now."

Still raw with grief, having lost not only my twin brother but the only family I had left in the world, I allowed Carol to persuade me that the call was nothing to be concerned about.

I wanted to believe her. I needed to believe her. She was right about one thing. Nick's death was more than I could cope with.

She led me into the bathroom, where she washed my hands, spread Neosporin on the wounds, and bandaged them, making me feel five years old again.

Then she put me to bed, giving me another sedative and closing the blinds on the afternoon sun as she had done the day before. She still wore the same rumpled clothes and hadn't left me for a waking moment, taking only a few minutes to talk with Sam and her children while I'd slept.

"I've called the caterer," she said, "and made all the arrangements for Saturday. Sam is bringing me some clothes later, so I'll be here whenever you need me."

She pulled the comforter over me and smoothed my hair in a gesture I had seen her use countless times with her children. "Hold on, Alex. Everything is going to be all right."

I closed my eyes, unable to look at Carol or to speak without weeping because nothing was ever going to be all right again.

Three

The next morning I awoke, feeling rested, rose and stretched in preparation for my daily workout. Then the knowledge of Nick's death closed in on me once more, and I sank back to the edge of the bed, trying to block away the blackness and the pain. The sound of Carol clattering about in the kitchen brought me to my feet again.

I found her on her hands and knees, rummaging through the lower cabinets.

"Coffee filters?" She hoisted her pudgy frame with effort from the ceramic tile floor.

I opened a drawer beneath the coffeemaker, removed a filter, and began fitting it into the basket. I had my back to Carol, but I could feel her watching me.

"I know this sounds ungrateful," I said, "but I need to be alone today."

"You could never be ungrateful." She handed me the coffee canister with an understanding smile.

I dumped coffee into the basket and switched on the coffeemaker. Carol leaned against the counter, arms folded, studying me with the look of a mother who worries over her children.

I plunged ahead with my explanation. "You're the one who told me I've got to face this."

I paused, waiting for a reaction.

"Guilty as charged," she said with a smile.

"I can't live the rest of my life on tranquilizers avoiding the truth. I have to deal with Nick's death. The longer I put it off, the harder it's going to be."

She started to speak, then hugged me instead and left the kitchen. A few minutes later she was back, carrying her belongings stuffed in a shopping bag.

"I'll go in for my morning classes," she said, "but if you need me, call. I can have my teaching assistant take over in an instant."

The edges of my carefully mended self-control unraveled, and I couldn't stop the tears that slid down my cheeks. "Thanks for everything, you and Sam both. And thank the kids for me for lending me their mom."

"You can save your gratitude there, honey. They were glad to be rid of me. Teenagers!"

She rolled her eyes in mock dismay, and I smiled through my tears.

She patted my cheek. "I'll call you as soon as I get home this afternoon, okay?"

I gave her a gentle push out the door. "Okay. And Carol . . . thanks again."

As I watched Carol's car circle the driveway and pull onto the street, all the pain I had held at bay overwhelmed me. I raced into the bedroom, tore off my nightgown, turned the radio to full volume, and stepped into the shower. There, where the sounds of pounding water and light rock drowned out all other noise, I wept. I cried and screamed until I vented the pain, fear, and anger that had been my constant companions for the past two days.

Clean and exhausted, I dressed in a cotton skirt and blouse, slipped my feet into low-heeled sandals, and went back to the kitchen.

Over a cup of coffee, I struggled with a list of things to be done over the next few days. Work, at least, was taken care of. Dean Koenig had sent word that Kevin McDermott, my graduate teaching assistant, would take over my classes until my return.

I jumped when the wall phone beside me rang and picked it up. It was Carol. "I know you wanted to be alone, but you've got to keep up your strength. Promise me that you won't forget to eat?"

"Don't worry about me. I'll be fine. And don't call again until this afternoon. Promise?"

I hung up, thinking Carol was the proverbial mother hen and loving her all the more for it. The phone, still in my hand, rang again, and I snatched it up in irritation.

"Carol—"

"Dr. Garrison," a male voice said. "This is Major Lowery. I'm going to be in your neighborhood today, and I thought I'd drop off your brother's belongings . . . save you from making a special trip to the station."

"I'll be at home all day, Major."

I returned to the kitchen table and my unfinished list, staring at the crescent-shaped wounds in the palms of my hands. Nothing had prepared me for what I was experiencing. When my mother had died, there had been sadness but also a sense of release, of freedom.

My mother had been elderly, seventy-five years old. She had worked long, hard years as the city librarian, retiring only when forced to at seventy. Even then she had returned to the library daily to work as a volunteer, and that was where she had died, stricken by a heart attack, slumped over a book cart in the reference section.

But Nick had just turned thirty-five, healthy and vibrant, and his death made no sense. He had been an accomplished driver, accustomed to getting himself out of dangerous situations, to driving rough terrain vehicles over primitive roads with the skills of a stunt man. I couldn't accept his being run off Interstate Four as an accident.

Someone knocked at the door, a young man delivering two huge arrangements of flowers. I placed them on the foyer table.

The card on a spray of brilliant anthuriums held a message

of sympathy from the faculty of the American Studies Department.

Inhaling the pungent scent of long-stemmed white roses in a crystal vase, I opened the envelope that accompanied them. The card read: "Deepest sympathy, Burke."

For a long moment I stared at the familiar handwriting. I hadn't seen Burke for almost two years. It had been six since I had broken our engagement, but now I would have to add an appointment with him to my list in the kitchen. Burke Fairfield Brock, although no longer my fiancé, was Nick's attorney. I tucked the card back among the roses, placed the vase on the coffee table in the living room, and tried to dispel the flood of memories Burke's name conjured up.

I poured fresh coffee and sat again at the table, gazing at my list, but remembering the last time I saw Nick. We'd had dinner two weeks ago at our favorite Italian restaurant.

"I'm going to try something new," Nick had announced.

"Everything you do is new," I had countered with more than a trace of irony, "travel, adventure, meeting famous people, wading into the heat of battle. Staying home and putting your feet up would be new for you."

He had shaken a breadstick at me playfully, and his dark eyes, so like my own, had danced with excitement. "I'm serious. I'm writing a book."

I'd stopped twirling my fettucine and considered him with surprise. "You're not leaving the *Courier?*"

"No, this is something I'll do on my own time. Now that I'm stateside for a while, I'll have more time for other things. I received a request to do some writing about a subject that intrigued me, and I've been checking it out."

The subject had to be exciting to generate so much enthusiasm in my globe-hopping twin. "I know all about your famous nose for news, Nicky, but a whole book? Sounds like a snootful."

He'd grimaced at my feeble attempt at humor and taken another bite of his veal scallopini.

"This book, what's it about?" I'd asked.

"Un-uh, no previews," he'd said. "It's a secret . . . for now."

"Since when do you keep secrets from your only twin?"

"I want to get the format straight in my mind before I start talking about it. Let's just say it's a timely topic with possibilities. I'll tell you all about it when I get back off the road in a couple of weeks."

"Well, be careful, will you? I grew a head of gray hair while you were in Eastern Europe."

Remembering, I folded my arms on the table and buried my head in them, experiencing a pain too deep for tears. I'd never know what he'd wanted to write about.

Again, there was a knocking at the front door, and I was beginning to regret having sent Carol, my buffer with the public, away.

Major Lowery stood at the door with Nick's suitcase, his battered portable typewriter, and a manila envelope. He held out the envelope.

"Your brother's wallet, watch, and gun."

When he handed me the envelope, the contents rattled loosely.

"I took the precaution of unloading the gun for you," he said.

"Would you like to come in while I answer your questions?"

"Questions, ma'am?"

"You said yesterday you didn't know if Nick's death was an accident. Aren't you continuing your investigation?"

The trooper shook his head. "No need for that, Dr. Garrison. We've studied the crash site, and the medical examiner confirmed your brother's death resulted when he was ejected as the vehicle rolled."

"And that's it?" I needed more reassurance than those meager facts gave me.

"We've got a bulletin out for the hit-and-run vehicle, but with no other description than the color and possible collision damage, frankly, we don't expect to find it."

Anger rose within me, anger at Nick for dying and leaving

me alone and anger at the man who stood complacently before me. *"I'm not convinced it was an accident. I need some answers."*

The major's sigh was audible. "Let me get the report, and I'll tell you what I can."

I waited impatiently in the doorway while he went to his car and returned with a clipboard stuffed with forms. I began firing questions before he reached the door. "Are you sure Nick hadn't been wearing his seat belt, that it wasn't torn loose somehow by the force of the crash?"

"Dr. Garrison."

I could hear the weariness in his voice, the kind I sometimes felt when dealing with a student who hadn't been paying attention.

"The seat belt was retracted and in perfect working order. Any other questions?"

He was impatient to be gone, but I had to find out all I could about the circumstances of Nick's accident.

"This gun," I dangled the envelope gingerly between my thumb and index finger, "where was it found?"

He flipped through the pages on his clipboard. "In the unlocked glove compartment."

I digested that information as Major Lowery shifted his considerable bulk from one foot to the other.

"Anything else, ma'am?"

Hampered by emotional fatigue, I wrestled with the puzzle of Nick's accident. "How fast was Nick going when his car flipped?"

Again, the trooper consulted his forms. "Over eighty miles an hour is our best estimate."

"Eighty! Are you sure?"

"As sure as we can be in cases like this. Anything else?"

My mind went blank. "I know there's more, but I can't think straight."

He looked at me with compassion, dug in his shirt pocket,

and pulled out a card. "I have to go now, but if there's anything else you want to know, here's my number. Give me a call."

I lingered on the front steps, the manila envelope still dangling in my fingers, Nick's suitcase and typewriter at my feet, and watched him go. Then I dragged the cases inside, shoved them into the entry closet, and put the envelope in the drawer of the foyer table.

I couldn't rid my mind of the image of Nick traveling at eighty miles an hour with his seat belt unfastened. My brother had been obsessive about automobile safety. As a young reporter he had come home sick from accidents he'd had to cover, ranting about the senselessness, how if people would only obey the speed limits, not drink and drive, and wear their seat belts, reporters would be spared a lot of bad news and carnage. Years before Florida's mandatory seat belt laws, Nick would refuse to start his car until all passengers had buckled up.

That the same man should die under the circumstances described by Major Lowery was inconceivable.

I wandered through the house out to the deck and sank into a chair in a pool of sunlight. Although the day was warm, I shivered. I sat with my knees drawn to my chest and my arms wrapped around them, attempting to conserve body heat. Was I losing my mind from grief, or was it rational for me to believe Nick's death could not have been an accident?

Guiltily, I recalled my promise to Carol to eat, and I returned to the kitchen to fix breakfast. As I placed bread in the toaster, I glanced out the window that overlooked the street. A strange car was parked just beyond my house. I couldn't see through its tinted windshield, but as I leaned toward the window for a closer look, the car pulled away.

I watched uneasily as it turned in the cul de sac and slowly passed the house again. The car didn't belong to anyone on the block, and although it could belong to anyone—a tourist who was either lost or sightseeing, a visitor, a salesman—its presence on my street filled me with uneasiness.

The same intuition that told me Nick had been murdered

warned me that I somehow was in danger, too, just as the strange phone call had warned.

Carol had insisted that the disturbing phone call was just some sick person's idea of a joke. So, why, lacking logical reasons, did I believe Nick's death had been no accident?

Disgusted with myself for being irrational, I chalked up my fears to grief. I forgot about the strange car in front of my house until days later. By then it was too late.

Four

I switched on the outside lights to make it easier for the caterers to load the stacks of chairs and dishes into their van. Spending the last few hours sharing memories of Nick with his crowd of friends had exhausted me. Their stories and reminiscences had touched me, bringing Nick back to me in a transitory, bittersweet way, but their sympathy and attempts at comfort had been hard to bear without losing control of my fragile emotions.

Relieved that one ordeal, at least, was over, I kicked off my shoes, slumped into a chair, and propped my feet on the coffee table beside Burke's roses, which looked as faded as I felt.

Carol shoved a plate and a glass of milk into my hands. "You haven't eaten a thing. I've watched you spend the entire day sipping club soda, and I'm not leaving until that plate is clean."

She settled onto the sofa across from me, while I nibbled at a sandwich that tasted like soggy cardboard. I set it down and drank the milk instead.

Sam came in with two glasses of white wine, handed one to Carol, then sat next to her. Side by side, the two reminded me of Jack Sprat and his wife. Carol was short, and round like a dumpling; Sam was tall and lanky, with his brown hair rapidly giving way to baldness and his kindly, craggy face becoming more wrinkled with age.

"It was a very fitting tribute, Alex," he said. "Nick would have appreciated Tom's remarks, spoken like a true journalist—concise, insightful, and accurate—nothing sentimental."

Tears welled. I had managed to hold them back for the past few hours. "Nick would have loved it when Carol read from T. S. Eliot, especially that line about how making an end is making a beginning. This certainly is both an end and a beginning for me. I couldn't have endured today without you two."

As I sat, too exhausted to move, I caught sight of an arrangement of red carnations and red roses with red bows on the mantelpiece, creating a garish stain of color against the white wall.

"Do either of you know someone named Gideon?" I asked.

Carol shook her head. "A friend of Nick's?"

"I suppose so, although Gideon was the name that crazy caller used."

"What crazy caller?" Sam leaned forward, concern adding extra wrinkles to his brow.

I shrugged, not wanting to make too big a deal of what was probably only a prank. "The day after Nick died, someone called. He didn't identify himself, and I couldn't recognize the voice. He told me to bring a file, a Gideon file, to Seaview Mall that night at some ungodly hour."

"What's a Gideon file?" Sam asked.

"I haven't a clue. I was hoping you might know."

"I don't like the sound of that," he said. "Did you report it?"

Carol nudged him with her elbow. "Don't be such an alarmist. It was just a crank. Nick's obituary was in all the papers. Because he'd won a Pulitzer Prize, it even made the wire services. Someone must have thought they were being funny. People have cruel senses of humor these days."

Sam didn't look convinced. "And the flowers?"

I avoided the garish sight. "Those came with a sympathy card addressed to me, but it was signed simply *Gideon*. I called the florist, but whoever ordered the flowers paid cash, and no one there could remember him."

Sam looked thoughtful as he cleaned his gold-framed bifocals with an over-sized white handkerchief. "Did you know everyone here today? I'm thinking specifically of that white-haired, older fellow I saw hovering around the fringes of the group while Tom was speaking."

"That was a student of mine," I said, "Paul Stephanos from my American history class. He spoke to me right after that, until Kevin ran interference for me, or he might still be here."

I set down my glass. The milk had a funny taste to it, but so did everything I'd eaten since Nick died.

"Kevin has been a godsend through all of this," I said. "With everything else I have to worry about, at least I know my classes are being taught well."

"Kevin is a dear, but I think the old fellow, Stephanos, was sweet to come," Carol said.

"Sweet! He gives me the creeps." I shivered at the thought of him.

"That harmless old man? Why?" Carol always rooted for the underdog.

"He studies me while I'm teaching as if I'm some kind of specimen on a slide. I'm afraid he might be a nut case."

"Aren't you being a tad paranoid?" Carol asked.

Her words reminded me of my suspicions about Nick's death. I told them about Major Lowery's visit the previous day and what I had learned about Nick's accident.

"Only it couldn't have been an accident, could it?" I insisted. "Nick would never have been driving at that speed, especially without his seat belt fastened."

I wasn't sure if I wanted confirmation or a good argument. It would certainly be simpler if I was wrong.

Carol extracted herself from the depths of the cushions and sat on the arm of my chair, hugging me. "Let it go, Alex. You're trying to explain away something for which there is no explanation. It helps you avoid the reality that Nick died in a senseless accident. But you have to face it and stop dancing around it with theories and excuses."

The ringing of the telephone saved me from a reply.

"Stay put," Carol patted my arm. "I'll get it."

She returned a minute later. "That was the police. There's a problem at Nick's condo, and they'd like you to come. Sam and I will drive you."

"What kind of problem?" I asked.

"They didn't say. Just asked that you come over to answer a few questions."

I felt myself being sucked down once more into a maelstrom of fear. "Why do I get the feeling this isn't going to be easy?"

We were silent during our drive across the causeway to the beach. Sam drove and Carol sat beside him in the front seat.

Alone in back, I leaned against the headrest and closed my eyes, seeing a bright summer's day and ten-year-old Nick on the causeway ahead of me, his long, thin legs pumping away at the pedals of his American Flyer. He wore only a too large T-shirt over his swimming trunks, and every so often he would glance back to make sure I was still following.

We hadn't been able to escape very often. Our mother firmly believed that idle hands were the devil's workshop. Most of the time she would draw her lips into a hard, thin line and respond with a punishing silence to our requests to go swimming at the beach, but that day, for some unfathomable reason, she had relented.

When we reached the beach, we splashed, dove, and floated with the abandon of captives just released, and when the blistering sun reached its apex, we retreated to the shade of Australian pines to sit cross-legged on damp towels and eat the lunch of peanut butter sandwiches we had packed ourselves.

I lay back on my towel to wait the prescribed thirty minutes after eating my mother had always insisted upon before we swam again. Her horrifying description of the agonizing cramps we would suffer, resulting in death by drowning, had made enough of an impression on us that we never broke that edict.

Sand ground between my skin and the elasticized back of my cotton swimsuit, a bright turquoise garment as shapeless as my child's body, with the exception of a pouf of ruffles across the buttocks. I plopped over onto my stomach to face Nick, who sat a few feet away.

"Nick, does Mother love us?"

" 'Course she does."

He hadn't hesitated in his reply. He squinted at me with his eyes almost shut in the sun's glare. The peppering of freckles across his sunburned nose was repeated on my own face.

"How do you know?" I demanded.

I wasn't afraid to ask Nick questions. He always tried to answer, unlike my mother, who would snap at me or, more often, not say anything at all.

He sighed with all the mature wisdom being two minutes older provided. "Because she's our mother, and mothers love their kids. That's their job."

His logic had not convinced me. "But she never says she loves us."

"She never says much of anything, but that doesn't mean she doesn't think it."

I considered the possibility of a silent, secret love as I watched a family down the beach. A mother tenderly rubbed a small child dry, wrapped him in a towel, then pulled him to her and covered his face with kisses. I started to ask Nick why our mother never touched us, but a more significant question occurred to me instead.

"Why did our daddy go away?"

Nick had been burrowing in the sand, building a fortress with a moat, and creating stacks of cannonballs from pine burrs. He dusted the sand from his hands and sat back on his heels.

"All she'll ever say is that he didn't want to be a daddy anymore." He scrunched his face with concern. "Don't keep asking her, because she won't tell you, and talking about it just puts her in one of her moods."

I sighed and looked back wistfully at the family down the beach. "Don't you ever wish we were a real family, Nicky?"

"We are a real family," Nick said, but we both knew it wasn't so. He smiled with the lopsided grin that always made me feel warm inside. "I'm a real brother and you're a real sister. What more do you need?" He'd been right, but now he was gone.

I thrust the painful memories away and opened my eyes as Sam pulled up to the security gate of Nick's condominium complex. We showed some I.D., and the guard waved us through. We passed two patrol cars on our way to the elevator, and a uniformed policeman was waiting for us when we exited on Nick's floor.

Kitty Flanagan, Nick's neighbor who watered his plants whenever he was away, was speaking quietly to an officer, who wrote her responses in a small notebook.

When she saw me, she hurried over. "I'm so sorry about Nick, dear. And now this." She wrung her hands. "I have no idea who or when. I only thank God I didn't walk in on them."

With my emotions on overload, I could make no sense of Kitty's ramblings. The front door of Nick's condo opened, and another officer emerged.

He looked toward us. "Ms. Garrison?"

I nodded numbly.

"Would you step inside, please, while we talk?"

He opened the door and stepped aside for me to enter, but the sight made my knees buckle. I would have stumbled if he hadn't caught my elbow.

The room looked like a refuse dump. Books and papers were strewn over the floor, cushions ripped apart, and their stuffing scattered among the broken lamps and overturned tables. Draperies hung in shreds, file cabinet drawers stood gaping and empty, and plants lay dying, their roots shriveled, white and exposed where the soil had been beaten from them.

In the kitchen, the cabinets' contents had been dumped on the floor, and the oven and refrigerator doors stood ajar. In the bedroom, the mattress and chair cushions had been slashed, bureau drawers removed and tossed in a heap, Nick's clothes had been ripped apart and trampled, and the dresser mirror had been shattered by the large ceramic sculpture that lay in pieces beneath it.

RELATIVE DANGER

I viewed the damage in shocked silence, then returned to the living room and collapsed on a chair from the dining set, one of the few pieces of furniture still in one piece.

I turned to face the officer. "What happened? It looks as if a bomb went off in here."

My voice shook with fatigue and rage. Nick was gone, and now even his belongings had been destroyed. Was I to have nothing of him left?

Carol and Sam had joined me, looking as dazed as I. They stood by protectively as the officer asked his questions.

"Did Mr. Garrison keep money in the apartment? Valuables?"

I shook my head.

"Is anything missing?" the officer asked.

"It appears everything, or what's left of everything, is still here. But how can I tell?" Stunned by the magnitude of the destruction around me, I struggled to concentrate on what the officer was saying.

"Sorry you have to go through this, ma'am. Unfortunately, we see it too often. When someone dies, thieves strike while the funeral is being held."

"But this was no ordinary robbery," I said. "Just look at the place!"

"I've seen worse," the officer said. "They were searching for something valuable, like jewelry, money, or furs. When they didn't find it, they got mad and trashed the place. It happens a lot."

"If they were after valuables," Sam said, "why didn't they take the television or the VCR?"

The officer shrugged. "Maybe they were scared away, or maybe they thought bigger items would be too conspicuous to carry."

Carol pulled me from the chair and toward the door.

Sam turned to the officer. "What's the procedure now?"

"We'll wrap up our investigation in an hour or so. We're

dusting for prints now. After that, I suggest you contact the insurance company."

Carol pushed me into the hallway and punched the elevator button. "You're going home to bed, ducky. You've had a day I wouldn't wish on my worst enemy."

While we rode the elevator to the ground level parking lot, my mind churned, sorting out the significance of what I had seen. When we stepped from the elevator, I turned and faced the Donahues.

"Do you believe me now?" My voice was shrill with weariness and desperation. "Someone killed Nick and now they've destroyed everything he owned."

"Sure, ducky."

Carol's tone was soothing, but I saw the look that passed between the couple. They thought grief had affected my mind.

As I settled into the back seat for the ride home, I wondered if they might be right.

Five

The blast of a boat horn, signaling the bridge-tender to raise the causeway drawbridge, awakened me, and I lay listening to the Sunday morning sounds, drifting through my open window, of boats and boaters in the channel.

All I wanted was to lie still, to ignore the hollow feeling that caused such pain. Like a soda gone flat, my basic substance remained, but the effervescence had disappeared. Nothing appealed to me, and I could think of no good reason to get out of bed.

I turned over and buried my head among the pillows until the persistent tone of the telephone pulled me from their soft depths into reality once more.

"Alexandra?"

Strange how a certain sound can evoke such memories. I would recognize that smooth, cultured voice for the rest of my life. At one time that voice alone had been enough to flood me with happiness.

"Good morning, Burke."

I had seen him briefly the day before at Nick's memorial service, but I had been surrounded by so many people, all waiting to speak with me, that he had simply offered his condolences and said he would call. And now he had. Burke always kept his promises.

"I hope I haven't wakened you."

"No, I was awake."

"Then I hope you haven't had breakfast."

I rolled into a sitting position to read the clock on my bedside radio. The red digital numbers winked ten o'clock. I would be admitting my laziness.

"No, no breakfast yet."

"Good. I'll pick you up in thirty minutes for breakfast on the beach."

The receiver clicked before I could protest. That was another of Burke's characteristics, never taking no for an answer, usually by not giving me the chance to say it.

I waited for my old resentment to bubble to the surface, but my numbness allowed nothing to intrude on it. I psyched myself up for the meeting with the hope of attending to some of the details of Nick's estate, saving myself from a private visit to Burke's office.

Twenty-five minutes later, I studied my image in my closet mirror. A liberal application of makeup covered the violet shadows beneath my eyes, but the deep vertical line between my brows seemed permanently etched there. My inner hurt was invisible beneath a pale yellow dress of Indian cotton, and when I clasped a long strand of cinnamon-colored wooden beads in graduated sizes around my neck and added matching earrings, I looked pale but fashionable. Not that I cared, but I remembered enough of Burke to know that dressing appropriately would spare me his disapproval and perhaps make our meeting easier.

A car pulled into the driveway, and I met Burke at the door. Punctuality was another constant of his, and he expected me to be on time as well. I shook away irritating memories and tried to be civil.

"You have a new car."

I slipped onto the seat of the sleek Jaguar. Burke always bought the best.

"You look more beautiful than ever, Alexandra." He studied me for a moment before starting the car, causing me to squirm with embarrassment.

"And you're as silver-tongued as ever," I shot back, realizing too late that seeing him was a mistake, that I should never have given in to his invitation.

My shot missed the mark. Burke laughed, showing even white teeth, put the car into gear, and pulled away from the house, driving expertly but too fast. I knew from experience that protest was futile, and somehow the dangerous speed seemed less important now.

In the clear, bright morning, the hollowness still gripped me. The brilliant sunlight on the waters of the bay; the graceful palms; the masses of zinnias, marigolds, and nasturtiums in the causeway median—a scene for a tourist's scrapbook—gave me no pleasure.

"This is the hour of lead—" The line from Dickinson leapt into my mind. Before Nick's death, I would never have believed I could sit so close to Burke once more and feel no anger, no regrets, no sadness, nothing.

He turned the car smoothly into the broad, sweeping drive of the Seashell Hotel, an elegantly restored building, built during the economic boom years of the early 1920s, and yielded his keys reluctantly to a parking valet. We passed through the spacious lobby into the restaurant, where we sat in fan-backed rattan chairs. Our table beneath the tall windows overlooked the swimming pool and gulf waters, framed by palms. Above, suspended from the open beams of the high ceiling, fans stirred the air languidly with long, wooden paddles.

As Burke knew, the hotel was a favorite of mine, with atmosphere worthy of F. Scott Fitzgerald and his decadent friends; but today its impressive ambience, its furnishings and carpets in trendy colors, its gleaming white walls, left me cold. I shivered in the air-conditioning. Ever since Nick's death, I could not seem to get warm.

I studied Burke as he scanned the menu. He was exactly as I remembered: tall, blond, tan, and physically fit, a living image from the pages of *GQ* with the chiseled good looks of an actor. He dressed, as was his custom, in the style expected of a senior partner in the city's most prestigious law firm, wearing a custom-tailored, gray pin-striped suit with his signature paisley silk tie as casually as some men wear jeans and sweatshirts.

When the waitress came, he ordered without asking my preference. "We'll have mimosas, eggs Benedict, and coffee—decaffeinated."

He leaned forward and placed his hand over mine. His voice, the one I'd once loved, was gentle, consoling. "I hear there was a problem at Nick's condo yesterday."

"How on earth did you know? Oh, God, it wasn't in the paper, was it?"

Burke smiled, an expression that at one time would have melted me away. Today my coldness shielded me, and I withdrew my hand.

"I'd like to say I'm a powerful man with connections in the police department," he said, "but the truth is I learned about the break-in when I called Kitty Flanagan late yesterday."

"Why did you call Kitty?"

"To arrange to pick up Nick's key."

"Why?"

He glared at me with another expression I remembered well, one that made me feel like a mentally deficient child to whom he was showing extreme patience.

"Alexandra." Even the way he spoke my name was a reprimand. "I need access to Nick's place. As executor of Nick's estate, one of my responsibilities is to make an inventory of his belongings."

"Yesterday someone made your job a lot easier. There's not much left to inventory now." The bitterness in my voice surprised even me.

The waitress brought our drinks. The icy mixture of orange juice and champagne slid down my throat like a blessing.

When Burke raised his glass, a massive gold ring set with an unusual design of black onyx and rubies caught the sunlight. "Yes, Kitty told me very little was left intact by the vandals, so I've arranged for a cleaning service to take care of the mess."

"Burke—"

He held up his hands, palms outward, to ward off my protests. "Don't worry. I'll have them set aside anything that's the least bit salvageable for you to go through. Also, as his sole heir, you'll need to let me know whether you wish to sell the place or keep it."

Just as part of me rebelled at his interference, another part, vulnerable and wounded, encouraged me to yield, to place all those bothersome matters in Burke's capable and willing hands.

He was watching me for a reaction, but seeing none, he continued. "Considering today's market and the lack of tax advantages for rental property, I recommend you try to move the property right away."

I squirmed in my chair. His advice was sound—Burke was nothing if not brilliant about such matters—but my old resentment of him and his manipulations surfaced with a vengeance, crushing my desire to be taken care of. Six years ago, when I broke our engagement, I had decided to no longer allow Burke Brock to tell me what to do with my life. I would not go back on that decision now.

I smiled to soften the blow of my independence. "I don't believe there's any hurry, is there? If I haven't decided by the time you're ready to close out the estate, you can transfer the title to me. I can always sell later if I decide that's what I want."

He liked to be in total control. He resented my self-reliance. A momentary triumph at the flicker of annoyance in Burke's gray eyes shot through me. It was the first emotion I'd truly felt since the grief of Nick's death had settled around me.

Our breakfast arrived, and my stomach revolted at the sight of eggs and cream sauce. My appetite had vanished with my other feelings when Nick died.

Burke ate with all the relish good manners allowed. When his plate had been removed and coffee served, he returned to the subject of Nick's estate. "Do you have anything of Nick's I should add to the inventory?"

"No—" I hesitated, remembering Nick's suitcase and typewriter in my foyer closet—and his gun.

Burke sat very still, waiting, his legal eye registering every nuance of my expression.

"I mean, yes . . ."

His scrutiny made me nervous, and my hand trembled as I reached for my coffee cup. As I drank, I pondered whether to tell Burke of my belief that Nick's death had been no accident and about my threatening phone call.

"Do you know anyone named Gideon?" I asked.

"No, why?"

I couldn't tell if it was my own wariness or if his denial had seemed too quick. "Someone named Gideon sent flowers and a sympathy card. I want to thank him, but all I know is the name Gideon."

His wintry gray eyes narrowed, watching me with an intensity that wearied me. I'd had enough of Burke's intrusion into my life. His intensity was part of the reason I'd broken off our engagement in the first place. I'd be foolish to revive his involvement with me by sharing my concerns with him now.

"Never mind," I said. "I'll check with Nick's editor. I'm sure he'll know."

"Alexandra, you still haven't answered my question." Burke's good looks dissolved into a snarl when he became impatient. "Do you have anything else of Nick's for the inventory?"

I set my cup down so firmly it rattled loudly in the saucer, making a dissonant clatter among the muffled tones of the dining room. "All I have is the suitcase and typewriter that were in his car when he—"

I couldn't bring myself to say it. Instead, I patted my lips with the large square of peach-colored linen, laid it beside my plate, and rose. "Thank you for breakfast, Burke, but I have to go home now. If you wish to stay, I'll call a cab."

He was on his feet almost as quickly as I. "Don't be ridiculous, Alexandra."

He smiled, his tone warm, but I could read the irritation in his eyes. I had taken charge, an act he hated, particularly in a woman.

"You're my guest," he said. "I'll take you home."

On the drive back, Burke talked about mutual friends, the Tampa Bay Buccaneers, and the weather; but I tuned him out, wrapping myself in the numbness that enabled me to survive.

When we reached my house, I jumped from the car as soon as it stopped.

"Don't bother to get out, Burke. Thanks again for breakfast."

I waved before I shut the door of the house, while Burke still sat in his car, taken by surprise by my assertiveness.

Inside, I leaned against the door, waiting until I heard the Jaguar roar down the street. Then I collapsed onto the chair beside the foyer table, exhausted by the spurt of energy that assertiveness had cost me.

"Oh, Nicky," I cried aloud in the stillness of the house. "Who did this to you? And how will I ever manage to live without you?"

Six

I dragged myself off the foyer chair, tugging off my yellow dress as I headed to the bedroom to change. I wanted nothing more than to lie on my deck in the cool October air and watch the frigate birds with their wide wings silhouetted against the sun as they rode the updrafts of the wind currents above the bay.

Aunt Bibi had told me years ago about the frigate birds that soared high over the gulf waters near her cottage on Longboat Key. Because of their eight-foot wingspan, she had explained, they had great difficulty taking off from the ground or water, so most of their flights began and ended in the tops of large trees or tall-masted ships.

"You can learn a lot from the frigate birds, Alex," my mother's sister had said. "Never let yourself sink so low that you'll find it hard to get up again."

As a child, I had wondered what she meant, but now, faced with the desire to give in to smothering depression, I understood.

Settling down into my chaise longue on the deck that stretched across the back of the house, I reflected on my morning with Burke. Nothing he had said couldn't have been handled with a phone call or by letter. Was he merely trying to be kind, or did he hope that in my grief I would turn to him for consolation?

I lay back and closed my eyes against the sun, remembering how Nick had tried, for my sake, to conceal his intense dislike of the man. Nick, with his sharp reporter's eye and instinct for people, had Burke pegged right away. It had taken me a great deal longer.

In spite of his feelings, Nick had been loyal from the beginning of my relationship with Burke. He had even gone to Burke for the closing on his condo and to have his will drawn up, doing both as peace offerings to me, his way of showing that, even though he would have chosen differently for me, he would support my choice.

That spring in the year before my mother had died, Burke and I had planned for a Christmas wedding, complete with poinsettias, holly, and red velvet ribbons. I recalled with a strange clarity the evening we had studied travel brochures for our honeymoon cruise to Bermuda.

"The timing is perfect, Burke," I'd said. "With the break between sessions, I'll have a week off before the wedding, then a week and a half afterward for our cruise."

He had looked at me then with the condescending expression I had come to dread. "Perhaps you haven't been paying attention, Alexandra, dear. I have no intention of allowing my wife to work. If you submit your resignation now, the university will have ample time to find a replacement."

I had sat motionless with shock. When I had finally found my voice, it shook with disbelief. "We talked about my taking leave when the children came, but I never agreed to give up my position."

I had stood and strode across the room, as far away from him as I could move. "I'm a tenured professor, next in line to head the department. And I love what I do. How can you ask me to give it up?"

His gray eyes had turned hard and frigid, and the obstinate lines of his jaw had appeared chiseled from stone. "I've made myself quite clear. No wife of mine is going to work. The choice is up to you."

He had sat back then and relaxed with a confident smile, as if the matter had been settled.

I would never forget his fleeting expression of stunned disbelief when I pulled the large, pear-shaped diamond, flanked with emeralds, from my finger and handed it to him.

"It's obvious you love the woman you want to make of me, not the woman I am. I'm sorry, Burke." I had turned and walked away but not soon enough to avoid the look of contempt that replaced his disbelief.

In retrospect, I could see how much Burke was like my mother, both of them with an insatiable need for control, both of them inflicting an unyielding silence upon those who refused to bend to their wills. I'd had a close call. Most women supposedly marry someone like their fathers. Since I had never known my father, I had been unconsciously drawn to someone more like my mother instead.

The warmth of the October sun began to draw the chill from my bones, making me drowsy. I slipped into sleep, pursued by dreams of Nick. He was driving, and I was with him in the passenger seat. His seat belt kept coming unbuckled as the car sped faster and faster, and I would reach over him to clasp it shut again. Suddenly, we were hurtling across a long, high bridge. As we reached the top of the span, the bridge disappeared below us, and the car began to fall into nothingness. Both our seat belts came unfastened, and we were falling—

I awoke with a start, bathed in perspiration, my heart pounding. The dream was a variation of one I'd had all my life, a dream of being on a bridge that suddenly ended, pitching me into the chasm below.

As a child, I would awaken, crying in terror, but my mother either slept like the dead or chose to ignore my cries. Nick had always been the one who had crept into my room with his pillow and blanket to sleep on the floor beside my bed, knowing I was too frightened to go back to sleep alone.

Still jittery from my strange dream, I went into the kitchen for a glass of water, wandering like a lost child through the empty rooms of what had once been my refuge. My nightmare had returned, and there was no Nick to comfort me.

What about Nick's nightmare? What had he thought when he'd been forced off the road? How had he felt when the car had begun to roll? Like an abyss had opened up beneath him with no one there to save him? I owed it to Nick to find out what had happened. I would have no peace unless I could convince myself his death had really been an accident.

Feeling more purposeful than I had since before Nick's death, I changed into navy slacks and a chambray blouse, knotted a sweater around my neck, and searched for my car keys. It was after two o'clock, the Sunday afternoon football games had already begun, but I would go to Tom Stanislaus to learn what I could about the last two weeks of Nick's life.

Tom's wife, Lila, led me into the living room and went off in search of Tom. I could hear her talking over the noise of the television set in their family room.

Tom was grinning when he entered the room. He settled his weighty frame into a chair across from me as I perched on the edge of the sofa, unsure how to ask what I needed to know.

"I wanted to thank you again," I began, "for your tribute to Nick yesterday. He admired you as a colleague and loved you as a friend. Your words would have meant a great deal to him."

Tom's grin faded, and he looked haggard, older than his age. "I still can't believe he's gone. We had some good times on assignments before I decided my family responsibilities were better served behind a desk. Reporting can be a risky business, but, Jesus, I never thought it would end like this for Nick."

The big man rubbed a large hand over his face, lost for an instant in his memories. Then he shot me a piercing gaze from beneath his graying eyebrows. "You've got something on your mind, haven't you?"

His directness made it easier.

"I'm not satisfied Nick's death was an accident. You know how he was about safe driving. The highway patrol says he was going over eighty miles an hour, with his seat belt unfastened, when his car rolled. Does that sound like the Nick you knew? And was it just coincidence his condo was searched and vandalized during the service yesterday?"

Tom sat quietly for a moment, digesting what I'd said.

"Speeding and no seat belt, that's very unlike Nick," he said, "but we all at some time or another do things out of character, for whatever reason: we're tired, in a hurry, a little tipsy. And the break-in at his condo, that's not unusual when someone has died, especially if there's been newspaper coverage. The circumstances seem odd, but that's all they are, just circumstances."

I nodded. "I agree with everything you say. At least my head agrees. But my gut tells me they're more than circumstances."

"I know the feeling." Tom leaned forward, his hands clasped before him, elbows resting on his knees. "It's like a reporter's instinct, a feeling that leads you to a story when most other people would insist there's no story there."

"That's it, exactly."

"But often those instincts are wrong," Tom added. "Things don't always turn out the way you think they might. I wish I had a dollar for every instinct of mine that ended up nowhere."

"But didn't you have to follow through, just to be sure, so it didn't constantly nag at you? And I'm not talking about just any story here but Nick's life!"

Tom leaned back in his chair and sighed. "I hear what you're saying, Alex. You want to investigate this to satisfy yourself." He shook his bearlike head. "I guess it's no use trying to talk you out of it?"

"Not a chance." I stood and paced the length of the room. "So you might as well help me."

I stopped before him, arms folded across my chest, looking down in mute appeal.

"There's not much I can do," he said. "You already have more information than I do."

I returned to the sofa and sat down. "Think back, please. When did you talk with Nick last, and what did he say?"

He wiped his large hand in a washing motion over his face again. "He faxed in a story early last week, a piece on the AIDS epidemic among Haitian cane cutters in Clewiston, near Okeechobee. Right after that, he called to ask if I'd track down a name for him."

"Was it Gideon?"

"No. Gideon who?"

"Someone sent flowers and signed them Gideon. I don't know who he is, but I'd at least like to be able to thank him."

Tom shrugged his meaty shoulders. "I don't know anyone named Gideon."

"What name did Nick ask for?"

"A psychic. One the Miami and Jacksonville police departments have used to help locate missing persons."

"A psychic? Nick wanted the name of a psychic?"

My pragmatic brother had never held any credence in the paranormal.

Tom nodded. "Said he lost track of one of his sources, as if the man had disappeared off the face of the earth. He was afraid something might have happened to him and wanted some help tracking him down."

"A source? For what?"

Tom shrugged again. "Don't know. Nick said it wasn't newspaper business, that it had something to do with a book he was working on, so I didn't ask. Anyway, I had our librarian do a computer search that came up with the woman's name and address, and I passed them on to Nick when he called in the next night." His eyes, like a sad old dog's, glinted with tears. "I never heard from him again."

His sadness disappeared as he scowled at me. "You don't have to ask. I remember the name and address and I'll tell you, but I think you're asking for trouble to fool with psychics, especially now."

"Come on, Tom, I can take care of myself. Besides, I might learn something about Nick's accident. What harm could it do?"

Lila came in, carrying a tray with a coffeepot, mugs, and a

plate of brownies. "I couldn't help overhearing, Alex, and Tom's right. You're in a very vulnerable emotional state, and you have no idea what kind of character this psychic might be."

She poured a mug of coffee and passed it to me. "I'm no expert on psychics, so I can't say if any of them are legitimate, but I'm sure more than a few are ready to take advantage of someone in your situation."

I refused the offered brownies, wondering if I would ever desire food again. Tom and Lila both looked at me with concern.

I forced a smile. "Thanks for the warning—"

"It's more than a warning." Tom smacked the upholstered chair arm with his fist. "It's good common sense. Go to her, if you must, but don't get her involved with solving your dilemma. What you don't need right now is more pain caused by getting mixed up with the occult."

"And if you go, take a friend," Lila said. "Someone like Carol, who can be objective. You're too fragile right now."

I shook my head. "Thanks, but if there is danger, I don't want Carol or anyone else involved. This is something I'll have to sort out for myself."

"If you're that determined—" Tom said.

"I am."

He shoved himself to his feet and crossed to the Windsor desk beside the fireplace, pulling a pad and pencil from one of its cubbyholes. He scribbled a few words on the pad, tore off the sheet, and handed it to me.

"Bella Ionescu, Macy Avenue, Cassadega," I read aloud. "Where's Cassadega?"

"It's a little community off Interstate Four north of Orlando. There's a Spiritualist church campground there, and some spiritualists make it their year-round home, but that's all I know. Never been there myself, but we ran a feature on it in one of the Sunday sections a few years back."

"Looks like I'll be making the trip." I held out my hand as I rose to leave. "Thanks, Tom, for everything."

He grasped my hand in both of his. "You'll let me know when you're going and when you plan to return?"

I was touched by his interest. "I'll call you."

As I unlocked my front door, I could hear the telephone ringing. I raced to the kitchen to answer it, leaving the door standing open with my keys in the lock.

"Alexandra, my darling girl, how are you? Herman and I were so sad to read in the paper about your Nicky. What a terrible thing! I wish we could be there with you. I've been trying to call you all day, but nobody answers. Are you all right? You're not eating like you should, I know—"

"Hello, Rosa." I smiled through tears, warmed by the sound of Rosa's voice. Herman and Rosa Myers from Long Island had bought the house next door as their winter home shortly after my mother died, and they treated me like one of their own daughters.

This conversation would not be difficult. Rosa, in her vivacious, non-stop style, would do all the talking. All I needed was to make the appropriate murmurs as I listened to the reassuring chatter of one who loved me.

"I'm so sorry we can't be there with you now with what you're going through, darling, but it will be after Christmas before we can come to Florida. Our Rachel is having her first baby—our fifth grandchild—in December, but the doctors have put her to bed until then and she wants her mama with her. Such problems the poor girl has . . ."

I listened uncomprehendingly to the comforting, lilting notes of Rosa's voice as she recited a litany of her daughter's troubles with her pregnancy.

"So we've rented the house for the next three months to this nice young man—"

"What?"

"I'm sorry, darling, is there a bad connection? No? Well, as I was saying, since we can't come down until after Christmas anyway, we've rented the house to Mitchell Lawton. He's a detective with the New York City Police Department, but he's had a bad time, a nervous breakdown, poor boy. His partner was killed, and he took it very hard. So they gave Mitchell three months' leave to rest and put himself back together. He's a good-looking boy, about your age—"

"Now, Rosa, you know better than to play matchmaker with me."

"Who's talking matchmaker, darling? I'm talking friend. He's lost someone close and so have you, so I think you two can help each other. Anyway, I wanted to tell you—"

A rapping at the front door distracted me. "Hold on a minute, please, Rosa."

"Anybody home?" A voice sounded in the front hall, and before I could move, a tall figure stepped into the kitchen doorway from the foyer. Sunlight streamed into the hallway behind him, outlining a familiar form.

"Nick?" I attempted to move, but could not.

"Nicky?" I whispered and crumpled onto the cold ceramic tiles. The last thing I heard before losing consciousness was the sound of the receiver, bumping against the wall.

Seven

Struggling to throw off the blackness that engulfed me, I felt someone lift me from the floor before unconsciousness closed in again. Sometime later, the sounds of voices, footsteps, and the opening and closing of doors penetrated my oblivion.

When I opened my eyes, a strange man sat next to where I lay on the sofa in the living room. He smiled with a pleasant expression that crinkled the skin at the corners of his dark brown eyes, and the attractive angles of his face reminded me of Harrison Ford. I thought for a moment I was dreaming.

"Who are you?" I tried to sound indignant, but my voice came out a hoarse croak.

"Mitchell Lawton. Rosa Myers was telling you about me when you put her on hold."

"Rosa!" My motherly friend would be sick with worry. I tried to sit up but was too weak. Only the slightest pressure of his hand restrained me.

"Don't worry about Rosa. I told her you'd fainted, that I'd take care of you, and you'd call her back in a while." He looked puzzled. "For some strange reason, she sounded delighted."

I lifted myself on my elbows. "You'd better be careful. Rosa will have us married by tomorrow if she sets her mind to it. She thinks of herself as a world-class matchmaker."

I slumped back against the cushions, thinking my dizziness had loosened not only my tongue but my brain as well.

He grinned. "Thanks for the warning. By the way, I go by

Mitch. If we're threatened with matrimony, we should be on a first name basis."

"I'm Alexandra, but my friends call me Alex."

His expression sobered. "I apologize for frightening you. When I saw the door open and the key in the lock, I thought there might be trouble." He shrugged, looking embarrassed. "The policeman in me, I guess."

"You didn't frighten me. I thought you were . . . someone else. I don't know why I fainted. I'm not the type." I attempted to rise again, but dizziness washed over me. I closed my eyes and sank onto the sofa cushions.

"I can make a good guess why you passed out," he said.

His fingers gently probed the pulse at my wrist. "When did you eat last?"

I thought for a moment. "I can't remember."

"Bingo," he said. "Lie still, and I'll bring you something. Maybe by the time it's ready, Carol will be here. Rosa gave me her name and number, and when I called, she said she'd be right over."

I waited gratefully, too weak to protest or be concerned about the presence of a stranger in my house. I could hear his movements in the kitchen and wondered why I felt so at ease with a man I'd met only a few moments ago.

I dozed off, and in what seemed only seconds, he was back at my side, arranging a tray of food on the coffee table.

"Drink the orange juice first," he said, "to raise your blood sugar. Then maybe the dizziness will go away."

Obediently, I drank the tumbler of juice.

"Now the rest."

Surprisingly, my lightheadedness began to clear, and I was able to sit up. He had toasted an English muffin and spread it with cream cheese and a dollop of strawberry preserves. There was also an apple, cored and sliced and sprinkled with sugar and cinnamon, and a steaming mug of lemon tea.

"I hope you don't mind, but I made tea for myself, too. They say it's dangerous to drink alone." He sat across from me, sipping his tea in easy silence while I ate.

I finished the muffin and polished off the last slice of apple, surprised to find my appetite had returned. "You seem to know your way around a kitchen."

"A necessary by-product of my bachelor existence."

His smile warmed me, and I liked his friendly banter. As I studied him more closely, I could see why I had mistaken him for Nick. He was tall, like Nick had been, with the same slender, well-muscled frame. He had Nick's dark eyes but his hair showed more gray at the temples than Nick's had. Although his mouth was wider than Nick's, he had the same crooked grin.

Even his clothing, khaki Dockers and a plaid cotton shirt with the sleeves turned back at the cuffs, reminded me of Nick. Maybe the resemblance explained why I felt so comfortable with him, or maybe it was his ease with himself. If he was depressed over his partner's death, he kept his pain well hidden.

A car pulled into the drive, and seconds later, Carol swooped into the living room, stopping short at the sight of Mitch.

He scrambled to his feet when Carol came in. "Now that reinforcements are here, I should finish my unpacking. Maybe when you're feeling better, you can give me a tour of the area." He wiggled his eyebrows and rolled his eyes. "Rosa would like that."

I couldn't help laughing, and the experience felt strange. I hadn't laughed since Nick had died.

Carol walked with Mitch to the door, then returned to fling herself into the chair where he'd been sitting.

"What a perfectly mah-velous man," she said. "Thank God for making me short and fat, or I'd be a nymphomaniac for sure!"

"Don't you ever think of anything but sex?" I tried to sound appropriately shocked but found myself laughing again at her lascivious expression.

"Hyperbole, I assure you," she said with a sigh. "My bark

is worse than my bite. I'll just have to resign myself to taking more cold showers."

I hugged her, knowing she was trying to keep things light for my sake. "I'm sorry to drag you away from your family again. I really am fine, now that I've eaten. Go home. You've been away too much already on my account."

I picked up the tray and carried it into the kitchen. Carol trailed along behind me.

"Away from my family. Ha! That's a good one. Sam is neck-deep in tax forms, Jillian has a phone growing from one ear, and Trevor doesn't realize there is life beyond Nintendo. But you don't fool me, Alex Garrison. You're just trying to get rid of me so you can sneak that gorgeous man over from next door as soon as I'm gone."

I unloaded the dishes from the tray. "My dear Carol, it may have slipped your attention, but not everyone is as oversexed as you are."

She ignored my jibe, opened the container on the kitchen table and sampled its contents. "Ummm, good brownies! Who made them?"

She munched contentedly while I loaded the dishwasher.

"Lila Stanislaus. I was over there earlier today, and she sent them home with me." I filled the kettle and set it on the stove to boil for tea. "Tom gave me the name of a psychic near Orlando Nick was going to visit last week. I'm driving there tomorrow to see what I can find out from her about Nick's accident."

"You're kidding?" Carol stood staring with a brownie suspended midway to her mouth.

"No, I'm absolutely serious."

A look of apprehension flitted across Carol's face.

"Don't worry," I said. "Nick may not have gone there. And even if he did, his visit might mean nothing. Whatever the outcome, the trip will get me out of the house and give me some breathing room to sort things out."

I set my jaw, silently daring Carol to try to talk me out of it.

She must have seen my resolve because she returned her attention to the brownies.

Just as the kettle began to whistle, the telephone rang.

"That's probably Rosa, calling back," I said. "Pour the water in the teapot while I answer it, will you?"

Expecting Rosa's cheerful voice, I picked up the phone.

"Dr. Garrison?" an unfamiliar voice asked.

"Yes." I grew cold, wondering if the voice on the other end of the line was the crazy caller who'd demanded the Gideon file.

"This is Max with security at the university. I called Dr. Donahue's house and was told I could reach her here, too. Could both of you come to the campus? Your offices have been broken into, and we need to know what, if anything, is missing."

"We're on our way."

I replaced the receiver, and a familiar chill took hold of my body once more as I relayed the message to Carol.

"This is too much." I shivered from the cold. "How much more do I have to take?"

For once at a loss for words, Carol didn't answer.

I sat at my desk, surveying the chaos around me with a dreadful sense of *déjà vu*. Every file folder had been pulled from my filing cabinets and its contents dumped on the floor. All of my books had been knocked from the shelves. They lay heaped on the floor with their covers spread like the wings of injured birds. My desk had been ransacked and its contents emptied.

Carol's office was in the same state as mine, as were Moira Rafferty's and Emmett Nyagwa's. The only difference among the four ruined offices was the small memo pad positioned neatly in the center of my desk with the name *Gideon* written on the top page in neat block letters. Although nothing appeared to be missing from the offices, several of Emmett Nyagwa's valuable West African artifacts had been smashed beyond repair.

When Carol and I had first arrived at the Arts and Letters

Building, we found Moira and Emmett shouting at one another in the lobby. A security guard stood nervously nearby, looking unsure whether to intervene.

"Don't think I don't know why my artwork was ruined." Emmett spoke between tightly clenched teeth. "It isn't just coincidence tomorrow is the vote on the multicultural curriculum."

"Are you accusing me . . ." Moira's question disintegrated into a sputter. "My office was wrecked, too!"

"Yes, a very convenient alibi, particularly since you've lost nothing," Emmett said. "What I have lost is irreplaceable."

He sank into a chair in the lobby, holding his head in his hands as if fearing it might slip from his shoulders if he released it.

I went to him and placed my arm around his sagging shoulders, while Carol attempted to cool Moira's fiery temper.

"I'm sorry about your artwork, Emmett," I said, "but no one on this faculty would do such a thing. There has to be some reason the four of us were targets."

He looked up in surprise. "Your office, too?"

I nodded. "And Carol's."

He stood, squared his broad shoulders, and took both my hands in his. "Forgive my anger. This curriculum issue has all of us at the flashpoint. What I have lost is art of great value, but it is nothing beside the loss of your brother. I must learn to keep things in perspective."

His gentle dignity reminded me why I admired the man.

With Carol at her side, Moira approached us with her hand extended. "I'm sorry, Emmett. We've all been under a great strain recently, and I'm not known for my sweet disposition, even under the best of circumstances."

Emmett nodded coolly, ignoring her outstretched hand. They were still adversaries in the curriculum debate, regardless of who had vandalized our offices.

Carol and I had left them to go off to our respective offices to assess the damage. When we returned to the lobby, Dean Koenig had arrived.

"I have the campus security police and the city police both trying to find a common thread," he announced. "My staff will be running a computer search for all students presently taking classes from you four. I suspect the theft of exams might be the motive."

When I reported the name from the memo pad on my desk, Dean Koenig said he would expand the computer search for any student named Gideon.

As I returned once again to the shambles of my office, I feared that, although Dean Koenig might come up with a few students whose schedules included all four professors and might even turn up a Gideon or two, the senseless destruction around me was not the work of students out to steal exam papers. Midterms had been graded and returned over a week ago, and finals were still six weeks away. Many professors had not yet compiled their final exams.

No, whoever had wrecked our offices had been looking for something, and, like those who had vandalized Nick's condo, they'd lashed out angrily when it wasn't found. The residue of that rage hung in the air like a fine mist.

"Dr. Garrison." Kevin McDermott, my teaching assistant, stood in the doorway.

"Kevin, what are you doing here?"

"I saw the police cars from my dorm window." He surveyed the office, shaking his head in disbelief. "Why would anyone do this?"

He entered the room and began picking up the strewn books and papers.

"I have no idea," I said wearily. "Dean Koenig thinks it was a student looking for exams, but I don't think that's likely."

"Is anything missing?"

I scanned the chaos. "Not that I can tell."

I rose from my desk and began helping Kevin replace books on the shelves.

"There's really nothing here but lecture notes and resource materials," I said. "All the exams in my files are essay exams, so advance copies wouldn't be very helpful. The thief would still have to study."

Kevin removed the heavy volumes of Shelby Foote's history of the Civil War from my arms and placed them on the shelves beside the door. "You're all done in, and you don't need this on top of all you've been through. Why don't you go home? I can re-shelve your books and reconstruct your files before you come back to work next week."

"But—"

"This office is the last place you should be now."

I sank into my desk chair, observing my teaching assistant with new appreciation. Kevin, ruggedly good-looking with a spate of freckles across his nose that reminded me of Nick as a child, was a cut above the average teaching assistant. At thirty-something, close to my age, he was older and more mature than most assistants, in addition to being intelligent, well-mannered, and now, as I discovered, thoughtful as well.

I shook my head. "Cleaning all this up would be above and beyond the call of duty. I can't ask you to do that."

"You didn't. I volunteered, didn't I?"

A boyish smile wreathed his face, and I struggled not to weep at his kindness. I would accept his offer because I didn't have the emotional energy to deal with the chaos around me.

"Thank you, Kevin. I find myself deeper in your debt every day." My mind still reeled, wondering who'd done the deed, and I wanted to be alone with my thoughts. "Why don't you just leave this until tomorrow? Maybe it will seem less ghastly in daylight."

He set down the load of books in his arms. "Whatever you say. Just promise you won't worry about your office. I'll have it back in shape by the time you get back to work next week."

He closed the door softly behind him as he left.

A week from tomorrow would be the end of my bereavement leave. I despaired at the task of pulling the pieces of my shattered life back together in so short a time. Swiveling my chair, I gazed across the moonlit bay and picked out the outline of

Nick's condominium among the monoliths that edged the skyline.

Carol might think I was paranoid, but I knew that whoever had broken into these offices was the same person who had made the phone call demanding the Gideon file, the same one who had trashed Nick's apartment, the same one who had sent the blood-red sympathy bouquet to my house, and possibly even the same one who had driven Nick off Interstate Four to his death.

If the same person hadn't been responsible for all those things, then they had all been coincidence. I didn't believe in coincidence.

Who was this Gideon and what was he searching for? If I knew the answers to those questions, I could begin to make some sense of Nick's death. I needed to find Gideon to find answers.

As I sat staring into the blackness of the night, a cold tentacle of fear reached out, traced down my spine, and gripped my heart. Whoever Gideon was, he already knew me, and he knew where I lived.

I stumbled to my feet, turned out the light on my desk, and locked the door on the chaos. Kevin could deal with my office in the morning. I was going to seek out Gideon.

I was going to pay a visit to Bella Ionescu in Cassadega.

Eight

I waited until mid-morning the next day before starting out for Cassadega, hoping to miss going-to-work traffic. The late start gave me time to call Tom and Carol with my plans. Tom seemed resigned to my going, but Carol tried once more to talk me out of it.

"I give up," she finally said, "but if you must go, at least call to make sure the woman's going to be there. Maybe she's out of town, and you'll have made a long trip for nothing."

"I don't plan to take more than a few minutes of her time. Besides, I'd rather see her reactions firsthand, not give her time to plan what she's going to say. If she isn't there, maybe a neighbor can tell me where to reach her."

"She'll probably be there," Carol said. Satire dripped from her words. "If she's what she claims to be, she has to know you're coming."

I gathered my map and sunglasses and locked the deadbolt on the front door. As I was backing out of the driveway, I searched the house next door for signs of Mitch Lawton, but the shades of Rosa's house were still drawn.

Driving across the causeway and bridges that spanned Tampa Bay, I experienced again the disorientation that had hounded me since Nick's death. The brilliance of the autumn day was a strange companion to my grief, mocking my loss. I derived no satisfaction from the beauty of the drive across the lone strip of land flung across the bay's wide expanse, the harshness of its asphalt lanes softened by cabbage palms, pampas grass, and banks of oleanders.

Once on Interstate Four, I inserted Dvořák's Slavic dances in the tape player and tried to sort through all that had happened over the past few days.

My formerly quiet but satisfying life of teaching, research, and time with friends no longer existed. Death, violence, and destruction dominated my existence, along with too many apparent coincidences and unanswered questions. There was the question of Nick's death, an unlikely accident, and the ransacking of his condo. Nothing of value had been taken, so I couldn't believe robbery as a likely motive, and the unrestrained destruction of everything he owned had seemed too intense, too personal to be random.

I pondered whether the same person had broken into the four offices at the university. Why those particular offices? The rooms were not contiguous, so what was the connection? It and the mysterious Gideon continued to elude me.

Glaring sunlight, the stress of driving in heavy traffic, and efforts to find a common thread among a muddle of information took their toll. I detected the onset of a migraine.

Just past Lakeland, I pulled into a rest area and drank a cup of vile-tasting vending machine coffee. My medication, as always, was in my pocket, but I dared not take it and drive. Caffeine and relaxation techniques would have to provide relief.

I bought a second cup of coffee, climbed a grassy rise to one of several covered picnic tables, and settled there to wait for the pounding in my left temple to abate.

A few cars and minivans, loaded with families headed to Disney World, had also stopped at the rest area. A small girl and boy played tag among the picnic tables, working off the energy pent up after long miles in the family car.

They reminded me of Nick and myself at that age and how we'd played together. We had relied almost solely upon each other for friendship the first dozen years of our lives. Insecure and tentative about trusting others, we had felt keenly the differences that set us apart from other children our age. We had no father at home, and our mother, while providing us with food, clothing, and shelter, had been physically present but emotionally distant, never loving us, incapable of loving even herself.

My mother had been a lonely, frightened woman, lacking in self-esteem and inhibited by an emotionally crippling religious fundamentalism. Her job as librarian had provided her with the security she had never been able to attain from her religion or her relationships. If she had not found happiness in her work, at least she had found order. With her Dewey Decimal System, her library rules, and time schedules, she handled any situation that arose. Nick and I, her creative, imaginative children, didn't conform to those rules and categories. We were the bane of her existence.

Ours had been a paradoxical childhood. On the one hand had been our mother, a woman who consecrated her home and life to frugality, practicality, and emotional restraint, whose only recorded flight of fancy had been naming us after Russian royalty.

On the other hand had been the part that formed us as much as, if not more than, our mother's influence, the hours Nick and I spent in the library, immersed in fiction, while Mother worked. Somehow we had learned, possibly through books like *The Secret Garden* and *Anne of Green Gables,* what it was to love and be loved and that love needn't come from parents in order to be real.

As we grew into our teens, Carol had rescued me from solitude, and Nick had found his niche on the school newspaper and at the *Courier,* where he'd worked after school and on Saturdays. He remained mostly a lone wolf but a contented one. He had joined the *Courier* staff full-time after college and went on to win a Pulitzer Prize for his coverage of the ethnic conflicts in Bosnia.

Tears oozed from beneath my closed lids. There would be no more stories filed by Nick Garrison.

I stood and stretched, rolling my head in a circular motion to ease the tension in my neck and shoulders. As I walked back to my car, I spotted a gray sedan with tinted windows parked at the opposite end of the rest area. The car looked exactly like the one that had circled the cul de sac in front of my house a few days after Nick had died.

Carol was right, I thought, feeling foolish over the rush of fear the vehicle caused me. I was paranoid. Hundreds of cars like that one traveled Florida's crowded highways every day.

I climbed back into my car and fastened the lap belt. The shoulder belt on my Toyota engaged automatically when I started the engine. I needed to check the map for the exit number for Cassadega before starting out again, but when I leaned toward the glove compartment, the seat belt pulled taut, restraining me from reaching it.

Like a flashbulb exploding, a picture clicked in my mind. I shook my head to clear the troubling image, but it held fast. Confused and frightened, I turned off the ignition and gripped the wheel, trying to blot out the picture, but the logic of it, a credible explanation for my brother's uncharacteristic behavior, would not let go.

I pictured Nick driving down the interstate and realizing he was in danger. He leaned toward the unlocked glove compartment for his gun, but his seat belt prevented him from reaching it. In my mind's eye, I watched Nick unclasp the combined lap and shoulder harness of his American-made car and saw the seat belt retract, but before Nick could reach his weapon, he was forced by his pursuer onto the shoulder of the road. His car overturned, rolling in terrible slow motion in my mind.

I replayed the scene again, trying to make sense of what my imagination had conjured up, and found too many blanks in the picture with no *who,* no *why.* Then I glimpsed myself in the rearview mirror: a wild-eyed woman with disheveled hair and flushed cheeks. I had news for Carol. Not only was I paranoid, I feared I was stark, staring crazy—or if not now, I soon would be, unless I found answers to my questions about Nick's death.

I removed the map from the glove compartment, located the exit number for Cassadega, then started the car once more. As I merged back into traffic on the interstate, I hoped Bella Ionescu would have some answers.

The gray sedan pulled into traffic behind me. It was probably heading for Disney World. My mind returned to Nick and the void his death had left in my life.

Most people who are not twins have little idea of the connectedness twins share. When we were eight, I broke my ankle jumping out of a camphor tree. Nick had walked with a limp until my cast came off. His limp hadn't been an affectation. His ankle, like mine, had ached from the injury. Maybe that connectedness explained the numbness and disorientation I'd suffered since Nick's death. A part of me was dead, too.

The road became more congested the closer I came to Disney World, but the tourist traffic thinned after I passed through Orlando, with its placid lakes, green stretches of parks, and art deco skyscrapers. I followed the interstate north across the broad St. John's River.

At the Cassadega exit, I turned onto a narrow, winding, two-lane road that meandered for a few miles through uninhabited woods. A strange stillness pervaded the landscape. Mine was the only vehicle on the road, and although I saw dwellings, I saw no people. Ancient oaks and thick shrubs crowded the roadway so that, even at noon, the narrow highway was deep in shade.

When I came over a rise in the road, a cluster of buildings and the sprawling Spiritualist Convention Center, whose huge sign advertised a psychic medium on duty (inquire within), spread before me.

Only a few ordinary-looking young people walked the empty street, and the tiny community seemed like any other small settlement tucked away off the main roads, with the exception of numerous signs in the windows of shops and houses announcing the availability of psychics and open readings.

As I drove slowly along the abbreviated business district, I was struck by the town's unearthly quiet—like Brigadoon, suspended in time.

I drove on toward the first through-street, intending to turn around and return to the bookstore for directions, but when I reached the corner, the sign indicated I'd found Macy Avenue. I turned onto the narrow road that ran downhill, reading names on mailboxes as I passed. Where the street began to rise once more, I discovered the name I was looking for.

I turned into the driveway of the neat, white clapboard house with a deep, broad front porch nestled among tall azaleas. Beside the porch, a woman on her hands and knees weeded a bed of Gerbera daisies. Tiny and fragile, with birdlike bones, she wore her thick white hair cropped in a pixie cut. A pink smock covered her polyester slacks and cotton blouse. At the sound of my car on the gravel, she stood, brushed dirt from her hands and knees, and waited for me to approach.

I climbed from behind the wheel and followed the brick walkway, neatly lined with low junipers, to where the woman stood, studying me with eyes the color of seawater.

"Bella Ionescu?"

"I am Bella." A strong Eastern European accent colored the woman's words.

"I'm—"

"You are Alexandra Garrison. I thought you might be coming."

Bella started up the porch steps, leaving me standing on the walkway, motionless with surprise.

"Well, do not stand there in the hot sun. Come up and sit down in the shade."

I followed her up the stairs. "Forgive me, but your . . . your gift is truly remarkable."

"My gift? Oh," Bella laughed, a crystal sound like water tumbling over smooth stones. "You misunderstand. I saw your brother's picture in the paper." Her expression turned sad and her green eyes clouded. "I am very sorry, my dear."

She motioned toward a cane-backed rocking chair, asking me

to sit, and eased herself into a second one. "It is not my 'gift,' as you call it, that told me about you. Your brother's obituary said he had only one survivor, his sister Alexandra. You look very much like him, and that is how I recognized you."

"Then he did come to see you?"

"Yes, he was here, and that is how I knew you would come. Your brother was a man of many questions. That was how he earned his living. And if you are like him, you, too, have many questions."

"Oh, yes, I have entirely too many questions."

"Well," Bella stood up, "you have had long ride, and it is lunchtime. It is not good to ask 'too many questions' on an empty stomach. You sit and rest from your journey, and I will bring us sandwiches and tea."

I started to decline, then remembered my fainting spell from the day before. "Thank you. A sandwich and tea would be very nice."

An unexpected peacefulness descended on me on Bella's porch. A light breeze cooled the noonday heat, and the only sounds were mourning doves, calling to one another in the surrounding woods, and the wind rustling in the trees. No traffic passed on Macy Avenue, and no neighbors were visible in the tiny shuttered homes across the way. I felt as if the delightful Bella and I were the only two people on earth.

Bella was nothing like what I had imagined. I'd been expecting an aging hippie with long hair, ironed straight and secured Indian-style by a headband, dressed in a tie-dyed granny dress, puka beads, and sandals. Bella could be anyone of thousands of charming grandmothers retired to Florida.

She returned with sandwiches, sliced breast of chicken and crisp romaine lettuce on homemade whole-grain bread, and tall glasses of iced tea. While we ate, Bella chatted about her flowers and her fall vegetable garden, and for the first time since Nick had died the knots of tension and pain eased within me.

When we finished the sandwiches, Bella brought out another

plate, heaped with cookies plump with raisins and macadamia nuts. I ate three.

"It is good for you to eat." Bella's sea-green eyes twinkled. "You have not eaten well for a while, yes?"

My eyes widened in surprise, and I nodded.

"Again, it is not my gift that tells me, but my memories. I, too, have lost loved ones, and I know the empty feeling."

I returned her smile and rocked gently in the cane-backed chair, sipping iced tea and absorbing the serenity of my surroundings like dry ground soaks up water. As I sat, I became more curious about this woman I had driven so far to see.

"Where did you live before you came here, Bella?"

The little woman reached into a sewing basket at her feet and pulled out a shuttle and a spool of fine thread. While she talked, her fingers flew, tatting out delicate lace as her voice spun out her story.

"I lived until I was young woman in Romania. My family was what you call gypsies, and we traveled in caravan across country. My father was blacksmith and my mother told fortunes. I had seven brothers and sisters. When Hitler's SS came, we were all taken to concentration camp."

She rolled back her sleeve, exposing a tattooed number, its dark ink an obscene stain on her pale forearm.

"Of all my family, only I come out alive. So I come to this country to escape memories. I work for a while with circus, telling fortunes like my mother, but it is hard life and a sad one. There is much in the future is better not to know. The present is trouble enough."

She seemed about to say something more about the future but apparently thought better of it and went on with her story.

"So I leave circus and go to work in department store, selling ladies dresses. When time to retire, I take pension and come to Cassadega. Here I sometimes help police find missing children. Also, here I am not—what you call it—a freak?"

I gazed out over the well-cut lawn, the beds of carefully

tended flowers, and the cool depths of the sheltering forest. "I think you've found a bit of paradise here."

Bella patted my hand, reminding me of Rosa Myers. "But you did not come to hear of me."

I set down my glass and wiped my hands nervously on a paper napkin. "I'm trying to understand how and why my brother died. Much about his accident makes no sense, so I'm trying to piece together the last few days of his life. Can you tell me why Nick came to see you?"

She shrugged. "Your brother was searching for someone, that is all I know. He did not say the name, but he brought a man's cap, a military hat made of mottled fabric—"

"Camouflage?"

"Yes, that is the word. He brought the hat to me because, you see, if I hold article that belongs to someone, it tells me about that person."

My pulse quickened. "What did the hat tell you?"

"That the man your Nick sought was dead."

"Is that what you told Nick?"

Bella nodded solemnly. "When he heard, he had all he wanted to know. But I tell him one thing more."

Chill bumps rose on my arms. "What else?"

Bella shook her head slowly, and salt tears ran down her cheeks from eyes the color of the sea. "I tell him he must take great care, that he, too, was in much danger. But my warning was not enough. It did not save him."

Her words dissolved into a low, moaning keen, an eerie sound that made the hair rise on the back of my neck.

I stood to leave, sorry to have upset the lovely old lady and to have shattered the serenity I'd found there. But I had another question to ask.

"Did my brother mention anyone named Gideon?"

Bella seemed not to hear the question. She looked up through her tears. "I am only one to come out alive, so I come to this country, but now is not safe here either."

Her words made no sense, and, not wanting to upset her further, I thanked her for lunch and extended my hand. When Bella stood and grasped it, a sensation like a small electric shock coursed through me.

Bella's eyes widened as she gripped my hand. "Beware, beautiful Alexandra. You also are in great danger."

"What kind of danger?"

"They come for you, too."

I assessed her in alarm, wondering if the woman was crazy after all. After disengaging my hand from Bella's firm grip, I hurried to my car. I had enough worries already. I was anxious to put Cassadega and Bella's prophecies behind me.

Backing onto Macy Avenue, I glanced back to see Bella, kneeling in the same spot, tending her Gerbera daisies, that she had occupied when I arrived, creating the disturbing illusion that our meeting had never occurred.

Nine

As I drove back through the tiny Spiritualist settlement and down the narrow winding road toward the interstate, the passing scenery registered only on the periphery of my consciousness while I wrestled with the significance of the information Bella had given me.

Bella had been a nebulous character. She hadn't appeared untruthful, but her mystical, otherworldly quality, combined with her bizarre behavior at the end of our visit, made a pragmatist like me doubt the substance of her words.

Bella had spent her early adult years in the horror of a Nazi death camp, had lost her entire family, and had moved to a strange, new land. She might have been mentally and emotionally unbalanced by her experiences, and I wondered whether I dared believe anything she'd said. Everything, even the account of Nick's visit, could have been the fabric of an old woman's tortured imagination, constructed from newspaper pictures and stories.

I was not a believer in what Carol called New Age pseudo-psychobabble, and I endeavored to analyze my visit with Bella. What had caused the jolt of current that ran up my arm at her touch? Static electricity from her polyester slacks, or something else?

I entered a stream of heavy traffic on the interstate, noting the contrast of the crowded highway to Cassadega's deserted streets. Bright sunlight shimmered off the rear windshield of the car ahead of me, and, too late, I realized the intensity of the glare had triggered my dormant migraine. Blossoms of light exploded in my head, and my vision blurred as unbearable pain shot through my left temple. I would never make it home in this condition.

At the Altamonte Springs exit, I turned off the interstate and circled around to a Hilton Inn where I had attended a conference on Florida history a few months before. I had no choice but to take my medicine and sleep before I was in any shape to drive home. A gray sedan with tinted windows followed me into the Hilton parking lot, but it was a common model, and I was too ill to be curious or afraid.

When I entered the elegant, softly lit hotel, the presence of so many people was comforting after my visit to Cassadega, which had left me with an overriding uneasiness. Professional men and women in suits; tourists in neon-colored shorts, theme-park T-shirts, and thong sandals that flip-flopped as they walked; and children in mouse ears mingled together in the lushly carpeted lobby.

I waited behind a group of German visitors at the reception desk, then registered for a room in the Towers, where experience informed me I would find everything needed for an overnight stay.

My visit to Cassadega still preyed on my mind as I rode the elevator to the seventh floor, and Bella's final warning echoed like a sinister mantra through my pounding head: *they come for you, they come for you . . .*

Shaking from the pain and nausea of the migraine, along with anxiety from the morning's encounter with the strange little Romanian, I took comfort in my room's proximity to the concierge's desk. After fumbling in my purse for change, I purchased a diet cola from the machine across the hallway, then inserted my room card into the door lock.

Inside the spacious room, I drew the drapery on the bright light streaming through the large picture window overlooking the interstate, turned on a bedside lamp, and slipped out of my clothes and shoes. Dressed in the soft, one-size-fits-all terry robe with its Hilton emblem that I found in the closet, I washed down my medicine with cola and collapsed in a broad armchair, waiting for the pills to do their work.

Again, I tried to make sense of what I had learned from Bella. According to her, a woman who was a possibly unreliable source, Nick had visited her, searching for someone, probably a military man, whom Bella believed was now dead. She claimed to have seen danger in Nick's life and to have issued a warning so vague, if valid, it could have meant the danger of a car accident and nothing more.

Also, if Bella was to be believed, "they" were coming for me, too, whoever "they" were. Bella seemed to have them confused with Hitler's SS who had carried away her family, but she had made no connection there with Nick.

I still had no explanation for Nick's death. And none for Gideon.

The pain in my head eased, and with its passing, drowsiness encroached. I turned back the bedspread on the king-sized bed and crawled between the smooth, freshly laundered sheets, concluding that nothing Bella had told me was of any use. I knew no more than I had before, and I could almost hear Carol saying, "I told you so."

Ill and frustrated, I turned out the light, snuggled beneath the covers, and went immediately to sleep.

Hours later I awakened in the dark room, disoriented, unsure where I was. I heard pounding, and it took a moment to realize it was no longer my head throbbing. Someone was beating on my door.

"Who is it?" I called out, still half-asleep.

"I've come for the Gideon file," a muffled voice answered.

I shrugged into the terry robe and stumbled to the doorway in the dark. Anxious to confront the mysterious Gideon and too groggy from sleep and medicine to be cautious, I slipped the security catch off the door and flung it open.

No one was there.

The long hallway was deserted, and the concierge was not at her desk.

I secured the door and fumbled to turn on the bedside lamp. Deep sleep and medication left me feeling hungover, and I decided I must have dreamed I'd heard someone.

Slowly my mind cleared. The clock on the television console read nine forty-five, and my migraine had left a ravenous hunger in its wake. I called room service for a club sandwich and house salad, then phoned Carol.

"My God, Alex, where've you been? I was ready to call out the National Guard to look for you, I've been so worried. I thought you'd be home before dinner. Now it's almost ten, and when you didn't call—"

"I'm sorry I worried you, but I'm okay. And if you'll calm down, I'll tell you about Bella."

Anxious to hear her opinion of Bella's statements, I told her everything about my visit.

"What do you think?" I asked when I'd finished.

"She sounds more than a bit loony. Nothing she said about Nick makes much sense. Do you suppose he only went there to do a story on her? She'd make a great feature."

"It's possible, except Nick told Tom she wasn't newspaper business. Uh-oh, I promised Tom I'd call him."

"Don't worry, I'll give him a call—"

"First, tell me what's happening on campus. Have they discovered who vandalized our offices?"

"The computer came up with two dozen students who are taking classes from the four of us this semester. The police are questioning each of them, but frankly, Alex, I've seen the list, and there's nobody I can believe as a suspect."

"For instance?"

She giggled. "Can you imagine Peregrine Smyth-Phillips in his bow tie, blazer, and Reeboks daring to perform such an act?"

Peregrine, better known as Perry, was the campus intellectual and eccentric, with an IQ off the scale and the assertiveness of a noodle. A wet paperbag, much less a locked office door, would be an effective barrier to that timid soul.

"What about Gideon?" I asked.

"The computer came up with a blank on that one. Checked first, middle, and last names. Koenig showed some interesting initiative when he had them check the names of hometowns and places of birth, but even then they came up with zip."

I sighed with frustration. "So we're back to square one."

"And on the curriculum committee as well. Dean Koenig announced that with the disruption caused by the break-ins, now is a bad time for making major decisions, so he's postponed the vote on the curriculum changes."

"I needn't have felt guilty about missing today's vote, then." Conflicting emotions washed through me. Now I would be able to cast my vote, but I had also been looking forward to having the issue resolved.

"There's more," Carol said. "In the interest of faculty camaraderie, which has suffered major casualties in the fallout over this curriculum issue, the dean's holding a little party for the arts and letters faculty, and their significant others, next Saturday night."

"Count me out." I dreaded the grand scale affair the dean's little party would turn out to be. "I'm not up to schmoozing. You know I don't like faculty get-togethers, even in the best of times."

"Nonsense, ducky, it'll do you good. You could even bring along Rosa Myers' gorgeous gift she so kindly set on your doorstep—"

"What?"

"Mitch Lawton, of course. A party would be good for him, too. Give him a chance to meet people. I can tell you right now Moira will love him. If you don't want him, she'll be delighted to take him off your hands."

"Good grief, Carol, he's not mine to start with!"

"Promise me you'll at least think about going to the party?" Carol's voice had taken on the pleading note I could never resist.

"I promise I'll think about it. I should be home around lunchtime tomorrow. I'll call you then."

When room service brought my supper, I settled back and watched television while I ate. Wide awake after my afternoon of sleep, I watched the late news and waited for the movie that followed, an old black-and-white classic that reminded me of the movies I'd loved as a child at Aunt Bibi's.

Aunt Bibi had been my childhood link to reality. People who knew both women found it hard to believe Bibi and my mother were sisters. Bibi had been everything Mother was not: extroverted, generous, loud, loving, uninhibited, and, in my mother's eyes at least, more than slightly scandalous.

Nick and I had adored her, and although our mother seldom allowed us to visit her, for two glorious weeks every summer of our childhood, she relented and permitted us to stay with Aunt Bibi at her beachfront home on Longboat Key. For us, it was two weeks in heaven.

When Aunt Bibi's air force husband had been killed over Germany in World War II, she had invested his life insurance in the small beach cottage. Then she had taken a job as a cocktail waitress at one of the beach's watering holes, a rustic establishment frequented by characters who would have been comfortable bending elbows with Hemingway's Key West crowd. There, Bibi earned good money and the undying disapproval of my puritanical mother.

I missed Aunt Bibi. Unlike my mother, Bibi had managed to live life to its fullest. When I was in my teens, Bibi had married a customer from her bar, a wealthy widower from Sarasota, who owned a Cadillac dealership. She had moved from her humble cottage to his palatial home on St. Armand's Key, but they seldom stayed there. They had traveled the United States and the world, inseparable and incredibly happy.

Just over a year ago, a car crash in Greece killed them both, and while the money and the St. Armand's house had gone to his children, Aunt Bibi left her cottage at Longboat to Nick and me.

The opening titles began to roll for *Heaven Knows, Mr. Allison,* and I lost myself in its South Pacific setting, pushing Nick, Bella, Gideon, and everything else from my mind.

I had mixed feelings as I prepared lunch in my own kitchen the following day. Being home again felt good, but it also brought back the pain of Nick's death and the irritation of unanswered questions. Since I was on bereavement leave for a week, I decided some time at the beach cottage would help me come to terms with all that had happened in the past few days.

I walked into the living room to switch on the weather channel. Although October was usually clear and mild, hurricane season didn't end until December, and I wanted to check the tropical forecast before heading for the beach. I turned the volume up loud enough to be heard in the kitchen while I finished lunch.

I was walking back toward the foyer when something out of place caught my eye. Opened wide in the center of the glass coffee table was my mother's Bible, a pulpit-sized, leather-bound volume with pages like tissue paper.

I had always kept it on the top shelf behind the television, and I hadn't moved it. I kept it only for its record of family births and deaths going back a hundred years, and I was certain it hadn't been on the coffee table yesterday morning when I'd left for Cassadega. I trembled, realizing someone had been in my house while I was away.

Nervously, I checked doors and windows, finding them all locked. A cursory inspection of the other rooms showed everything in its accustomed place.

I tried to figure out how my unknown visitor had entered the tightly locked house and why he had placed the Bible so conspicuously in the middle of the room.

I approached the coffee table, intending to snatch up the Book and return it to its place, but I stopped short when a portion of the text caught my eye. The Bible lay open to the Book of Judges.

> *And they said to one another, Who hath done this thing? And when they inquired and asked, they said, Gideon, the son of Joash hath done this thing.*

Gideon had been in my house.

Ten

While my lunch lay untouched on the kitchen table, I grabbed up the telephone to call the police. I had dialed the first two digits when I slammed down the receiver in frustration. What would I have said? That I wanted to report a suspicious Bible? They'd think I was crazy. If I wanted them to believe me, I'd have to give them more than that.

I rechecked every door and window, searching in vain for any sign of forced entry or something missing that I could report stolen.

As I made another sweeping inspection of the house, I began to suspect Gideon had done more than leave the Bible out for me to find. A closet door I always left open had been closed, books in my study were arranged in a different order on my bookshelves, the contents of my bureau drawers had been shifted almost imperceptibly, and the Monet waterlilies print above my bed hung slightly askew.

Gideon was still searching for something, but what? The phantom file the anonymous caller and the voice outside my hotel room had requested? The evidence seemed clear to me, but how could I go to the police with such unsubstantial proof that an intruder had been in my house?

Whoever Gideon was, he was clever, covering his tracks so thoroughly that any complaint by me seemed not only groundless but bordering on hysterical. How could I expect anyone to take my fears seriously when even Carol, my closest friend, thought I was overreacting in my grief?

RELATIVE DANGER

I jumped as the phone sounded, then let it ring a few times before reluctantly answering it. My calls lately had meant bad news.

"Hello, how are you?" a vaguely familiar voice responded to my tentative hello.

I waited before speaking again, trying to identify the voice, until the caller saved me the trouble.

"It's Mitch, next door. Remember me?"

"Of course." I'd forgotten all about Rosa's renter.

"Mind if I drop over for a few minutes?"

I started to say I did mind but remembered his kindness a few days before. "That's fine. I'll be here."

I had taken only a few steps across the kitchen when the phone rang again. This time the caller, delivering a terse message in a strangely distorted voice, gave me no chance to speak.

"You still haven't given me what I want, but I'm giving you another chance. Meet me at the west entrance of Seaview Mall at ten forty-five tonight. If you're not there with the Gideon file, you'll live just long enough to regret it."

"Wait! Don't hang up! I don't know what you want."

"The Gideon file," the deformed voice snarled.

"How can I give you something if I don't know what or where it is?" I demanded.

"You're a smart lady, so I suggest you get busy and find it," the threatening voice hissed again. "And if you bring the police into this, you'll be responsible for the consequences."

"But how—" The connection broke, and I slammed down the receiver in frustration.

I trembled uncontrollably and clutched the edge of the kitchen counter to keep my legs from giving way beneath me. I hadn't recognized the voice, couldn't tell if it was male or female. All I could be certain of was the deadly menace in its tone.

I had to find out who this Gideon was. I had to know whether he was merely some perverted soul getting his kicks by making random telephone threats or if the caller, his demands for a mysterious file, and the vandalizing of my office were all somehow connected with Nick's death.

The obvious way to find out would be to meet him at ten forty-five as he'd demanded. I pictured the mall parking lot, dark and deserted, and I remembered horror stories of women abducted from such areas and their battered bodies found days or weeks later in distant orange groves. I couldn't chance a face-to-face meeting with a possible killer, no matter how desperate I was to know Gideon's face and motives.

"They come for you, too." Bella's warning sounded in my memory.

"If you're not there, you'll live just long enough to regret it," the caller's voice echoed.

I clapped my hands over my ears in a futile attempt to still the inner voices. I wanted to go to the police, but my story sounded so bizarre, so irrational, even to me, I was convinced no one else would find it credible.

More certain than ever that I needed to get away, I dumped my untouched sandwich into the trash bin and began gathering clothes and supplies for a stay at the beach. Longboat Key was less than two hours from home, far enough away, with any luck, to be free of Gideon and his threats.

Best of all, the cottage had no telephone.

Halfway through my packing, someone knocked at the French doors. Startled, my nerves already frayed by Gideon's intrusion and my threatening caller, my heart raced with fear, as I wondered if Gideon had returned. But when I approached the door in the dining room, I recognized Mitch. Again, I'd forgotten all about him.

"I won't come in. I've been trimming Rosa's hedges." He smiled his crooked grin and indicated his grimy, sweat-stained attire. "I hadn't seen you around and wanted to make sure you were okay."

I stepped out onto the deck, tweaked with remorse at having let Rosa down. She had told me Mitch had gone through a bad time and needed a friend, so what had I done? Wiped him completely from my mind since the night he had rescued me so gallantly from my kitchen floor. And now I was going to desert him again.

"I've been out of town." My mind still grappled with the fear that gripped me. "And I'm leaving again today until Saturday."

"Then I guess there's no point in inviting you to dinner this evening?" He didn't try to hide his disappointment.

His smile faded, and traces of dark circles were visible beneath his eyes, the imprint of sleepless nights. His entire body appeared suddenly weary and older.

I could hear Rosa berating me in her gentle, logical way: "So what are you doing to a nice young man who knows no one and needs company? Be friends with him, darling. What could it hurt?"

I longed to get away, but within that longing lay a reluctance to be alone. My thoughts and memories were too uncomfortable to be my only company, and the threat of Gideon, although it might not seem so to others, was all too real.

"Mitch," I hesitated, knowing how my suggestion might be interpreted. "I don't want you to get the wrong idea."

I paced across the room, groping for the right phrase. "I don't usually—"

He watched, his expression quizzical, as he waited for me to continue.

I took a deep breath and plunged ahead. "Rosa told me you'd recently lost someone close to you and you'd come here to recuperate, but I'm finding from my own experience it's not good to be alone all the time."

I was babbling like a teenager, and Mitch's crooked grin had returned.

I'd started it, so I figured I might as well finish. "So why don't you come to my cottage at the beach with me? That way neither of us will be alone. You'd have your own bedroom and bath, rustic but clean, and a stretch of beach that isn't strangled with motels and condominiums. But you'd have to do your share of the cooking."

Mitch's grin expanded wider as I spoke, and his weariness disappeared. Then his smile faded. "Aren't you taking a chance, inviting a stranger? How do you know I'm not an ax murderer?"

I laughed. "Rosa Myers has been anxious to get me married ever since we met, but even Rosa's not desperate enough to recruit ax murderers—yet."

Mitch's dark eyes reminded me of Nick, and when I spoke again, my tone was serious. "This invitation isn't something I usually do, but my whole life has been turned inside out the past week, so you can chalk my radical behavior up to that. I'd like some company, but I won't take offense if you say no."

Mitch wiped a grimy palm on the front of his shirt, then extended his hand. "I'll be happy to accept your invitation, but only on one condition—that I be allowed to do *all* the cooking, to earn my keep, so to speak."

Experiencing a strange mixture of relief and regret, I grasped his hand and shook it to seal the bargain. "Who can resist a man who cooks? I'd like to leave as soon as you're packed."

An hour later we were driving through southbound traffic, skirting St. Petersburg on the interstate bypass. When we reached the mouth of Tampa Bay, the gigantic span of the Sunshine Skyway Bridge rose above the waters before us. The golden cables of its twin suspension peaks shone in the autumn sunlight like giant celestial harps in the cloudless blue sky.

I flung a handful of quarters into the toll basket and drove onto the causeway approaching the high span. Oil tankers and cruise ships passed beneath its immense arch, following the channel that led east to the port of Tampa and west to the Gulf of Mexico.

"God, it's beautiful," Mitch said.

From the corner of my eye, I watched him taking in the diving pelicans, sailboats with their brightly colored spinnakers puffed full in the wind, and the slender lighthouse at the bay's mouth on Egmont Key.

As we started up the incline of the portion of the bridge that spanned the channel, I kept my eyes riveted to the road ahead. My knuckles turned white on the wheel as I fought against the compulsion to look to my right.

To the west of the new Skyway, up until just a few years ago, had been the horrifying manifestation of my worst nightmare. The original Sunshine Skyway Bridge, two separate spans, looking like toys built from a giant erector set, had stood there, but for the last twelve years of their existence only one span had been whole. At its apex, the western arch had gaped open where the entire center section had once been.

For those twelve years, I'd had to travel the eastern span of the old bridge to reach Aunt Bibi's, driving past the yawning space where the road ended in nothingness. When the new bridge was built, both spans were abandoned. Finally, a few years ago, the state allocated the necessary funds to demolish both old spans, but that soaring bridge with its gaping hole, like all the nightmares I'd had as a child, was etched forever in my memory.

My hands slipped on the steering wheel from the nervous perspiration that drenched my palms. As beautiful as the drive across the Skyway was, it was the part of the trip to Aunt Bibi's that I hated.

"Alex? You okay?" Mitch had abandoned the scenery and was studying me, the fear written on my face and the tension in my body.

"Over there, to your right," I said, "almost fifteen years ago, a huge tanker, the *Summit Venture,* was navigating through the channel, when a severe thunderstorm struck. The tanker was empty, and the force of the storm threw it against the supports of the bridge. The collision caused the center section to break loose and fall into the bay."

I inhaled a deep breath, trying to steady my voice and ease my irrational fear.

"The falling span took cars, trucks, and a bus down with it. Thirty-five people died that morning in the space of a few minutes. One man survived the plunge. Another managed to stop his car at the edge just in time."

By now I was trembling violently and breathing in short, tortured gasps. My heart pounded with panic, even though we had cleared the main span and were approaching the southern end of the Skyway.

"You'd better pull over." Mitch pointed to a rest area exit sign.

I turned off the road onto a narrow strip of landscaped causeway with picnic tables and restrooms. I parked the car, got out, and walked to the water's edge, where I stared off into the distance, avoiding the sight of the bridge.

Mitch followed and stood by silently, waiting for me to speak.

Slowly my breathing returned to normal, and the brisk offshore breeze dried the perspiration from my skin. Embarrassed by my loss of control, I turned to find Mitch watching me.

"Better?" he asked.

I nodded. "It's silly, letting the bridge affect me like that, but when I was a child, I had terrible nightmares of driving across such a bridge, one that would disappear beneath me, just as it did for all those people years ago. I'd wake up screaming, terrified, but Nick was always there . . ."

"You're not silly." He reached out to me, but something in my expression must have stopped him because he dropped his hands to his sides.

"I read in a book once," I said, "one that gave interpretations of dreams, that my dream was a manifestation of my fear that those I relied on were going to let me down when I needed them."

My words surprised me. I'd never shared my dream or its meaning with anyone, not even with Nick.

"The story of that broken span would be frightening to anyone," he said. "It reminds us how vulnerable we really are."

"And you?" I asked. "Does anything frighten you?"

"Oh, yes." His face contorted in a strange expression that held both anger and fear before it relaxed once more into his engaging smile. "If I went through my list of things that frighten me, we'd never make it to your cottage before dark."

He walked back to the car, and I followed him, still avoiding the sight of the bridge that loomed above the bay.

Eleven

I left the interstate, driving through downtown Bradenton and across the bridges of the Intracoastal Waterway. At Anna Maria Island, I turned south, traveling along the gulf beaches. The Gulf of Mexico sparkled like emeralds in the late afternoon sunlight, and on its jeweled surface, colorful windsurfers and wave runners glided close to the white sand beaches.

When I crossed the bridge onto Longboat Key, hedges of oleanders lined the road and the feathery leaves of Royal Poincianas and dense umbrellas of banyan trees shaded the landscaped lawns of resorts and condominiums from the sun's heat.

"This is fantastic," Mitch said. "Sure beats New York City as winter approaches."

His enthusiasm made me smile. "Sounds like damning with faint praise to me, but you ain't seen nothin' yet."

I slowed the car and turned into a driveway that wound through a forest of pines, fiddle-leaf figs, sea grapes, and palms to a small, one-story, board-and-batten cottage sprawled on the edge of a broad expanse of beach.

We couldn't see or hear the highway behind us, and before us the afternoon sun glinted off the white sands and jade green waters that stretched to the horizon.

As we carried our bags from the car, the crash of surf and the calls of seagulls filled the air. The soothing rhythms of the gulf began to ease the tension from my mind and body, and I experienced the same rush of excitement I had felt as a child every time I visited Aunt Bibi.

After opening windows and doors to the fresh salt breeze, I guided Mitch through the simple layout of the cottage. The living room and kitchen encompassed one large area, with windows and double doors that opened onto a deck built out among the dunes and sea oats, overlooking the water. From every window of that large common room, the Gulf of Mexico stretched into the distance, creating the illusion of a cabin of a ship at sea.

Memories waited everywhere I looked. On the wall above the sofa hung a twisted branch of driftwood, draped with fishnet. The collection of shells Nick and I had gathered as children was entwined in the netting. On the table by the double doors, next to a framed color photograph of two skinny youngsters nut brown from the sun, sat a huge conch shell on which Aunt Bibi had blown short trumpet blasts to call us from the beach to the dinner table.

Mitch stowed his bag in Nick's room, then began putting away the box of foodstuffs I had brought.

"Looks like we should go shopping soon, unless you want a dinner of mustard sandwiches, diet cola, and brownies," he called through the open doorway.

I stepped in off the deck, where I had moved the ancient but sturdy Adirondack chairs from the utility shed. "I've eaten worse, believe it or not."

I opened the doors of the pantry. "We also have pork and beans, tuna fish, and coffee, but we have to shop eventually, so might as well do it now. Then we can settle in for the rest of the time. Being here's like being on a desert island. I even had the phone taken out."

An unreadable expression raced across his features, then was gone. "What about emergencies?"

I gestured north and south of the cottage. "You can't see through the thick undergrowth, but there are houses on both sides, less than a hundred feet in each direction. And if anyone needs to reach me, the Longboat Key police know where I live."

With his back to me, he stowed away the last of the supplies.

When he spoke, his tone seemed strangely neutral. "Does anyone else know you're here?"

"Carol." I smiled at the thought. "I wouldn't dare leave town without telling her. Otherwise, she'd have the paramedics or the police beating down the doors of my house when she couldn't reach me. I told her I'd be back in time for Dean Koenig's faculty party Saturday night."

He grinned, again reminding me of Harrison Ford. "In that case, I suggest we do some serious shopping if I have that many days to exhibit my culinary skills."

We climbed back into my Toyota and drove south down the narrow key, occasionally glimpsing the gulf to our right and the Intracoastal Waterway on the left.

"What happens in a hurricane here?" Mitch asked.

"After the severe storms of the last few years, anyone with any sense will evacuate to shelters on the mainland. All the new construction, built on stilts with breakaway walls, should survive a minor storm surge, but if Longboat gets a direct hit, Aunt Bibi's cottage will be history."

I remembered that conversation later that evening, after a dinner of grilled fresh grouper, when we sat on the deck watching waves cresting into curls of white foam that caught the moonlight before crashing onto the silvered beach a few yards away.

The sand pulsed with the dormant power of the ocean and I shuddered, as I pictured it, rising up in a mighty surge and washing over the cottage where we sat. I had never considered the ocean a threat before, always feeling somehow strangely invincible when I sat at its edge, as if I might live forever.

Nick's death had changed all that.

I shivered again and turned to Mitch, who stared at the sea, his profile outlined against the night sky. I wondered what he was thinking and what kind of man the stranger at my side really was.

"Have you always lived in New York City?" I asked.

His gaze remained fixed on the water, and I could not see his eyes.

"Ever been there?" he asked.

I shook my head, but he didn't see me. "Only passing through one summer on my way to visit Rosa and Herman. Nick was the traveler in the family."

I waited, but when Mitch volunteered no more to the conversation, I tried again to draw him out. "How do you know Rosa and Herman?"

"Herman used to work with my father. They've been friends as long as I can remember."

His answers, short and to the point, discouraged any more questions.

We sat for close to an hour, watching the waves break on the beach, before he finally turned and spoke again. "Tell me about Nick."

"What's to tell? He was my twin brother, my friend, my only remaining relative." A yawning emptiness opened inside me every time I thought of Nick, frightening me with its blackness.

"They say when you lose someone it's good to talk about them, to remember, that as long as you have those memories, that person will never really die." Mitch's voice was soft, kind. "What do you remember most about Nick?"

I considered for a moment. "His sense of justice . . . and his courage. He was always so brave. Not reckless, but sure of himself."

Mitch nodded. "He must have been brave to have covered the stories he did."

I smiled, remembering. "I'm sure when others think of Nick's bravery, they recall his war coverage and the stories he wrote about organized crime, but I believe he was the bravest one summer day when we were nine years old."

Mitch stared at the waves before turning to me again. "I'm listening. Tell me about him."

"We were spending the day at the library—that's where our mother worked—downstairs in the basement in the children's section. Sometimes we read there all day, waiting for Mother to finish work."

"I can think of worse places to spend a summer day in Florida."

"I'm not complaining. We both loved books. Nick had brought an anatomy textbook from the adult section downstairs with him. That was during his I-want-to-be-a-doctor-when-I-grow-up phase, and he was learning Latin names for the parts of the body. When Mother came down on one of her breaks and found him with it, she was furious."

"Why?"

I scowled at the memory. "My mother had her own puritanical morality that said knowledge of the human body was corrupting to the nine-year-old mind. She decided Nicky had to be punished, so she shut him in a storage closet off the basement. It had no windows, and the overhead light fixture had a pull switch neither Nick nor I could reach."

"That was a harsh thing to do to a little kid." The neutrality in Mitch's voice clashed with the condemnation in his words.

"My mother was a harsh woman." My hands clenched in anger as I relived the helplessness and anguish I'd felt that day. "The closet door locked from the outside, and she took the key away with her. She told him he'd have to stay there all day to pay for his sin.

"I spent the day crouched against the door, crying. Nick, locked in that horrible, airless blackness, spent the whole time assuring me through the keyhole that he was okay."

I gripped the arms of the chair and my nails gouged the layers of old paint. "When Mother let him out that night, he was pale as a ghost, but he hadn't shed a tear. I believe that experience was one reason he chose the life he did. After that, Nick could never stand to be closed up, hemmed in. He wanted to be outdoors, traveling, always on the move."

Tears coursed down my cheeks. My itinerant brother was never coming home again. "Being locked in that closet is also why he wanted to be cremated and his ashes scattered to the wind. He couldn't stand the idea of his body closed up in a box underground."

Those ashes rested in an urn in my bedroom, waiting for me to commit them to the wind and water off Longboat Key, but I couldn't let Nick go until I'd found answers to the questions that surrounded his death.

"So, you see, when others reminisce about a courageous investigative reporter and war correspondent, I remember a stoic nine-year-old with wide eyes and a pale face, more worried about his sister than himself."

"I'd like to have known him," Mitch said.

"I wish you could have."

Afraid I had talked too much, I went inside, brewed a pot of tea, and carried the tea tray onto the deck, where Mitch sat, unmoving, studying the gulf. I poured his tea, and he grasped my hand as I passed him his cup.

"Your cure is working, Dr. Garrison. When Dexter, my partner, died, I thought I'd never be able to unwind again. Every muscle in my body was constantly on alert. Tonight I feel rested for the first time since he died, able to concentrate on something besides—"

Wariness flashed in his eyes, and he released my hand. "I owe you my thanks."

I settled back into my chair, cupping my hands around the warm china mug. "Wish I could take the credit, but it's this place. It always has that effect on people. Everyone, that is, except Burke. All this tranquility sent him scurrying for civilization as fast as his Gucci loafers would carry him."

My talkativeness astonished me. I'd never been so open with anyone but Nick. Either grief or Mitch Lawton's easy manner had loosened my tongue.

"Who's Burke?" he asked.

I couldn't keep the bitterness from my voice. "The man I almost married, until I realized I'd rather be single the rest of my life than married to the wrong man."

"And you've never found the right man?" Friendly interest colored his words.

I avoided his eyes. "I haven't been looking. Too badly burned by my poor judgment with Burke, I guess. Not that Carol hasn't tried to remedy my singleness. She has some kind of internal device that homes in on unattached men. She and Rosa are a lot alike that way."

"It must frustrate them you're so comfortable being single." He grinned at me over the rim of his cup.

"I suppose, but I have my work and my friends. I have a good life. At least I did until Nick died."

The emptiness was still there and the overwhelming feeling of loss, but now I could talk about Nick without weeping.

"And before Gideon," I added.

Mitch sat up and placed his cup on the tray. "Who's Gideon?"

Far removed from my vandalized office, the misplaced Bible, and the threatening phone calls, I began to think Carol was right, that I had been overreacting to everything that had happened. Maybe my fears were foolish.

"I don't know who Gideon is, but if I could find out, maybe I'd know the truth about Nick's death."

"I thought he died in a car accident."

"If it was an accident." I turned my chair away from the water to appeal to Mitch for an objective opinion. "You're a detective. Tell me what you think."

While the moon rose over the Australian pines, I related all that had happened since Carol and the highway patrolman had appeared at my door last week. He listened without interrupting, until I came to the part about my mother's Bible.

"Does anyone else have keys to your house?"

"Mrs. Baxter comes to clean every other week—" I stopped, embarrassed at not having thought of her myself. "She isn't due until next week, but she might have come yesterday while I was away, knowing I had all those people in for Nick's memorial service. It would be easy enough to check with her."

"Do it," he suggested.

"Mrs. Baxter may have moved the Bible, but what about the phone calls?" I described the call I had received after Nick had died and the one earlier in the day.

"Do you have something this caller wants?"

"No, nothing," I said. "The caller mentioned a file, but I don't have it. And everything Nick had was either with him when he died or in his apartment. Unless he left something with someone else, but that's not likely."

"Why not?"

"As twins, we shared a closeness most brothers and sisters don't have. Nick told me everything. If he had given something that important to someone else, he would have told me."

Unless he hadn't had a chance.

I remembered the book he was writing and his promise to tell me about it when he returned. How many other things would I never know now that Nick was dead?

"The call was probably a nuisance one," Mitch said. "People who make those calls often pick a page in the phone book at random or names from the newspaper. They go down the list until they find someone at home or, better yet, someone who reacts in a way that plays to the caller's sense of power."

I shuddered. "You mean they feed on fear?"

"Fear, outrage, any intense emotion. Indifference is what they can't stand. If someone hangs up without saying anything, the caller rarely tries that number again. The statement your caller made was provocative, encouraging an unsuspecting person to be drawn into a conversation, to ask questions. That's how these telephone terrorists get their thrills."

I was shaking my head before he finished. "But he, or she, didn't give me a chance to talk. He hung up before I could ask any more questions."

"Maybe he was interrupted. I arrested a guy like that once who'd placed hundreds of harassing calls from his desk at work."

I wasn't convinced. "Okay, the phone calls aside, what about the name Gideon on the memo pad, the sympathy card, and the open Bible?"

"You have an interesting pattern there, but it's circumstantial, nothing concrete."

He shifted in his chair and leaned toward me. I could see his grim expression in the moonlight.

"If this was my investigation," he said, "I'd have to say there's no real evidence of a crime, except the vandalized condo and offices. And those events could be totally unrelated. Equally important, without this elusive and possibly nonexistent file, there's no motive, no apparent reason for anyone to harm Nick or to threaten you."

I sighed, frustrated by his logic. "So, if it was your investigation, you'd drop the whole thing?"

Mitch grinned. "I didn't say that. I'd watch and wait to see if any hard evidence turns up."

"Great! If Gideon kills me, you'll have hard evidence of a murder. That's reassuring." Frustration laced my sarcasm.

His look sobered. "Try not to worry. Just let me know if anything else suspicious happens. In the meantime, I'll be right next door. I'll keep an eye on you."

A strange expression, like a spasm of pain, crossed his face, and he rose abruptly and paced to the water's edge. He shoved his hands in his back pockets and stood looking out to sea.

I set my cup down and followed him. "Forgive me. I know you're on leave, and I shouldn't have bothered you with my troubles."

He turned and took my hand and together we walked up the beach in the bright moonlight.

"You haven't done anything that needs forgiving," he said. "Offering to look out for you reminded me I wasn't able to look out for Dexter."

My grief recognized his. "You miss him, don't you?"

"We'd been partners for eight years. He was my closest friend, and I'm godfather to his three children."

We walked north through the sand. A night heron skittered

through the breaking waves ahead of us, and a brisk sea breeze showered us with a fine mist of salt spray. Neither of us spoke until we reached an immense log, half buried in the sand.

Mitch pulled me down next to him. "I'd like to tell you how Dexter died. I keep playing it over and over again in my mind, searching for a way I might have prevented it."

He picked up a handful of small shells and pitched them one at a time into the water as he spoke. The violence of his movements contradicted the gentleness of his voice.

"Dexter called to say he had come across a lead on a new case he'd been working on. Asked me to meet him downtown. I left right away, but traffic was rerouted because of a broken gas main, and it slowed me down twenty minutes. When I finally reached our rendezvous point, a crowd had gathered around a police barricade. I showed my badge and went through."

He stopped pitching shells and dropped his hands to his knees, sitting with his head and shoulders bent in a crumpled posture of despair.

"Dexter was lying on the sidewalk, covered with a sheet, but it didn't hide the blood. Witnesses said he had been approached by a gang of about twenty young punks, who shoved him and shouted racial epithets—Dexter was African-American. They knocked him to the ground and kicked him. Several wore heavy, steel-toed boots. They kicked him in the head, the spine—"

Mitch sucked in a long ragged breath.

"And they just kept kicking him and kicking him, until a shopkeeper ran from his store with a double-barreled shotgun. When they saw him, they ran, but it was too late for Dexter. He was already dead." The beads of moisture on Mitch's face could have been salt spray or tears.

"Why torture yourself?" I asked. "What could you have done if you'd been there? If there were that many of them, they might have killed you, too."

The beads of moisture rolled down his cheeks.

"But I'll never know, will I?"

His question was an agonized cry, and I had no answer.

We sat silently, observing the gulf, where occasional running lights flashed from a fishing boat far off on the horizon.

Finally, Mitch spoke. "All I can do now is find the people responsible for Dexter's death."

The deadness in his voice frightened me. "And once you've found them?"

"I may commit murder myself."

I shivered in the night air, struck cold by the determined look on the face of the stranger at my side.

Twelve

I dove into the breaking waves, swimming with long strokes straight out to sea. The warm waters of the gulf, heavy with salt, buoyed me as I turned, treading water, to witness the sunrise streak the sky behind the beach house with bands of gold and coral.

From my vantage point in the water, I could see the large Bermuda-style house to the north of my cottage being renovated. In the cool of early dawn, landscapers dug in the gardens, and a large crane lifted a tall palm over the house to be planted on the gulf side. On the three-story house to the south of the cottage, a zigzagging outer staircase led to a widow's walk atop the roof.

Aunt Bibi's simple cottage sat between the two like a poor relation at a wedding.

I floated on my back with my hair fanning out upon the water like dark seaweed and observed the changing colors of the clouds. How simple it would be to drift out to sea and into nothingness. The paralyzing numbness of grief had erased all emotional peaks and valleys from my life so that even as I considered the mysterious Gideon I felt strangely insulated and untouched.

The fear I'd experienced the night before at Mitch's expression, the face of a man who could kill, dissipated in the morning light, replaced by a consuming hollowness.

Listlessly, I swam back to shore and trudged through deep

white sand that sucked at my ankles. The aroma of coffee brewing filled the cottage, but Mitch was nowhere in sight.

In the bathroom, I stripped off my swimsuit and stepped into the pulsing warmth of a hot shower, washing the salt and grit from my body and hair. As I dressed, I experienced again the sensation of not belonging in my body, of seeing my hands and feet, even my face when I stared in the mirror, as the alien features of a stranger, as if Nick had taken the best part of me with him and I didn't know what was left behind.

The thud of pounding feet sounded on the drive, and Mitch, wearing running shorts and an NYPD sweatshirt, jogged up to the cottage. I ran a comb through my wet hair and waited for him as he knocked sand from the treads of his shoes before entering.

"Your morning paper." He presented me a copy of the *Courier*. "I found a rack at the convenience store a mile or so up the road."

"Thanks." I studied him a moment, searching for signs of the threatening stranger of the night before. But this morning he seemed relaxed and content, and I was glad once more I had invited him.

I poured a cup of coffee and carried it and the newspaper to the deck. Behind me, the patter of the shower running and occasional fragments of songs drifted out of the cottage, barely audible over the crashing of the surf. In spite of Mitch's despondency over Dexter's death, he showed, on the surface at least, a remarkable resilience I wished for myself.

Later that morning Mitch worked beside me, raking the beach beneath the Australian pines and carrying trailing armloads of delicate needles to mulch the shrubs around the cottage. We worked in comfortable silence until the beach was clear of debris, then moved the chairs and a small table from the sun-washed deck onto the neatly raked sand in the shade.

At noon Mitch filled pita pockets with tuna salad and shredded lettuce and I made a pitcher of iced tea with key lime juice, and we ate a quiet lunch under the pines on the beach, while sunlight danced on the water and fishing boats passed.

At another time I would have been uncomfortable with so much silence, but for now it seemed right, a space for healing. I sprawled in my chair after lunch and drifted almost to sleep.

"Why history?"

Mitch's out-of-the-blue question caught me off guard and brought me fully awake. "What do you mean?"

"Why did you choose to teach dates, people, and places? Sounds like pretty dry stuff to me."

I was too relaxed to take offense. "I admit teaching history doesn't have the glamor and excitement being a detective has."

I had tried not to sound defensive but must not have succeeded because Mitch started to protest. "I didn't mean—"

"It's true. When was the last time you saw a movie or a television series based on a history professor? Not a very action-packed, scintillating occupation, is it?"

"There's more to it than I can see, or a woman like you wouldn't have chosen it." Mitch stared as if he were seeing me for the first time.

I avoided the temptation to ask what kind of woman he thought I was and returned to his original query. "If you approach history as a grocery list of dates and events, it is pretty dry stuff. Too many in my field do just that and turn people off of history for life."

"What do you do that's different?" he asked.

"I teach history as an exercise in critical thinking, a way of examining cause and effect, understanding why things happen."

"Isn't that still just a list of people, dates, and events?" He stuck his nose in the air and peered over imaginary glasses. "Class, list the major causes of the Civil War."

His triumphant look said he'd proved his point, but I wasn't about to concede.

"The student mustn't stop at the list. That's just the beginning." I leaned forward, eager to discuss my favorite topic.

"What comes after the list?"

"Take your Civil War example," I said. "During the colonial period, the diverging directions of development taken by the North and South guaranteed the eventual emergence of sectionalism in this country."

His brown eyes widened. "The Civil War was destiny?"

"North and South differed in ethnic origin, religion, social customs, government, and economy. Those differences were the reason slavery, the spark that started the blaze, was practiced—and accepted—in the South and not the North."

"So far it sounds pretty much like the history course I took," Mitch said, "except you're much prettier than Dr. Schlosser. But don't let that go to your head. That bush," he indicated a small, scraggly sea grape, "is prettier than Dr. Schlosser."

Mischief danced in his eyes before his expression sobered. "Sorry for interrupting. Please, go on."

I didn't know if his interest was serious but decided that if I bored him, he'd asked for it. "Knowing the causes is only the beginning. Next, I ask students to speculate on who or what might have turned the course of events. The better students understand the motivating factors, the better chance they have of coming up with plausible ways that might have changed history."

I stopped, self-conscious. "Had enough?"

He sat watching me. With his head cocked to one side, he reminded me again, as he had the day I first saw him, of Nick. "I've never seen anyone quite so enthusiastic about history. What next?"

"It isn't enough to see cause and effect in the past. If you study history closely, you can project the effect current actions and policies might have on the future. That ability enlightens citizens—voters—and makes them more active participants in government."

His forehead wrinkled in concentration as he tried to follow my reasoning.

I searched my memory for an example. "For instance, in 1820 Representative Cobb of Georgia predicted the verbal battle over the Missouri Compromise had kindled a fire that 'all the waters of the ocean could not put out, but only a sea of blood could quench.'"

He nodded. "A sea of blood is an accurate description of the carnage forty years later."

"That's the point. Forty years before the Civil War, people saw it coming. If they had acted on their knowledge, perhaps the war could have been avoided."

"I'm not sure I follow you. Isn't what you're saying a close cousin to fortune-telling?"

I shook my head. "Not fortune-telling but understanding that action, or inaction, always carries consequences. Which proves the old adage that those who do not learn from history are doomed to repeat it."

Mitch looked thoughtful. "Okay, how do you apply what you've learned about history to what's happening today?"

I scuffed my bare feet through the sand beneath my chair and chose my words carefully. "Take the issue that has polarized our entire campus: the adoption of a multicultural curriculum."

He raised his brows. "Why is a multicultural curriculum so important?"

His question echoed one my colleague Moira had posed often. "Demographers project that in fifty years the majority of residents of the United States will trace their ethnic origins to Africa, Asia, the Hispanic world, the Pacific, or Arab countries. Today's descendants of Northern Europeans will no longer be the majority. So shouldn't we adopt a curriculum that teaches the diversity of these expanding cultures?"

He thought for a moment before answering. "Taking into consideration the separatist movement that caused the Civil War, you should vote against a multicultural curriculum and work instead toward assimilating everyone into a common culture."

I smiled. He had answered exactly as I'd expected him to.

"Take another example." I said. "Germany at the end of World War I had a ruined economy and a population divided into haves and have-nots. Those in power projected the blame for the hardships onto the Jews, who eventually became not only scapegoats, but sacrificial lambs."

Mitch looked more puzzled. "You've lost me this time."

"Look at the parallel. Today we also have a widening chasm between the haves and the have-nots. The poor have no access to health care and little chance of advancement through education and are most often the victims of crime. A large majority of these poor are whites, looking for a scapegoat. They vent their anger on ethnic minority groups or the government, which they feel is giving unfair breaks through affirmative action programs."

Mitch nodded. "That anger and frustration explains the rise of militia and neo-Nazi groups and the expansion of older white supremacist groups like the Klan."

He had picked up my line of reasoning. "It even accounts for misguided individuals like the ones who bombed the federal building in Oklahoma City."

"I see where you're headed now, professor."

"The other side of this potentially explosive equation is the ethnic groups. Some resentfully see all power and wealth in the hands of a white male establishment."

"But there have always been opposing factions within society," he said.

"If we don't work at reconciling those factions and opening real opportunities for them, we are headed straight into civil war, race against race, religion against religion."

Mitch made a scoffing noise. "Civil war's a pretty radical prediction."

I held my ground. "Look at what happened in Los Angeles after the Rodney King verdict. Other such outbreaks are almost certain unless measures are adopted now to effect change."

"What kind of measures?"

"There's an epidemic of hate in this country," I said, "fed by ignorance and resentment. At the university level, we can't solve the problems that cause that resentment. Only educational opportunities, jobs, health care, and freedom from crime can cure that. But treating the ignorance is a different matter. People fear what they don't know or understand, and what they fear long enough, they also begin to hate."

"So you believe the multicultural curriculum would help alleviate fear and hate by creating acceptance and understanding among cultures."

"Exactly." I leaned back in my chair and closed my eyes, as the sea breeze caressed my skin. "If we can understand the traditions, symbols, and values of other cultures, we'll be less likely to fear or misinterpret the actions of others. By recognizing and respecting ethnic origins, we lessen resentment among all ethnic groups."

When he didn't comment, I brushed my hair back from my face and stared unseeing at the far horizon, searching for the right words to explain why I felt so strongly about the issue.

"Years ago," I said, "when I was a teenager, Gene Roddenberry, the creator of 'Star Trek,' came to St. Petersburg, and Nick and I went to hear him speak. He presented a wonderful vision of the future, one that he exemplified in all his television series and movies."

"You're a Trekker?" Mitch grinned at the revelation.

"Yes, and proud of it. Roddenberry's view wasn't so much a vision of new worlds to be discovered as a blueprint of a world we can fashion for ourselves, where men and women of all backgrounds and races live and work together with mutual understanding and respect. I want to help build such a world."

Mitch regarded me with an expression I couldn't interpret, and I felt exposed, having shared my deepest convictions with a man I barely knew.

"I know I've condensed my viewpoint until it sounds simplistic," I said, "but I'll spare you and get off my soapbox now. You asked a simple question and I responded with a lecture. Sorry."

Mitch turned away and gazed out over the gulf. The prolonged silence began to wear on my nerves.

"What are you thinking?" I asked.

Mitch turned to me with the same unreadable expression. "That a woman with so much conviction is a very dangerous thing."

Thirteen

The October day had been pleasantly warm, and after an afternoon swim, Mitch moved the dining room table out to the deck, covered it with Aunt Bibi's best cloth, and placed a trio of hurricane lamps in its center.

As the sun set in a montage of spectacular colors, burning the sky a bright orange above the deep blue of the gulf, we dined on Cornish hens with wild rice to the strains of Paganini and Grieg on the tape player.

Mitch raised his glass of chardonnay. "Thanks again for inviting me. It's peaceful, beautiful here."

"It's good to have company. And your cooking."

As he sipped his wine, his dark eyes studied me across the crystal rim of his glass, until, uncomfortable under his scrutiny, I glanced away to the last of the ocher streaks fading from the sky.

The darkness gathered quickly, and the flames of the hurricane globes spread a circle of light around us. When I looked back to Mitch, he was studying me still.

"You're quiet tonight," I said. "Did cooking this marvelous meal exhaust the chef?" I hoped the lightness of my tone concealed my uneasiness.

Mitch rotated his chair away from the table, stretched his long legs before him on the deck, and rolled his wineglass between his palms. "I've been thinking about what you said this afternoon, about history and your multicultural curriculum."

I waited for him to continue, but he sat, silent.

"And?" I probed.

"I was wondering if yours is a very popular position?"

I laughed at the irony of his words. "No, it's about as popular as a beggar at a wedding. Even Carol is against me on this one. And Moira Rafferty, too. They see my position as separatist and anti-intellectual. Emmett Nyagwa is the only other member of the committee who shares my views."

"Sounds like a hung jury, two against two."

"Dean Koenig will have the deciding vote. He hasn't made his position clear, but he worries about how not adopting such a curriculum will affect accreditation and federal funding."

"What about the students? How much do they know about the proposed curriculum?"

"There's been plenty of coverage in the campus press, and the minutes of our meetings are open record. Most of our students are conservative . . . and white. They'd like to maintain the status quo."

Mitch's brows knitted above dark eyes that burned like coals in the glow from the lamps. "So there are a great many students and faculty members unhappy about the stance you've taken?"

His penetrating questions made me uneasy. "Yes, I suppose so. I haven't given it much thought. I've been more concerned about how to resolve the issue."

He refilled our wineglasses. "Just for the sake of discussion, has it occurred to you that Gideon might have nothing to do with your brother's death? That he or she might be upset with your attitude toward the curriculum changes?"

I leaned toward him across the table, and the heat cast by the hurricane lamps bathed my face. "But who? Even if Nick's death was an accident and Gideon had nothing to do with it, who is Gideon and what is this file he wants?"

"Maybe someone is trying to spook you into changing your vote. Didn't you say your office was broken into the night before the scheduled vote, and your house after that?"

"Yes, but why wouldn't the person just come to me and say

what he thought, try to persuade me himself?" Lightheaded from the wine, I tried to comprehend this new picture of Gideon.

"Maybe he's already tried to talk you out of it," Mitch said. "Haven't you discussed this with students and other members of the faculty?"

"Of course, but so far no one has convinced me to vote differently."

"That's just my point. Whoever Gideon is, he knows talk alone won't sway you, so maybe he's hoping fear and intimidation will."

I contemplated this new twist to my dilemma while Mitch finished his wine. I was still lost in thought as he began to clear the table.

"Do you really think that's who Gideon is and that's why he's threatening me?" I picked up my dishes and followed Mitch into the cottage.

He took the plates from me, put them in the sink, then placed his hands on my shoulders and gazed into my eyes. "I've been playing devil's advocate. I just want you to realize Gideon could be anybody—or nobody."

"That's a big help," I muttered.

"One thing I've learned in all my years of investigative work is that people and events are seldom what they appear. The most obvious answer isn't always the correct one."

He released me and ran hot water in the sink. I was sorry he had let go. His touch had awakened a need in me, a yearning to be held and comforted, and I studied his back as he washed dishes, feeling bereft and alone.

He handed me a dishtowel. "How about a walk on the beach when we finish these?"

"You're on." My loneliness dissolved as we finished the washing up together.

I fell asleep immediately, tired from a day of physical exercise, but in the early morning hours, my nightmare returned. I was running as fast as I could, while a faceless Gideon chased me across the western span of the old Skyway Bridge.

In the distance, Bella Ionescu called, "Beware, beautiful Alexandra, they come for you, they come for you!"

Frantically, I ran faster and faster with the heat of Gideon's breath on the back of my neck. Just as he grabbed me, we fell together through the void left by the missing center section and into the bottomless chasm below. I screamed as I fought to extricate myself from his embrace, falling all the while.

I awoke screaming still.

Suddenly, Mitch was beside me, enfolding me in his arms, rocking me softly, as he would a child, and whispering in my ear. "It's okay, Alex. I'm here. I won't leave you."

His breath warmed my cheek, and I reached out, drawing him close, and the heat from his body eased my shivering.

He turned back the covers and slid into the wide double bed, pulling me against him until we lay like spoons, my back against the hardness of his stomach, his arms wrapped around me. He stroked my hair and whispered words of assurance until I fell asleep once more, feeling safe for the first time since Nick had died.

I awoke alone and wondered if I had dreamed of Mitch coming to my bed and holding me until I slept. When I spotted the indentation left by his head against the pillow next to me, I realized his presence had been real and felt a stab of disappointment at his absence.

I dressed in my swimsuit and a terry coverup, planning to slip out quietly for my morning swim, but Mitch was perched on a stool at the kitchen counter, reading the morning paper. When he saw me, his face crinkled into the slow grin I had grown fond of, and he stood and drew me to him.

I moved easily into his embrace, like coming home.

"No more talk of Gideon while we're here, okay?" he said. "You need your rest—without the nightmares."

He tilted my chin and kissed me gently. I yielded, returning his kiss with an intensity I had never experienced with Burke. Shaken by the power of my emotions, I pulled away, flustered.

"Want some company for your swim?" he asked.

His smile forgave my withdrawal, and his easy manner restored my emotional balance. We sprinted across the beach and into the surf, where I raced him out to sea, matching his long, powerful strokes.

The entire day was an odyssey back to my childhood. We swam, searched the beach for shells and driftwood, ate a monstrous brunch of gingerbread waffles and sliced apples, then stretched out in the Adirondack chairs beneath the pines, alternately napping and reciting snatches of poems from memory, a crazy-quilt, highly inaccurate anthology, from Shakespeare to Ogden Nash.

That night, after clearing and washing the dishes, we took a run on the beach. In the distance, lightning illuminated thunderheads in a squall line, approaching from the northwest.

"Rain soon," I said, "and cooler weather."

The wind rose, and waves swelled higher, crashing onto the beach with the roar of thunder. Salt spray hung in the air like fog, and we were soaked to the skin before we returned to the cottage.

Later, showered and in dry clothes, we snuggled on the sofa with a huge bowl of popcorn and watched classic movies on video, laughing at Bogart and Hepburn on the *African Queen* and sighing with regret when Bergman boarded the plane, leaving Bogey behind in *Casablanca*.

The hour was late when the second film ended, and as I stood to say goodnight, I wondered if Mitch would be coming to my bed again.

Almost as if he had read my thoughts, he took me in his arms and kissed me briefly. "We have to take things slow. We're both still walking wounded." He cradled my face between his strong hands. "Here's looking at you, kid."

He kissed me once more on the tip of my nose, turned me

around, and gave me a little push toward my door, then walked into his own room and closed the door.

My own feelings were so confused, I didn't know whether I was relieved or disappointed, but he was right. We both suffered still from our losses and were too emotionally damaged to know what we wanted. I felt certain of only one thing, that I wanted Mitch with me. I couldn't have stood the loneliness, the emptiness, without him.

I awoke the next day after a night free of dreams of Gideon and falling bridges to find the cabin a small, snug island in the rain that pelted the beach.

Mitch braved the weather in Aunt Bibi's oilskin poncho to buy a newspaper, but the rest of the day, we played canasta, baked chocolate chip cookies, and read, while rain obscured the beach and waves pounded along the shoreline out of sight.

That evening Mitch sat with one long leg hooked over the arm of his chair, reading an old P. D. James mystery he had found on the bookshelves.

He seemed too good to be real. He had warned that people and events were seldom what they seemed. We had spent days with only each other for company, but I knew little more about him than the day I had met him. He had talked, mostly about places, things, and ideas, but had said nothing about his family, friends, or work, with the exception of his story of Dexter's murder.

He appeared intelligent and compassionate, with a sense of humor, but I recognized him also as a man of secrets who kept a part of himself closed up, locked away. His barriers went up when I mentioned certain topics or asked certain questions, and even more subtly, at times he changed the subject or sidestepped an inquiry so artfully that only later did I realize a query had gone unanswered or the direction of a conversation had been skillfully shifted.

Nick had been so good with people. If only he were there to talk to about the mysterious Mitchell Lawton.

But if Nick were there, silly, I reminded myself, I would be teaching my classes at the university instead of spending a week at Longboat Key with a man I'd met less than a week before.

"The sister did it." Mitch unfolded himself from the chair's depths and returned the half-finished book to the shelf.

"How can you know? You're barely into it?" His assurance amused me. I was still struggling with the crossword puzzle from the morning paper.

"It's my job to know, and I'm good at what I do." He spoke, not boastfully, but in the same tone in which he might have called attention to the rain.

"Well, if you're so good, how about figuring out who Gideon is?" I teased.

He stood at the kitchen counter, his hand in Aunt Bibi's cookie jar, a ceramic facsimile of Porky Pig. His face was expressionless. "What makes you think I don't already know?"

His question stunned me. Was it coincidence that Gideon had left me alone the past few days? Maybe Mitch's presence was a deterrent. Or maybe Gideon had given up altogether.

A chilling thought struck me. Could Mitch be Gideon? Or was he teasing me with his remark? Before I could pursue the matter further, he changed the subject.

Piling cookies on a plate, he flashed his appealing grin. "Dr. Mitch prescribes milk and cookies before bedtime to insure a restful, dreamless sleep."

My moment of uncertainty passed, and the matter of Gideon was dropped once more.

The next morning, as we walked the beach a last time before packing up for the trip home, I remembered his comment about Gideon, but in the light of day, it seemed insignificant. In fact, everything about my time with Mitch had taken on a quality of unreality, making the days seem illusory and ephemeral, like mist in the air after the rain.

Everything that had happened since Nick had died seemed like a dream, and I wished I could awaken to my former life, with Nick alive and well, waiting to tell me about his latest adventures.

I wondered if I was losing my grip on reality or working through denial, a natural stage of grief. The stiff cold breeze dried my tears as soon as they touched my cheeks.

We wore jeans and jackets against the chilling blast of salty air. Our surroundings, a study in gray, from the dark gun metal hue of the crashing surf to the pale pewter sky and ashen sands, mirrored the coldness in my soul.

I was reluctant to return home to reality, to Nick's not being there, to the faculty debate, to living alone once more.

Beside me, his dark hair ruffled by the wind, his cheekbones reddened by cold, Mitch was a man of secrets whose mysteriousness only made him more attractive.

The direction of my thoughts embarrassed me. I'd been watching too many old movies. Next, I'll be hearing violins, I thought. I jammed my hands deeper into the pockets of my windbreaker, shoving romantic fantasies aside.

"Reminds me of Long Island when it's cold and gray like this," Mitch shouted above the roar of breakers.

"Like at Rosa and Herman's?"

"Don't know," he shouted back, "never been there."

"But I—"

I thought better of what I had started to say. I had believed Mitch was a close family friend of the Myers', but by his own admission, he had never been to their home.

Just how well did Rosa know this man she had rented her house to? For that matter, how well did I know him?

Fourteen

"How well does Rosa Myers know this man?"

Burke echoed my question the night of Dean Koenig's party. He had come as Moira's escort but wasted no time maneuvering me to a secluded corner of the terrace after I arrived with Mitch.

"I don't think that's any of your business." I struggled to keep my voice pleasant and looked around for an escape route.

"Don't be ridiculous, Alex. Of course it's my business. You broke our engagement, not me. I'll always care about you and your welfare. You have to admit you know practically nothing about this man you so recklessly went off alone with."

I couldn't defend myself with facts. What I didn't know about Mitchell Lawton would fill a library, and defending him would be a losing battle, especially with Burke. I kept a lid on my temper by reminding myself that Burke did care for me, in his own overbearing way.

"You're right, Burke. I'll see what else I can find out about him. How are you progressing with Nick's estate?"

"I know when you're trying to change the subject. Don't think I'm going drop this Mitchell Lawton issue. I care too much about you."

Burke launched into a detailed description of the probate process, while I tuned him out and observed the festivities around me. In the far corner of the garden, in a classical arbor covered with bougainvillea, a string quartet played Mozart, their polished notes blending with the splashing waters of a huge fountain, the centerpiece of the terraced back lawn of Dean Koenig's home.

On the opposite end of the terrace, Kevin McDermott sat alone, hunched over a plate piled high from the buffet. His shirt cuffs protruded from the too-short sleeves of his sports jacket, and his sandy hair had the rumpled look of a child awakening from a nap.

Poor guy, I thought, at least he's getting a decent meal.

I experienced a familiar surge of anger at the thought of some of my students from wealthy families who partied their college years away, while bright people on scholarship, like Kevin, had to scrape and do without to get an education.

"Excuse me, Burke. I'll set up an appointment to discuss the other details with you. I have someone I need to talk to."

I crossed the terrace, glad I had worn my long heather skirt and its matching shawl, because the night air was cool as it blew across the garden.

"Dr. Garrison." Kevin, juggling his plate and drink, attempted to stand at my approach.

"Don't get up. May I join you?"

He nodded and made room on the carved stone bench.

"How's the food?" I asked.

"Terrific, especially the roast beef. Can I get you something?"

"Not now, thanks. I just wanted to ask how my classes have gone while I was away."

"Everything's been . . . fine." He paused a fraction of a second. "Everything's fine."

"If there's been a problem, you can tell me."

"It wasn't a problem, more of a nuisance. I didn't want to worry you with it. That student in your morning class, Paul Stephanos—"

"What about him?" My old uneasiness returned.

"He's been hanging around your office, asking where you were and when you were coming back. Made a real scene. I was afraid he was going to get physical. Finally, I told him he'd have to talk to Dr. Donahue."

"Good thinking. Carol took care of him, I'm sure. Anything else?"

"All classes are on schedule, and I have your office shipshape again."

"You are a marvel. If there's ever anything I can do to repay—"

"I'm just doing my job, Dr. Garrison." He squirmed uncomfortably at my praise.

"Relax, Kevin, and please call me Alex. We're colleagues, after all."

"All right. Alex it is." He was handsome when he smiled and seemed less young than before.

A white-coated waiter came by with a tray of tall fluted glasses filled with champagne. Content away from the crush of people in the house, I sipped the fine dry wine while Kevin attacked his plate once more.

Carol had led Mitch off to introduce him to the others and Burke had gone back inside, so I sat with Kevin in the solitude of the cool night air, looking back at the lighted windows of the Mediterranean-style mansion and listening to the laughter drifting out across the garden, blending with the Mozart.

Inside, my friends and colleagues, and possibly Gideon, mingled, if Mitch's hunch about the curriculum issue was correct. The more I tried to imagine one of them resorting to anonymous threats and intimidations, the less likely it seemed. They were all too civilized, too intelligent and open-minded to engage in such behavior.

I considered the possibility that Gideon was a student. When I had returned from the cottage, there had been no message, no further intrusion into my home. Perhaps whoever it was had given up and left me in peace.

"Dr.—Alex?"

I flinched, so caught up in my thoughts I had forgotten Kevin beside me.

"All this—" he gestured with the hand that held his drink to indicate the house and grounds. "Does a dean make enough to afford all this?"

"A dean makes more than a full professor, but not enough to support this life-style." I leaned toward Kevin and whispered like a conspirator. "Dean Koenig earned his money the hard way. He married it."

I giggled. The champagne had made me giddy. I refused the waiter, who offered to replace my empty glass with a full one, then stood and shook out the creases in my long skirt. As much as I disliked the idea, it was time to go back inside and pay my social dues.

Kevin, looking self-conscious and out of place, stood. "You won't mind if I stay out here and don't go in with you? Crowds make me nervous."

"Me, too. I'd rather stay here myself, but duty and campus politics demand I speak to the others."

As I crossed the broad flagstoned terrace toward the house, Carol and Mitch met me.

"I wondered where you were," Carol said. "I've been introducing Mitch to everyone. Brought him out here to escape Moira's clutches. When she saw him, she had the look of a hound smelling blood."

"Don't let Carol scare you," I said to Mitch. "Moira's harmless, and charming as well. By the way, Carol, Kevin tells me he had to send Paul Stephanos to you while I was gone."

"What an old windbag. He came huffing and puffing, demanding I tell him where you were and when you were coming back."

"What did you say?"

She grinned her impish smile, revealing the dimples in her round cheeks. "I used the old Ann Landers response to inappropriate questions. Works every time."

"Ann Landers response?" Mitch asked.

"You look the person who's making an ass of himself straight in the eye," Carol said, "and ask sweetly, 'Why would you ask such a question?' Stopped him cold. He walked away without another word."

"So that's what you teach in your advanced communications classes?" I hugged her, realizing how much I had missed her wacky humor the last few days.

Mitch moved to the edge of the terrace and looked over the formal gardens, taking deep breaths of the cool night air. "This weather is perfect. At home they're probably sloshing through sleet and snow now."

Carol laughed. "Before you go into ecstasies over the climate, spend May through September here. Then you'll understand why they named it Florida. That's Spanish for 'land of perpetual perspiration.' "

"Careful, Carol, the Chamber of Commerce will lock you up as a traitor." Feeling a warm glow from the champagne, I took Mitch's arm. "Let's go back in. I'm not the best at small talk. Might as well get it over with."

We threaded our way into the house through the throng of guests and waiters, pausing to speak briefly with various members of the faculty before moving on again. The muted roar of conversation blended with a Marvin Hamlisch medley coming from the grand piano in the corner, and clinking glassware and an occasional burst of laughter punctuated the noise.

I introduced Mitch to Gilbert Trenwith, the classics professor whose profile resembled the imprint on an old Roman coin. His wife, Marcia, a short, barrel-shaped woman, dressed like a bag lady, was the university's poet-in-residence. They seemed an unlikely couple, but most couples usually were.

Reginald Hartwick, who taught art history, threatened to engage Mitch in an endless discussion of New York City's art museums, until his companion, an anemic-looking young man with haunted eyes, interrupted, jealously demanding Reginald's attention and allowing us to escape.

When we reached the library, it was less crowded, and I could speak to Mitch without shouting.

"I don't see how cramming everyone together until polite

conversation is impossible will ease tension over the curriculum issue. Probably Stephanie Koenig just wanted to give a party, which she does with style, I have to admit."

"Somehow I pictured college professors as more casual in their leisure time," Mitch said. "You know, gathered around a pitcher of beer at the campus pub, that sort of thing."

He was watching Moira work her way across the room toward us. She wore an abbreviated, fitted black satin dress with a matching jacket lined with red, and she moved with the suppleness and elegance of a jungle cat. She looked many things, but academic wasn't one of them.

"Alex, it's good to have you back," she said. "Perhaps now we can get this curriculum mess settled."

She snagged a glass of champagne from a passing waiter and gulped it down.

"But not in the way you would hope." Emmett Nyagwa said. He and his wife Jawole, both in colorful native African dress, joined us.

Moira sighed and pushed her thick red hair back from her face. "Oh, Emmett, we're never going to see eye-to-eye on this. You hang on so fiercely to a culture you've only read about. We're all *déracinés* in this country, so first we should consider ourselves Americans."

"Help me out," Mitch whispered. *"Déracinés?"*

"Uprooted people who come from somewhere else." My stomach knotted in nervous tension at the look on Emmett's handsome ebony face.

Moira, her voice slurred from too much champagne, continued her assault. "Take those ridiculous clothes you're wearing. My Celtic ancestors probably arrived in this country more recently than yours, but I don't go parading around in a kilt every day, for God's sake."

I winced at Moira's rudeness. Emmett, looking for a moment as if he would strike Moira down, wheeled and walked out of the room without a backward glance.

Jawole, projecting serenity and self-control, drew her perfect posture to its full regal height. When she spoke, her words were soft, and I strained to hear them above the surrounding chatter.

"Perhaps knowledge of the African-American experience, like the curriculum that's been proposed, would help your understanding, Dr. Rafferty. Then you would not alienate others with your ignorance." She followed her husband out of the library.

"Oh, Moira." I shook my head in frustration, wondering how we would ever reach an agreement with such animosity existing between committee members.

Moira's face contorted with anger. "Don't 'oh, Moira' me, Alex. You're as bad as he is, trying to ram all those irrelevant subcultures down our throats. I don't like it, and I'm not about to pretend I do."

She wobbled off in the direction of a waiter who had just entered the room with more champagne.

Carol and Sam had joined us in time to witness the blow-up between Moira and the Nyagwas.

"In vino veritas?" Sam asked.

"Oh, no," his plump wife challenged. "Sounds more like *in vino stupiditas* to me. I agree with her philosophically, but her methods are brutal."

An incipient pressure blossomed in my left temple, prelude to a migraine. Was this the civilized, open-minded group I'd been thinking of only a few minutes before? Too many emotions—grief, frustration, anger—converged on me at once. I feared I would break down and weep if I stayed in the charged atmosphere much longer.

"Would you mind leaving early?" I asked Mitch.

"You look whipped," he said. "Let's get out of here."

I climbed the wide marble staircase that spiraled to the second floor and entered the guest room to collect my handbag. Moira had passed out among the coats on the bed, looking vulnerable and sad with her dress skewed up around her garters and her thick hair fanned out on the pillows. I covered her with an afghan and turned off the lights, wishing she had passed out fifteen minutes sooner and saved us all from grief.

I was angry with Moira, but I also understood her. She had shared much of her background with me one night soon after she had first come to Suncoast University, when I had given a dinner party for her to meet some of the faculty. Moira had drunk too much and eaten too little, and I had insisted she stay over with me rather than drive home in her condition.

"I come by my drunkenness honestly," she'd said. "I'm the youngest of twelve children in a family of Irish Catholics from Boston."

She was the type whose inhibitions disappeared as the blood alcohol rose.

We'd sat in my living room, drinking coffee. I was keyed up from the night's entertaining and would have trouble sleeping, so I'd stayed up to keep Moira company. She'd shown no inclination toward sleep and had wanted to talk.

"My childhood was like those you hear about on the talk shows today—poverty, alcoholism, abuse."

She'd tilted her head on the low back of the chair, gazing at the ceiling. Her hair, flung over the chair's back, had glowed, a bright auburn cascade in the dim room.

"I got out of the house as soon as I graduated from high school. Lucky for me the nuns made me study hard, and my grades were good. I was able to get into college, but I had to work my way through."

She'd laughed with a deep-throated, sultry chuckle at the memory. "I worked every job I could find—waiting tables, delivering newspapers, selling doughnuts door to door, cleaning other people's filthy houses—but I made it straight through to my Ph.D."

"That must have been a tough time," I'd said.

She'd jumped, so caught up in her reminiscences she'd forgotten I was there.

"Not as hard as watching my brothers and sisters falling into the same trap my parents had—too many kids, too little money, too much booze."

She'd sat up and looked at me, as if suddenly aware of my presence.

"I'll tell you something I've never breathed to another soul. I've never had a real boyfriend. I've always run like hell in the opposite direction when I've met a man I'm attracted to."

"You had every man here tonight eating out of your hand," I'd said.

"I may play the *femme fatale*, but it's all an act. I'm terrified of ending up like my parents and brothers and sisters did."

"But don't you get lonely?"

"Sure I get lonely. Why do you think I drink?"

She'd laughed again, but her laughter had sounded forced, as if she'd recognized the irony of having wound up in her parents' trap after all.

She'd never mentioned her family or her difficult struggle through college again, but I had learned enough that evening to understand Moira's impatience with Emmett Nyagwa.

Few had ever had to work harder than Moira to attain their goals. She had pulled herself up from the depths of poverty and abuse, even without the proverbial bootstraps, and she believed anyone else with the same determination could do the same, without affirmative action or racial quotas. She insisted that achieving success had nothing to do with race or culture but everything to do with hard work, sacrifice, and patience.

Moira and Emmett would never see multiculturalism in the same way. Emmett claimed his ethnic heritage with fierce pride. Moira rejected hers as a trap to be avoided. I could only hope they would at least learn to respect each other's point of view.

By now the pressure in my temple had turned to pounding. I tugged my ever-present medicine from the pocket of my skirt and went into the adjoining bathroom for a glass of water. After I washed down my pill, I searched for the Koenigs to say goodnight.

Stephanie Koenig, looking fashionably thin and elegant in

her white cashmere gown belted with gold lamé, chatted with Burke at the foot of the stairs. Her long, expressive fingers sculpted pictures in the air as she spoke.

"Burke," I said, "Moira's waiting upstairs. I believe she's ready to go home."

Mitch joined me as I thanked our hostess, and we said our good-byes.

When we stepped outside into the cool night air, I sighed with relief, but the pain gathering in my head indicated the price I would pay the next day for the champagne I'd drunk.

I tried not to think what Moira's loss of control might cost us all.

Fifteen

Kristin Montgomery's car exploded several days after Dean Koenig's party.

After Gideon's threatening call, accusing me of causing the tragedy, I had combed through the events of the prior two weeks but had found nothing to identify Gideon or the file he wanted.

I gagged at the stench of smoke from the explosion in the parking lot, which permeated my office. Kristin Montgomery was dead, blown to bits, and at least seven other students were injured.

"You're the only one who can stop this. Somebody else is going to get hurt."

The words of his threat hammered in my brain like a pulse. Because I had not heard from him while I was at Longboat Key or since my return the night of the party, I had hoped Gideon had gone away. But now, two weeks to the day since Nick had died, the mysterious and deadly Gideon had returned, and I had no clue what or where the illusive file he demanded might be.

I remembered the call I'd received before I'd left for the beach cottage. "If you bring the police into this, you'll be responsible for the consequences."

Consequences? I couldn't imagine any worse consequences than the carnage in the parking lot. The blood of those students was on my hands. If I hadn't been so incapacitated by grief and indecision, today's holocaust might never have happened. It was time to act.

I hurried from my office and rushed directly to the parking

lot, where both uniformed police and crime lab technicians still worked. I'd had enough intimidation from Gideon. The police could think me insane if they wished, but they must deal with him. Whoever my crazy caller was, he was their job, not mine.

After threading my way across the wet, oil-slicked pavement, stepping over fire hoses, shards of glass, and other pieces of debris from the explosion, I waited behind the flapping yellow plastic tape of the police cordon, trying not to look at the twisted metal and burned out frames beyond or to breathe too deeply the choking stench of hot asphalt and scorched metal.

"I have to speak with someone in charge."

The uniformed officer I'd approached jerked his head toward a group of men inspecting the scene. "Detective Dillard's who you need, but he's busy right now."

"I have information important to his investigation." I inhaled slowly to remove the edge of hysteria from my voice before I spoke again. "I'm Dr. Garrison. My office is there."

I pointed to the multistoried glass structure of the Arts and Letters Building.

"Wait here."

The officer picked his way among the wreckage toward a bulky, red-faced man in green polyester slacks and a short-sleeved dress shirt. His thinning hair was combed in careful strands across the crown of his head in a futile attempt to cover his sunburned scalp. He was monitoring a technician, who was scraping samples into plastic bags and labeling them.

When the officer delivered my message, the detective looked impatiently toward me, then stomped his way across the lot.

"Yeah, what is it?" he asked.

He wore no sunglasses and squinted in the blaze of the noonday sun, like a parboiled mole. His abrupt, surly manner made me hesitate.

"Aw, come on, lady, gimme a break. I got an investigation to finish here. Whaddaya want?"

His voice, raspy and impatient, grated like metal on metal, and his rudeness jolted me into speech. "I'm Alex Garrison. I teach here, and my car is exactly like the one that . . . like that one."

I indicated the mangled metal that had once been Kristin's Toyota.

"So?"

The man was either too dumb to draw a parallel or purposely obnoxious. "I just received a phone call in my office related to what happened here . . ."

My voice trailed off lamely. Spoken aloud, my concern lost its menace. I could see Detective Dillard thought the same.

"What kind of call?" His voice was heavy with impatience and skepticism.

"He said I was the only one who could stop this." I nodded at the wreckage. "He said I had to give him a certain file or someone else would be hurt."

"Can you identify the caller?"

"No, but he was very serious about wanting that file." I had regained my conviction that Gideon was at the bottom of the day's event, and my voice regained its confidence.

"Look, lady, I got a dead kid here and seven more burned to a crisp. Are you trying to tell me some crazy did this all on account of some file, like an academic record or something?"

"Not an academic file. I don't think it has anything to do with the school. I don't know who he is or what he wants. That's why I came to you."

"For something that had nothing to do with the school," he said, "it did a hell of a lot of damage."

The detective squinted at me, as if assessing my reliability, then glanced impatiently back toward the wreckage. "Leave your name, address, and phone number with the officer there, and I'll get back to you."

He stomped back to the forensics team, muttering under his breath, while the officer took down the information.

Frustrated by the detective's scorn and the realization that Gideon was still my responsibility, I crossed the grassy quadrangle and headed back to my office. Several sheets of glass on the building's exterior had been damaged by the explosion. Some on the first floor had shattered completely, and maintenance crews were nailing plywood in place to secure the building.

When I reached the second floor, another team from maintenance was sealing the cracked glass outside my office with strips of duct tape.

"Ain't too purty, I know," the older of the two remarked as I unlocked my door, "but at least it'll keep the weather out 'til the replacement glass comes in."

Broken glass was the least of my worries. I closed my door and sank into the overstuffed chair in front of my desk, wondering what to do next. I couldn't deliver what the caller wanted because I didn't know what it was. I had gone to the police, with no results. Mitch thought I was paranoid, and Nick, who would have known what to do, was dead.

Tears of frustration rolled down my cheeks. I felt paralyzed, helpless. Emotions tugged at my memory until I became a little girl again, leaning against a locked door and crying for my brother in the dark on the other side.

A knock on my office door sent me scurrying for tissues. I was wiping my eyes when Carol peeked in.

"I thought I'd find you like this. Come home with me, ducky. I'll feed you lunch."

Food was Carol's universal prescription.

I wasn't hungry, but I didn't want to be alone. "Thanks. I'll get my things."

We walked together to our cars in faculty spaces near the building, several hundred feet from the cordoned area where police crews still worked. If I ignored them, I could almost believe nothing had happened.

A chevron of white ibis with long, curved beaks and red faces, soared above me, headed to their nesting grounds on the mangrove islands in the bay. The chimes in the bell tower pealed the hour, and their sweet tones floated through the clear autumn air, deceptively peaceful.

But for me, there was no peace. The parking lot was strewn with death and destruction, and Gideon's threats rang in my ears. I climbed into my car and hesitated before turning the key in the ignition, afraid of an explosion like the one that had killed Kristin, until I realized that as long as I supposedly had what Gideon wanted, he was not likely to kill me.

I turned the key and relaxed when my car started smoothly and I was still in one piece. I drove in behind Carol's gray Volvo and followed her home.

Carol and Sam lived in a sprawling modern house that backed up to the ninth hole of the golf course at the local country club. The interior of the house, filled with rose-patterned chintz, china knickknacks, and hunting prints, reflected Carol's love of all things English.

I grimaced at the pair of porcelain, pug-nosed Staffordshire dogs on the mantelpiece as I passed through the living room. I had always found them hideous, and Carol, knowing my dislike of them, had often threatened to leave them to me in her will.

I followed her into the kitchen and sat on a bar stool at the center island, while she assembled a salad of chicken, celery, and green grapes in thick crescents of honeydew melon. She worked without her usual running patter of conversation, an indication of how deeply the morning's tragedy had affected her.

We carried our plates and glasses of tea onto the screened lanai by the swimming pool, which overlooked the golf course. The only noise that broke the quiet was the occasional hum from the motor of an electric golf cart.

"Ah, this is the life." Carol sighed and kicked off the shoes with three-inch heels, which she wore in the desperate hope of appearing thinner.

I played with my salad, my appetite gone.

"Who would have thought we'd end up like this," she said,

"two respectable, middle-aged ladies enjoying lunch by the pool on a Wednesday afternoon?"

Carol was the sister I'd never had, but my mother had never approved of her. "Not Mother, that's for sure. She always insisted that unless we changed our wicked, wicked ways, which consisted of an occasional trip to the movies on Sundays and wearing too much lipstick, we'd end up either in jail or in a home for unwed mothers."

"Or dead." Carol's face crumpled in distress. "I'm sorry, Alex. I was trying to keep things light, but all the banter in the world can't change the fact that Nick is gone, or undo that awful accident on campus this morning."

I was glad she'd broached the subject.

"I think I'm going crazy, Carol. I keep getting calls with threats about a file I know nothing about."

I hesitated, not wanting to involve Carol, but, desperate for someone to talk to, I plunged ahead.

"I know Nick's death wasn't an accident, that there's something more going on here. The call I got this morning implied the explosion in the parking lot happened because I hadn't turned over some damned file I'm supposed to have."

"What?" The color drained from Carol's plump cheeks. "Then you have to go to the police. They must be told."

I tossed down my fork in disgust. "That's just it, and that's part of why I feel so stupid about this whole thing. I reported the call—and the fact that my car is just like Kristin Montgomery's—to the detective investigating the explosion."

Carol's pale face blanched whiter. "Your car is like Kristin's? What did he say to that?"

"He treated me as if nothing I'd said was important."

"Then you march right down to the police station and find someone who will think it's important. There's too much coincidence." Carol pushed her plate away, her unflagging appetite withered by my news.

I shook my head, racked by indecision. "I don't know. Even Mitch accused me of using poor judgment in drawing connections between today's explosion and the other events in my life. He thinks I'm jumping to conclusions."

Carol's image blurred through my tears. "You'd tell me, wouldn't you, if you thought I was losing it?"

"I'd have you locked up immediately under the Baker Act, so help me God." Her hazel eyes flashed with mischief before turning grim again. "Seriously, ducky, you know I always say what I think. And right now, I think you're under a terrible strain, what with Nick's death, the faculty tensions, your threatening phone calls . . ."

A strange look crossed her face.

"What is it?" I asked.

"You did have the phone company put a trace on your phone, didn't you?"

I shook my head. "I haven't received a call at home in over a week, so I assumed they were over. The last call came at my office. To put a trace on that phone, I'd have to tell Dean Koenig everything that's happened. I don't want him thinking I've been sent round the bend by Nick's death."

"Promise me you'll make a full report to someone in the police department," she said.

I raked my hands through my hair. "Thank God, someone is finally taking me seriously."

Her fair face flushed with embarrassment. "I admit, at first I thought you were overly affected by Nick's death and putting too much importance on insignificant things, but now? I don't know. The threats still might be a prank, but you should play it safe and report them."

The front door slammed, and in a moment cabinets banged in the kitchen.

"My walking bottomless pits are home from school," Carol said. "Jillian, Trevor, come say hello to your Aunt Alex."

Trevor, a thirteen-year-old masculine replica of his mother, dressed in the latest bizarre teenaged style of wild mismatched colors and name brands, kissed his mother in the martyred fashion of boys who believe they've outgrown such behavior and greeted me with a wave. I missed the hugs and sloppy kisses he had smothered me with when he was a toddler.

"Was somebody really killed at the university today, Mom?" he asked. "Larry Stewart in gym class said there was blood and guts all over the parking lot."

"Oh, gross, Trevor. Why do you always act so immature?" Jillian, a year and a half older, with the tall good looks of a model, draped herself on Carol's chair with her arm around her mother's shoulders.

"A car exploded," Carol said. "One student was killed and others injured. We don't know anything else yet. While we're waiting for more news, you two can get started on your homework."

The affectionate interchange between Carol and her children contrasted with the stiff formality I'd experienced communicating with my own mother.

"Now," Carol turned her attention back to me after the children had left. "Promise you'll tell the police what you've told me."

I promised, but as I left Carol's house for home, I felt more confused than ever.

Sixteen

I arrived home to find a battered green Chevy parked in my driveway. As I pulled up, Detective Dillard climbed out of the car and waited at my door.

"Dr. Garrison, can I talk with you a minute?"

My instinctive dislike of the man was tempered by my promise to Carol to tell the police everything. "Come in."

I unlocked the door, set my briefcase on the foyer table, and showed the detective into the living room.

"I'm glad you're here, Detective. I wanted to talk with you about the explosion on campus today and information that might be related to it."

Even in the dimness of my living room, the man's porcine eyes squinted as if in a glare. "I'll be glad to hear whatever you have to say, but first I wanted to tell you I reported your crank call and the others to the ATF. They're looking into them."

"The ATF?"

"The Bureau of Alcohol, Tobacco, and Firearms, a branch of the Treasury Department that investigates suspicious fires and explosions. I put in a call to their Tampa office."

So he hadn't written off my suspicions. "If they need to talk to me, I'll gladly drive to Tampa to get this thing cleared up."

"That won't be necessary, Dr. Garrison." He stood with his hands in his green polyester pockets, rattling his change. "They didn't seem very concerned about yours or the other calls."

"Other calls?"

He studied the room for a moment before answering, demonstrating either a tendency of his profession or a reluctance to look me in the eye.

"Yes," he finally said, "several other faculty members received a call similar to the one you reported."

"Which other faculty members?"

His change jingled louder. "That's information vital to our investigation I'm not at liberty to divulge, but you shouldn't worry about it."

"Shouldn't worry? A young woman was killed this morning, and I'm not supposed to worry about more threats?" The volume of my voice soared with my impatience.

"Of course you should be concerned about her death. But we're checking the calls out, and we don't feel they're directly related."

I liked the man even less than before. "If the calls are not related to her death, what are they? Figments of our collective imagination?"

He shook his balding head, and when he spoke again, his condescending tone reminded me of Burke. "We believe the calls are pranks, someone wanting to cash in on the excitement and notoriety of the event. Now, what did you want to tell me?"

I couldn't distinguish whether his attitude was total disinterest or subterfuge. Whichever it was, I didn't like it, and it made me hesitate. For a reason I couldn't identify, I didn't trust him. In spite of my promise to Carol, an overpowering reluctance to tell him more than I already had overcame me.

I astonished myself by lying like a pro. "Basically, Detective Dillard, it was what I'd told you before, about Kristin Montgomery's car being the same make and model as mine, but the more I think about it, the more I'm convinced it's just coincidence."

His pocket change silenced. "You're not going to file a report?"

"No, that won't be necessary." Another lie, but anything to be rid of him.

"If you think of anything else, let me know." He handed me his card. "There's the number of the PD and my extension."

I walked him to the door, consumed by a desire to have him out of my house. "Any idea yet what caused the explosion?"

He shrugged his bulky shoulders. "Whenever you've got gasoline, and maybe a cigarette or a match to spark it, there's all kinds of possibilities. We may never know for sure."

I closed the door on him with relief, anxious now to be alone with my thoughts. Although I could think of no logical reason why Dillard would lie to me, I hadn't believed him about others receiving the same threatening call. My intuition insisted that, whoever Gideon was, he was involved with Nick's death.

According to my anonymous caller, Nick had a file this Gideon wanted, would, in fact, do anything, including indiscriminate murder, to obtain. The rifling of Nick's car and belongings, the vandalism of Nick's condo and my office, and the careful search of my house had all been efforts on the part of Gideon to locate that file.

I went back into the living room and lay on the sofa, feeling sick and weak. Kristin Montgomery's death had been an effort to coerce me into turning over the file, a file I didn't have. If I was to get to the truth about Nick's death, I had to find that file. I closed my eyes, hoping to think of somewhere I might look for it.

"Of course!" I yelled aloud as the idea hit me, then raced to the phone in the kitchen to call Tom Stanislaus at the *Courier*.

"Tom, have you cleaned out Nick's desk?" I asked when I got him on the line.

"Sure, Alex. I have a box full of stuff here. Would you like me to drop it off with you?"

"Can you tell me what's in it?" I waited while he went to find it.

"Mostly personal stuff, a couple of photographs of the two of you, some copy of old stories, pencils, paper clips, a bottle of antacid. You know, the kind of stuff we all keep in our desks."

"Are there any files, notebooks?"

"Nick always kept whatever he was working on with him. Information on stories he had finished and names of old contacts he kept at home. He rarely used his desk here because he was always on the road. Are you looking for something special?"

I could hear the spark of interest in his journalist's voice.

"No." I tried to keep the disappointment out of my voice. "I promised his attorney I'd round up Nick's belongings for the inventory of his estate. Doesn't sound like anything important there, except maybe the pictures. I'll pick the stuff up later."

Appalled at how easy lying had become, I hung up, frustrated that my one idea had turned up nothing.

A noise emanated from the rear of the house, where someone was pounding on the French doors to the deck. When I went to investigate I found Mitch, holding a bouquet of flowers.

"A peace offering," he said. "I'm sorry if I upset you this morning. I wasn't questioning your judgment. I was just trying to keep you calm."

He grinned with that lopsided smile, so like Nick's, but beginning to be special in its own way, and I couldn't stay angry with him.

"I'm sorry I was rude," I said. "It's no excuse, but it's been a pretty horrible day."

He reached out and pushed a strand of hair off my face with a consoling gesture. I resisted the urge to throw myself in his arms and bawl my eyes out, afraid if I lost control, I'd never regain it.

"Will you reconsider having dinner with me?" he asked. "It's too late for me to cook, but I heard of a great little place on the beach we could try."

I was growing too fond of Mitch Lawton, maybe because he reminded me so much of Nick. And I was in no condition to make wise decisions involving emotions, but he was so appealing, standing there, holding the bouquet he'd brought me, I couldn't refuse.

We drove across the causeway and turned south on the beach,

driving its length to a small, rustic seafood restaurant, decorated with gray, weathered wood, fish nets, and brass lanterns. We ordered boiled shrimp, Greek bread, salad, and a pitcher of draft beer.

"Tonight you're going to relax," he said. "No talk of Gideon or what happened on campus today."

My mind went blank when robbed of those two alternatives. "What shall we talk about?"

"Music."

His choice of subject made me laugh because the old-fashioned juke box in the corner was blaring a medley of the Beach Boys' greatest hits.

"Not a very deep subject," I said.

"It could be. What's your favorite music?"

"I'm a romantic. I love Dvořák, Janáček, and Smetana, lots of strings and schmaltz. I cry every time I hear *Má Vlast*. And you?"

"Baroque is my favorite—Vivaldi, Sammartine, Albinoni—"

I giggled. We had finished half the pitcher of beer while we waited for our shrimp, and alcohol always makes me silly. "Sounds like the dessert menu at an Italian restaurant."

"It sounds like heaven if it's played on period instruments. I have two tickets to hear Christopher Hogwood's early music ensemble at Ruth Eckerd Hall Saturday night. Will you come with me?"

I hesitated, not in the mood for social occasions. The memory of the dean's disastrous party was too fresh. Being around others was an emotional strain, and I preferred to stay at home with my books and my stereo.

"Say yes," he said. "You need the distraction, something other than the routine of home and work. Besides, I hate to go alone. It's always more fun to share it."

As much as I preferred staying home, I couldn't say no to Mitch. By that time, he could have asked me to go with him to Siberia and I'd have said yes.

Later, Mitch kissed me goodnight at my front door, a lingering kiss that awakened desires long forgotten. I wanted him to come in, to stay the night, but before I could ask, he brought up the subject that had been taboo all evening.

"Are you certain you don't have the file this Gideon wants?"

As effective as a cold shower, the mention of Gideon doused my passion. "Yes, I'm sure. If I had, I'd have given it to him two weeks ago so he'd leave me alone. Why do you ask?"

"For the same reason." He smiled and brushed his lips fleetingly across mine. "To make him leave you alone. I want you all to myself."

Irritated that the mood of the evening had been shattered, I opened my door and stepped inside. "You'll have to wait until Saturday night. I have early classes in the morning."

When he'd gone, I wondered at his interest in the Gideon file and remembered my resolve to find it. My glance fell on the foyer table, where Nick's wallet and gun lay in the drawer. I took the envelope that held them into the kitchen and emptied its contents on the table.

The gun, a blued revolver, and bullets I put back into the envelope. Just the sight of them made me nervous. I searched his wallet and found credit cards, an old photograph of Carol and me taken in high school, his driver's license showing an unsmiling Nick, about a hundred dollars in small bills, and a few dog-eared business cards.

Although I hadn't really expected to find anything, I was frustrated at coming up empty-handed. I swept the wallet and its contents back into the envelope, and one of the business cards fluttered to the floor.

I picked it up and read, "Royal Palms Court, Okeechobee, Daniel Finley, Manager." As far as I knew, Okeechobee was the last place Nick had stayed before he died.

On impulse, I grabbed the phone and called the number printed on the card. Daniel Finley himself answered.

"You don't know me, Mr. Finley, but Nicholas Garrison, my brother, stayed at your motel a few weeks ago."

"I remember him. Real pleasant young man." The slow drawl

of the man's voice made me think of rednecks and Florida crackers.

"He was killed in a car accident shortly after he left your place, and I was wondering if you could tell me anything about how he spent his time there or who he saw in Okeechobee?"

"I'm real sorry about his accident, miss, but nope, 'fraid all I saw of him was when he checked in and out. Don't know what he did here or if he visited anybody, I wouldn't know."

My hopes plummeted. "I'm sorry to have bothered you, Mr. Fin—"

"Wait, don't hang up yet," he said. "Should I send the package to you?"

My breath caught in my throat. "What package?"

"The package your brother had me lock in the motel safe. It's not too big, just a manila envelope. Said he'd be coming back for it in a few days, but now he's dead, I guess you should have it."

I could barely hear him above the noise of blood pounding in my ears. My mouth had gone dry, and I had trouble speaking. "Do you have any idea what's in it?"

"Feels like papers. I can send it UPS tomorrow, if you like."

"No, I'll come for it." To Okeechobee and back was a six-hour trip. I'd have to wait until the weekend. "It'll be Saturday before I can get there. Will you hold it until then?"

"No problem. I'll keep it locked away until you get here."

I hung up and sat looking at the card, wondering why I hadn't thought to check Nick's wallet before. It seemed such an obvious place to look, in retrospect. I tried not to get my hopes up. The package could be the book Nick had been working on or a news story. Or, if there was such a thing, it could be the Gideon file.

Saturday, I would know.

Seventeen

"This whole idea of multiculturalism smacks of separatism." Moira's voice rang loudly in the small room, and I twisted uncomfortably in my chair.

Dean Koenig had called a special meeting to deal with the curriculum proposal, and, although it helped take our minds off the explosion and tragedy of the day before, the tension between proponents of opposing viewpoints mounted as the meeting progressed.

I had not slept well the night before, disturbed by Kristin's death and the possibility of locating the file of my tormentor. As a result, my senses were too finely tuned, and any stimulus affected them like salt in a wound.

Outside the second floor faculty lounge, visible through a wall of lightly tinted glass, sequins of light exploded in excruciating colors on the slightly choppy bay waters. Their reflections skewered my over-sensitive eyes like slivers of glass, and I feared developing another migraine before the meeting ended.

Beside me, Moira tapped the carmine tips of her porcelain nails in a torturous galloping cadence against the tabletop. "There's already too much emphasis on our differences and not enough on how we're alike. How will we ever learn to live in harmony if we don't begin to stress what we have in common?"

"If approached properly, multiculturalism isn't separatist," I said, "but a way of enabling people to see issues from different perspectives, to help them understand relationships among cultures."

"More than that," Emmett joined in, "it's power, power to prevent certain cultures from being excluded from a curriculum determined exclusively by a dominant class of white men."

"Oh, come off it, Emmett. What am I, chopped liver?" Moira glanced around the table at the predominantly female group. "Do those of us making this decision look like white men? Women are as disempowered as any minority."

Emmett's dark eyes flashed with anger, and the sharp angles of his ebony face hardened into stern lines. "As an African-American, I represent the only ethnic minority on this committee. And, Dr. Rafferty, you know full well we're discussing an issue greater than the composition of this committee. We're talking about a systemic racism that permeates American language, culture, and tradition."

"I acknowledge that racism, and I abhor it." Carol entered the debate, her eyes fierce with conviction. "But we have to consider what the role of the university is. And we have to be realistic. How can we justify additional requirements of multicultural courses when so many of our students are deficient in the basic skills of math and English?"

Although it was early morning, weariness seeped into my bones, urging me to ignore the turmoil around me, but I could not keep silent.

"Why does it have to be an either/or proposition?" I said with more energy than I felt. "Why can't we address basic skills and the responsibilities students must face in a country with a rapidly increasing ethnic population?"

"My sentiments exactly." Emmett nodded in agreement.

Moira leaned across the table and shook her finger in Emmett's face. Her voice was shrill with anger. "Even this university, as outstanding as it is, cannot be all things to all people. Like it or not, Emmett—"

Dean Koenig smacked the palm of his hand against the tabletop, squelching the chaotic discussion. The crack of the blow reverberated like a shot in the ensuing quiet of the faculty room.

Seeing that he had our full attention, he spoke, and his impatience at our inability to reach agreement added a biting edge to his usually mild voice. "We keep covering the same ground. Our backs have been pushed to the wall by ultimatums from the accreditation committee. If we don't make some hard decisions soon, we'll find ourselves operating a major university without accreditation and without federal funding as well."

He withdrew a sheaf of papers from a portfolio beside him and began distributing them around the table, like a dealer in a poker game.

"I have here three proposals, each a different approach to meeting the multicultural course recommendations of the accreditation team. Take them, study them, and come back to me Monday with your opinion as to which one we should adopt."

He stood to indicate the meeting had ended.

I wondered how I would make the six-hour trip to Okeechobee and back, attend the Saturday night concert with Mitch, and study all three of the bulky reports in front of me, all in the short space of a weekend.

"Two other announcements before you go," he said. "We haven't scheduled a campus memorial service for Kristin Montgomery yet. To be blunt, we're waiting to see if Chad Devereux will pull through. If he doesn't, we'll hold a double service. The other injured students are doing as well as can be expected under the circumstances."

He removed his glasses and pinched the bridge of his nose, the only sign he'd given of his own exhaustion. "The other news is that no cause of yesterday's explosion has been established. For those who've heard rumors of terrorism, that's all they are, rumors. No one has claimed responsibility. As far as we know, it was a terrible and tragic accident."

"No one has claimed responsibility?" I asked. "No one at the college has received any phone calls about the blast or its cause?"

Dean Koenig replaced his glasses and looked at me sharply. "Why do you ask? Have you heard something?"

Carol stared at me, as if waiting for me to divulge what I knew about Gideon.

I quickly shook my head, sorry to have called attention to myself. "It's just so hard to accept what happened as an accident..."

His statement provided substance for my hunch that Dillard had been lying. If anyone would know of faculty members receiving crank calls, it would be Dean Koenig. I trusted Dillard even less now than I had before.

As I left the faculty room, Moira followed and grasped my arm.

"You are going to vote with us traditionalists on this, aren't you?" She pushed back her dark red hair with her other hand.

I was struck then as I had been the first time I'd met her with how little her exotic beauty fit the mold of a university academic.

Her porcelain nails dug into my flesh. "If we start slicing our curriculum into a smorgasbord of mini-courses, none of our students will receive the broad overview of Western culture an educated person needs—"

I gave her hand a friendly pat before disengaging my arm. "I have to study the proposals first, but I'm open to discussing them with you when I've finished."

Classes were changing as I walked to my office, and students passed, wearing the stricken look of the young who, for the first time, have confronted violently and inescapably the fact of their own mortality. Yesterday's incident had left a deep scar on their psyches. Teaching for the next few weeks was going to be difficult.

Kevin McDermott waited at my office. "Do you have a few minutes to look at the changes I've made in my dissertation?"

I opened my door, glad to have company. I didn't want to be alone with my thoughts.

I spent the next hour discussing his research, losing myself in the problems of the past. We had almost finished when Paul Stephanos threw open the door and burst into the room.

"Dr. Garrison—" He stopped when he saw Kevin.

"Yes, come in, Mr. Stephanos."

The man's attentiveness still grated on my nerves, and I felt safer having Kevin there.

"No, it can wait." His expression looked like thunder beneath his bushy white brows, and he growled at me. "It can wait until you're alone."

He slammed the door as he left. Suddenly, I felt overwhelmed by all that had happened in the last few weeks. The tension of the faculty meeting and Stephanos' anger had stretched my self-control beyond its limits. I began to weep uncontrollably in hoarse, wrenching sobs.

Somehow I ended up in Kevin's arms with my head on his shoulder and his hand smoothing my hair.

"Go ahead and cry," he said. "Get it all out of your system, and you'll feel better."

I cried until I had no tears left. Kevin handed me the box of tissues from my desk, and, exhausted from weeping, I mopped my eyes and blew my nose.

"I'm sorry," I said. "I don't know what came over me. I hate helpless females who dissolve into tears at the drop of a hat."

"What you've been through is enough to make a stone cry," he said, "and Stephanos didn't help."

He smiled his boyish smile, and I noticed again the freckles across his nose that reminded me of Nick.

"Let's put a note on your classroom door," he said, "canceling your next class. These kids are in no shape for learning today anyway. Then we'll walk on the beach. Some fresh salt air will do you good, not to mention getting away from all this for a while."

This was a different Kevin from the one I thought I knew. His shyness had surrendered to an assertiveness that suited him and made him seem more mature. I remembered with a jolt that he was practically the same age as I was.

I could offer as an excuse that I wanted to encourage Kevin's newfound assertiveness, but the truth was I could not face my upcoming class with its sea of stricken young faces to remind me of Kristin and Chad—and of Nick.

I kicked off my dressy heels and slipped on the pair of walking shoes I kept in the bottom drawer of my file cabinet for treks across campus, then walked with Kevin to his car.

We drove a few miles north of the campus to Dunedin Beach, a state park where the island beach was maintained in its natural state, free of buildings and roads. There we walked along the hardpacked sand above the rolling surf.

Perhaps breaking down in front of Kevin had removed some sort of barrier between us because he seemed more comfortable, less intimidated by me, than before. We strolled in easy silence for a while, enjoying the solitude of the deserted beach.

"The winter tourist invasion doesn't begin for a few more weeks," I said. "That's why I love this time of year, when the weather's perfect and the beaches aren't mobbed."

"A day like today makes me realize I don't take enough time away from my studies. I've almost grown roots to my study carrel in the library stacks."

"It will be over before you know it," I said. "In another six months, you'll have finished your dissertation, passed your orals, and, Ph.D. in hand, you'll be looking for a job."

"When I get that job, will I have more time for this?" His sweeping gesture encompassed the beach and endless gulf.

"You'll have no more time than you do now unless you make time," I said. "Take it from the voice of experience. And you must make time if you don't want to burn out in a hurry."

"Taking things easy will be hard for me. I've never done it before."

I realized then that all I knew of Kevin's background was that he had attended the University of Alabama as a scholarship student and come to Suncoast with the highest recommendations of any teaching assistant I'd had.

"Did you grow up in Alabama?" I asked.

"No, here in Florida, on a farm outside of Two Egg in the panhandle. My daddy was a soybean farmer, so you could call me a country boy. I'm still more comfortable plowing fields with a tractor than doing research in the library."

"I haven't met many farmers. Farming is a disappearing lifestyle, especially in this part of the state."

A strange expression crossed his face, then disappeared so quickly I thought I'd imagined it. "That's why I'm working toward my Ph.D. There's not much call for tractor drivers these days, and I do like to eat."

"Does your family still work the farm?"

"My parents are both dead." His voice sounded strange and flat. "I'm the only one left."

We trudged to the northern tip of the island and back, then sat on the steps of a boardwalk leading to the bathhouses.

"Alex—"

"Yes?"

For a moment his boyish shyness returned, but he shrugged it off and gathered my hands in his.

"I've been really worried about you," he said. "You were devastated by Nick's death, but instead of coming to grips with it, you seem to be suffering more. Is there something going on, something bothering you that you'd like to talk about?"

The late October sun warmed me, melting away the tensions of the past two weeks. I faced the man, whose intellect I admired and respected, and hoped if I presented my dilemma to him, he might have some insight, some clue I'd overlooked.

Starting with the call I'd received the day after I'd learned of Nick's accident, I told Kevin all about Gideon. I held nothing back, including my suspicions that Nick had been purposely killed. I explained the other calls, the note on my desk, the open Bible, the most recent call after yesterday's explosion, and my distrust of Detective Dillard.

Just as I started to tell him about Daniel Finley at the Royal Palms Court in Okeechobee, he interrupted me.

"Good Lord, Alex, why didn't you tell me all this before? You're really in danger, aren't you?"

Being taken seriously was a new experience. Everyone else,

from Carol to Mitch, had treated my fears and suspicions with skepticism. I nodded, and my eyes filled with tears.

Kevin grasped my shoulders. "There's only one thing for you to do."

"Don't tell me to go to the police. I reached a dead end with Detective Dillard."

"No," he said. "You must find that file. It has to be somewhere, and, from what you've told me, handing it over is the only way you'll get this Gideon to leave you alone."

He pulled me into his arms. "You can't continue this way. This constant pressure will destroy you."

I started again to tell him about Okeechobee, but he leaned down and kissed me, closing his mouth over mine, stopping my words.

Taken by surprise, hungry for someone to take care of me, to shield me from Gideon's threat, I yielded, until my common sense kicked in again.

Gently, I pushed him away and disengaged from his embrace. I chose my words carefully to spare his feelings. "I like you a great deal, Kevin, but we can't endanger our professional relationship. I'd hate to lose the best teaching assistant I've ever had."

I smiled to indicate I wasn't angry.

He didn't return my smile, and his serious expression made him appear older than his years. "I won't always be your teaching assistant, Alex."

"No, but for now you are."

I stood and walked away, creating physical and emotional distance between us. His kiss had elicited a response in me, but whether because of my own emotional needs or a specific attraction to Kevin was beside the point. Any relationship beyond that of professor and teaching assistant was out of the question.

"Kevin." I struggled to find words to repair the rift his kiss had created. "I appreciate your listening to me. You're the first person I've told this to who hasn't treated me as if I've got a screw loose."

He stepped toward me. "If you're going to get this Gideon off your back, you must find that file. If you need me to help you search for it, just say the word."

Emotion charged his voice, and he stared with an intensity that made me uncomfortable. I could have kicked myself for encouraging him earlier. I had enough worries without having to fend off romantic involvement with my teaching assistant. Prudence prevented me from confiding in him further. The sooner we returned to our former association, the better.

I checked my watch. "We have just enough time to stop at Sea Sea Riders for a sandwich before my afternoon class. If you're hungry, I'll buy."

For an instant, I thought he would refuse. Then his boyish smile returned. "You're on. I'm starving."

Eighteen

Friday after my first class, Priscilla Gamble, Emmett's teaching assistant, rocked on the sofa in the faculty lounge when I entered, her arms wrapped around her and her petite frame racked with sobs.

"What is it, Pris?"

Without looking up, she shoved a wave of long black hair from her face and pointed to a memorandum tacked to the bulletin board above the coffeemaker.

"Chad Devereux died early today," she said. Her tear-strained voice came out in a hiccup. "He sat in the second row in my next class and asked the most intelligent questions of any student I have. He was such a good kid, it just isn't fair."

She beat the sofa cushion with clenched fists, then sat up and blew her nose forcefully.

I poured a cup of coffee and sat next to her, glad to see indignation had at last stopped her tears.

"Take it from one who knows," I said. "None of this is fair. Nick, Kristin, Chad, the others who were injured, all because of—"

Priscilla eyed me questioningly.

"All because of accidents," I finished lamely, but the deaths had not been accidents. I knew Gideon was to blame. Tomorrow I would recover the papers Nick had left with Daniel Finley. If they were the Gideon file, they were my only hope to stop the killing. I craved to see what was so important that three people had already died for it.

Priscilla regained her self-control. "The memorial service for Kristin and Chad is scheduled for Wednesday in the chapel."

I recalled Nick's service in my garden. "That's going to be tough getting through."

"I always thought your college years were supposed to be the most carefree, happy time of your life. What a joke." She uttered a snorting, mocking noise, then stared glumly into the bottom of her coffee cup.

I wanted to reassure her. She wasn't much older than the students she taught, too young to be so cynical. But how could I comfort her when I was riddled with cynicism myself?

We drank our coffee in uneasy silence until Pris glanced at her watch. "Back to the trenches."

She turned back at the door. "I dread my next class. The students were depressed enough before. I hate to think how they'll be when they learn Chad is dead, too."

She didn't expect an answer, and I didn't give her one. My heart ached for Nick and the two teenagers, killed so indiscriminately.

Saturday morning, on the drive to Okeechobee, I believed my life had reached a dead end. Nick was gone, and I had lost the zest I used to hold for my work. I wondered if I'd feel different when my life returned to its routine, or if I was experiencing the burnout I'd warned Kevin about a few days before.

At least my relationship with him had reverted to its former status. His attitude had lost its fervor of Thursday, and we had returned to the comfortable camaraderie of coworkers.

As I drove across the causeway toward Tampa, I remembered my recent journey to Cassadega, and Bella Ionescu's warning rang again in my ears: *they come for you, they come for you.*

I turned on the radio to drown out the chanting in my head and heard traffic control announce an accident in the causeway's eastbound lane, blocking traffic. At the same time, cars ahead of me slowed to a crawl. Within minutes, all movement in both eastbound lanes had stopped.

My ever-present briefcase, filled with papers to be graded and the curriculum proposals from Dean Koenig, sat on the seat beside me. I lowered the windows, switched off the ignition, pulled out the proposals, and began to read.

I lost myself in a curriculum based on Joseph Campbell's work, stressing the common mythology of cultures as well as their differences. I had tuned out my surroundings so completely that only the blare of a horn behind me brought me out of my concentration.

Ahead of me, traffic had begun to move once more. I glanced in the rearview mirror, shrugging an apology to a man in a red convertible directly behind me, and caught sight of a gray sedan with tinted windows two car-lengths back of me.

Call it paranoia brought on by my fear of Gideon, instinct, or a lucky guess, but I was convinced that the gray sedan was the same car that had prowled the street in front of my house, the same car that had followed me to Cassadega and to the Hilton at Altamonte Springs.

I had no idea who was in the car, but I couldn't let whoever it was follow me to Okeechobee. I had to see for myself whatever Nick had left there before I decided whether to let anyone else have it. I didn't want anyone taking it against my will, so as the traffic began to flow again, I pressed the accelerator, hoping to lose the gray sedan.

It kept up easily, following just two cars behind as I drove past Tampa International Airport and onto the interstate. In an effort to shake my pursuer, I exited into downtown Tampa, but the gray car stayed with me. I looked about for a way to lose him and saw the signs to Harbour Island, a complex of hotels and shopping malls.

Taking the winding streets and bridge that crossed over from the inner city to the island shopping complex, I thought I had lost him, but as I stopped for the light at the entrance to Harbour Island, I could see him several cars behind.

Hoping whoever followed was unfamiliar with the area, I pulled into the underground parking garage, a labyrinth of dark, twisting passageways. Ignoring the speed limit, I raced through the intricate maze and out again, stopping only long enough to pay the parking fee at the exit.

Once off the island, I turned up one street and down another, checking constantly for a sign of my pursuer. I zigzagged through the downtown business district until I reached Highway 60, then threaded my way through heavy traffic and road construction in Brandon, and finally hit open highway with no sedan in sight.

I sped past phosphate mines and citrus groves, turned south at Lake Wales, and followed the highway toward Okeechobee. The road wound in and out among gently rolling grazing land, paralleling the meandering path of the Kissimmee River. The highway was narrow and deserted, but I welcomed the loneliness. I was happy to have lost my pursuer, and on such a lonely road, I would spot him instantly if he reappeared.

When I reached the outskirts of Okeechobee, I soon located the flashing neon sign of the Royal Palms Court, a group of tiny cottages with peeling paint, set back from the road beneath the shade of a dense stand of melaleuca trees.

Nick's taste in lodgings brought a smile to my face. On his *Courier* expense account, he could have stayed anywhere without worrying about the cost, but most often he chose rooms that reflected the atmosphere of the story he was writing at the time. The story he had worked on here must have been a depressing one.

I turned into the dusty parking area and climbed stiffly from the car. I had left home at nine o'clock. The causeway accident and my circuitous route to elude the gray sedan had taken time, and it was now almost two. I had been behind the wheel the entire time. I was hungry and needed to use the restroom, but I would secure Nick's package first.

I entered the largest cottage, one with a sign marked "Office," where a teenaged girl with stringy blonde hair sat behind the counter. She was popping gum and reading a paperback novel, whose lurid cover showed a couple with remarkable, half-naked bodies writhing in a passionate but contorted embrace. So great was her absorption, I had to speak twice to get her attention.

"Yeah?" She raised her head as if coming out of a trance.

"I'm looking for Mr. Finley."

"He ain't here." She returned to her reading.

"I'm supposed to pick up a package he's holding for me in the motel safe."

"He ain't here." She didn't look up this time but kept on reading.

"Is there anyone here who can get the package for me?"

"Nope."

I was tired and hungry and my patience had worn thin. I tried the no-nonsense tone Nick had always referred to as my schoolteacher voice.

"Then will you please tell me when you expect Mr. Finley to return?" I snapped.

My words had the desired effect. She dropped the book and walked over to the counter. "He's over there."

She pointed across the highway to a building as dilapidated as the one in which we stood. "Jake's Cafe" was scrawled on a rough sign above the entry.

"He's having lunch," she said. "I don't know how long he'll be. If there's anybody to drink with, he could be there all afternoon."

Before I could get out the door, she buried her nose in her book again. I left my car parked at the motel and crossed the narrow highway.

Jake's Cafe was empty of customers, except for two men, deep in conversation, at the lunch counter. I went first to the restroom and was surprised to find it spotlessly clean. I decided I might not be risking my life to eat lunch there.

Back in the dining room, I sat at a small table near the window and, when the waitress came, ordered a hamburger and iced tea. She brought my food quickly, a plump, old-fashioned burger with fresh lettuce and tomatoes, pickles, and onions.

While I ate, I kept an eye on the two men, who were drinking beer from bottles and swapping fish stories. They were still drinking when I finished my meal, so I asked the waitress which one was Daniel Finley.

"The heavyset fellow on the right."

I approached him cautiously, reluctant to interrupt but anxious to retrieve the package and return home. I had told no one where I was going, and I didn't want Mitch asking questions if I was late for our concert.

"Mr. Finley?"

He swung around on the counter stool. "Who wants to know?"

"I'm Alexandra Garrison. I've come for the package my brother left with you."

He nodded to his friend. "Wait here, Jake, I'll be right back."

I trailed Finley back across the highway and into the motel office, where his young assistant did not look up from her reading.

"It's in the safe," he said. "Nobody's touched it since he left it here, just like I promised him."

He moved to a lone filing cabinet, tucked beside an old console television in the cramped room, and pulled open the top drawer.

I smiled at his euphemistic reference to the motel safe.

He removed a large, sealed manila envelope that looked like it held a manuscript and handed it over. He fixed his eyes on me expectantly.

I removed a ten dollar bill from my wallet and handed it to him. "For your trouble."

"No trouble at all." He held the office door open for me as I left, then followed me out. As I pulled away, he crossed the road again to Jake's Cafe.

The digital clock on the dashboard read three o'clock. I was dying to know what was in the envelope, but I hadn't wanted to open it in front of Daniel Finley. Now, I feared I'd have to wait until I reached home to check its contents.

Mitch had said he would pick me up at seven for the concert. If I didn't run into any more traffic problems, I would have just enough time to shower and change. I considered cutting across the state, through Arcadia and Myakka, to pick up Interstate 75, but going that way, I'd have to cross the Skyway again, so I stayed with my original route, too chicken to face the bridge alone.

My resolve to wait until I was home to open the envelope lasted about thirty minutes. By then, my raging curiosity refused to delay longer. In a small clearing ahead sat a tiny church with a deserted yard and adjoining cemetery. I turned into the parking area under the shade of an oak and stopped.

The peacefulness of my surroundings clashed with the turmoil in my mind. Using a nail file, I slit open the envelope with a shaking hand and withdrew a large accordion file.

A label, affixed to the front of the file, was marked in Nick's distinctive, left-handed scrawl: *The Sword of Gideon.*

Nineteen

The Sword of Gideon.

I thought at first it was the title for Nick's book as I flipped through what looked like manuscript pages. When I came across photocopied rosters of names, maps, charts, and a jumbled assortment of other data, I realized there was more than Nick's book there.

The file would require careful reading. Its assorted contents were not something I could assimilate in a hurry.

If there had been a telephone around, I'd have called Mitch and canceled our date, but the church was locked and there were no other buildings in sight. I jammed the papers back into the file, the file into the envelope, and placed the envelope in my briefcase with the curriculum proposals. I would read the file after the concert, even if it took all night.

No traffic snarls arose to slow my return trip, and I reached home with sufficient time to bathe and dress for the concert. Although the concert was the first real date I'd had since my break-up with Burke, my mind was distracted from the upcoming evening by the envelope that lay in my briefcase on the foyer table.

I dressed in a simple black wool dress with a Chanel jacket of nubby black wool shot through with gold threads. The dress hung loosely over my hips, drawing attention to the weight I'd lost since Nick had died. I might have lost body weight, but the burden I carried in my mind weighed a ton.

As I was fastening gold and jet earrings, my eye caught the

reflection in the mirror of the Monet print above my bed, and I remembered my suspicion that Gideon had searched my house. I had checked with Mrs. Baxter, my cleaning woman, who'd claimed she had cleaned only on her regularly scheduled day. Gideon had to have been the one who'd moved my mother's Bible.

I feared he might search again, and I did not want him to have the file—not yet. I needed time to study its contents, to see what was so important that my brother and two others had died.

Then I remembered the hiding place I'd used for Nick's gifts when we were children, one he'd never discovered, although he had taken the house apart inch by inch in the weeks before Christmas. At the bottom of the case of the grandfather clock that stood in the foyer was a small enclosure, a space for the heavy brass weights to drop as the mechanism slowly unwound.

I hurried into the hallway and wound the clock, raising the weights, slipped the envelope from my briefcase, and placed it in the bottom of the clock case. Even when standing directly in front of the glass door, I could not see the envelope secreted in the clock's interior. It was not as safe as a bank vault, but I hoped it would be safe enough until my return.

I was ready and waiting when Mitch arrived.

"You look terrific." He pulled me close and nibbled my ear. "Maybe we should just skip the concert."

Another night I might have taken him up on his offer, but I needed to spend the night alone with Nick's mysterious file.

"You did a hard sell on Hogwood Wednesday night, and I'm not letting you back out now," I said.

He let me go, though reluctantly, smiling with a hint of wickedness in his grin. "Then I'll save you for dessert."

I smiled back, groaning inwardly. I'd have to think of some way to get rid of him after the concert. If nothing else, I could always claim a migraine. I had them often enough for it to be a plausible excuse.

Riding to the concert, I studied him covertly in the darkened interior of the car. I had to admit I liked this man who had appeared in my life with such luck at a time when I needed someone. Besides liking him, I trusted him. Somehow I knew he'd be there any time I needed him, and it was a good feeling.

He turned, caught me watching him, and reached for my hand. "Where were you today? I stopped by your house a couple of times, but you were gone."

My first inclination was to hedge, to say I'd been working at my office, but I couldn't lie to Mitch. I'd begun to care for him too much to deceive him. But until I read Nick's file, I wasn't ready to acknowledge I had it, not even to him. I settled for half the truth.

"I drove to Okeechobee where Nick stayed for the last few days before . . . before the accident."

"And?" Mitch grew very still.

I tried to sound nonchalant. "And I had the best hamburger I've had since I was teenager. I ate at a dive called Jake's Cafe."

"You drove to Okeechobee for a hamburger?" His tone reflected his disbelief.

"The hamburger alone was worth the trip. Actually, I ate while I was waiting to see a Mr. Finley, the manager of the motel where Nick stayed. That part of the trip was fruitless. All he could tell me was that he liked Nick, but knew nothing of what he did or who he saw while he was there."

"Nothing about Gideon?"

I turned away and stared at the road ahead, unable to meet his eyes. "No, he said nothing about Gideon."

Mitch squeezed my hand. "I wish you'd told me so I could have gone with you. We don't know who this Gideon is or what he's up to. I want to keep you safe."

His concern made me feel guilty, but not guilty enough to tell him the whole truth.

"I feel safe enough tonight," I said, "in the company of one of New York's finest."

* * *

The concert was everything Mitch had promised. The ensemble of period instruments opened with Handel's "The Arrival of the Queen of Sheba" from *Solomon,* and for a short time I was able to lose myself in the beauty of the sound, forgetting all of the tragedy of the previous weeks.

At the intermission, we climbed the stairs to the Dress Circle Room, an elegant and comfortable mirrored lounge reserved for patrons of the hall.

"Good evening, Dr. Garrison." The young waiter in formal garb was a former student. He took our order for champagne, and we found a seat on one of the wide banquettes that rimmed the room.

"What do you think?" Mitch asked.

"It's indescribable. As many times as I've heard 'The Four Seasons,' I've never heard it played with such brilliance and vitality. The original instruments make it sound like a new piece."

"Wait till you hear the Bach. It'll knock your sachs off." He wiggled his eyebrows like Groucho Marx, just as he had the day I'd met him. It had been only days before, but I was beginning to feel I'd known him all my life.

The waiter brought our champagne, and as I lifted my glass, I caught sight of Burke in the mirrored wall. He saw me at the same time and began working his way through the packed crowd with a curvaceous young blonde in tow.

"Alex, Mr. Lawton, this is June." In his arrogant way, Burke managed to introduce and dismiss his companion with a single phrase. "I trust you're enjoying the concert?"

He also managed to imply by his tone that somehow he was responsible for its success. In a way, he was, being one of the largest contributors to the hall, a fact well-publicized in the concert program. Burke was not shy about promoting himself.

"Very much."

Mitch's answer was terse, and I could tell the two disliked each other. That dislike had nothing to do with me. Standing side by side, the two men projected such intrinsic differences in personality and style, I almost expected to see sparks fly.

Burke turned to me. "Did you investigate further that matter we discussed?"

He was referring to Mitch, and his rude, patronizing attitude infuriated me. "No, I didn't. And I probably never will."

"Alex." He shook his head sadly, treating me again like a mentally deficient child. "I suppose, as always, I'll have to do it for you."

"Suit yourself, Burke. Nice to meet you, June." I turned my back, and they moved away to speak to someone on the other side of the room.

"What was that all about?" Mitch asked.

"Just some details about Nick's will." I was too embarrassed by Burke's rudeness to make things worse by explaining the truth.

The bell sounded for the second half, and I forgot about Burke. The remainder of the program was as good as the first half, but I was preoccupied, wondering about the contents of Nick's file and the answers it might provide. I couldn't concentrate on Bach.

After the concert, when Nick walked me to my door, I had no need for my migraine excuse. Taped to the door was a folded paper, marked *URGENT* in big red letters. I yanked it down and read it:

> Alex,
> Why in the name of God don't you get an answering machine, and where the hell have you been? I've been calling all evening. No matter what time you get home come to my house. Moira was murdered in her office today.
>
> Carol

"Alex, what is it?"

Stunned by the note's contents, I had forgotten Mitch entirely. I handed him the note, which he read at a glance.

"I'll drive you," he offered.

"I can't ask you to do that. It's already late, and I may be awhile."

"No arguments. You're shaking like a leaf. How do you expect to drive in that condition? Besides, you're under the protection of New York's finest, remember?"

He was right. I couldn't drive because I couldn't stop trembling. Moira murdered? The thought was too horrible. She was abrasive at times, but she had a good heart. Why would anyone want to kill her?

Carol had every light in the house blazing when we reached her place. She met us at the door.

"Thank God, you're here and you're all right. I was afraid they'd find you somewhere murdered, too." Her full lower lip quivered.

I gave her a quick hug. "Hey, I'm okay. Tell me about Moira."

Sam called from the family room. "Come in here. I figure all of us could use a drink."

We settled on deep, chintz-covered sofas before the fireplace, where a fire crackled cheerfully, even though the night was mild. Sam poured us each a drink.

"I'm so glad the children are spending the weekend with friends," Carol said. "The police have been here most of the evening."

"Maybe you could start at the beginning and fill us in," Mitch said.

I appreciated his tact, but then digging out information was his job, and I was too distraught to think straight, much less ask the right questions.

Carol took a swallow of her vodka and tonic and set it aside. "It was about five o'clock. Sam and I were trying to decide whether to go out to eat or order pizza."

"The doorbell rang," Sam said, "and I answered it to find two detectives at the door. They said they had some questions involving the university, so I asked them in and went to find Carol."

"Was one named Dillard?" I asked.

Carol shook her head. "Sam made sure to check their identification before letting them in. The first question they asked was whether I remembered an argument between Moira and Emmett at a party last weekend at Dean Koenig's."

She twisted the rings on her fingers as she spoke, a nervous habit she'd developed in high school after we'd received our senior class rings.

"I told them I did remember it, and they asked me to describe the argument. I assured them it wasn't really an argument, just a difference of opinion. Then I related what I'd seen and heard at the party."

A log in the fireplace fell with a crack, and I jumped. Mitch moved closer and placed his arm around me. I moved gratefully into the security of his embrace.

"Next," Carol said, "they asked about the faculty meeting last Thursday when Moira shook her finger in Emmett's face."

"But why?" I asked. "Every meeting we've had, Moira has shaken her finger in somebody's face. That's just Moira."

"That's what I told them," Carol said. "But it didn't make any difference. They'd already arrested Emmett and charged him with Moira's murder."

"You can't be serious?" I cried. "Emmett Nyagwa has dedicated his life to a philosophy of nonviolence. He'd be the last person to murder anyone. How could the police make such a mistake?"

"Because of the evidence," Sam said. "They found Moira in her desk chair in her office, impaled by one of Emmett's African ceremonial spears right through the heart. They found his prints—and only his prints—on it. He was seen in the building this afternoon, on a Saturday, when only faculty and staff have access."

"It doesn't look good for him," Mitch said.

"There's more," Sam said. "They said the killer had to be someone she knew. There was no sign of alarm or struggle."

"And, thanks to my big mouth," Carol added, "they've given

Emmett a motive—his public disagreements with Moira over the past week. The police think they have an airtight case."

"You mustn't blame yourself," Mitch said. "Someone, probably Dean Koenig, had already told them about the arguments, or they wouldn't have known to ask you about them."

"Jawole and the children, how are they taking all this," I asked.

"You know Jawole," Carol said, "always projecting that wonderful aura of calm and control. Who knows what's really going on underneath? She had a friend staying with her when I called earlier, and she said she's thankful the children are too young to understand what's happening. I plan to see her in the morning."

"I'll go with you," I said. "Then I'll talk to the police. Maybe with enough of us as character witnesses, we can convince them they've got the wrong person."

Mitch got up and stood with his back to us as he stirred the dying embers of the fire.

"The question is," he said, "if Emmett didn't kill Moira, who did?"

"And why?" Sam asked.

Gideon, I thought instantly, praying he had not killed Moira as another warning for me. I felt ill, mourning the loss of my friend and wondering if I had somehow been to blame. If only I'd found the file sooner, perhaps I could have stopped all this from happening.

If there were any answers, I would find them in Nick's file. It was after one o'clock in the morning, but I would read all night if I had to, to find out what I needed.

"Take me home, please, Mitch. It's late, and if Carol and I are to visit Jawole in the morning, I'd better get some sleep."

Carol and Sam walked us to the car, and as Carol hugged me, she whispered in my ear. "What in God's name is happening, Alex? I feel like I'm living under siege."

Her voice caught, as if she might burst into tears. I couldn't remember a time in all the years I'd known her that Carol's ever-present, plucky sense of humor had disappeared, but that night she looked frightened, old, and tired as she watched us drive away.

I was quiet on the ride home, trying to make sense of Moira's death.

"You're thinking it's Gideon, aren't you?" Mitch asked.

I was reluctant to put my fears into words. "I know it wasn't Emmett. That much I'm sure of."

He parked his car in Rosa's driveway and walked me across to my door. "You're all done in. Try to get some sleep, okay?"

He held me close, and I longed for him to stay, to protect me from the madness that had haunted me the past few weeks, but I had to be alone to read Nick's file. I hoped it would reveal something that would be helpful to Emmett. I hated to think of him, sitting alone and abandoned in a jail cell.

"I'm sorry the evening ended like it did," I said. "Thanks for the concert. It was everything you promised. For a little while I forgot, and the pain went away."

"There'll always be other concerts, and if I can, I'll end your pain forever."

He kissed me, and I went inside, leaving him standing on my front step until I turned out the light.

Over five hours later, I set aside the last page of the file. The morning light was gathering outside my bedroom window, but I had not slept. I had read carefully every page of the manuscript Nick had written and every page of the Gideon file.

I did not discover who killed Moira, but I had learned another terrible and inescapable fact. Even if I turned the Gideon file over to my tormentor immediately, I was as good as dead myself.

Twenty

I contemplated Nick's *Sword of Gideon* file with a sense of fatal resignation. Events had been set into motion over which I had no control, events that would lead as inevitably to my death as they had to his.

I brewed coffee and went out onto the deck, wrapped against the dawn chill in a velour robe, and stared unseeing at the bay. The unfinished manuscript of Nick's book, the one he had been so excited about when I'd last seen him alive, had revealed the beginnings of Nick's end.

According to his manuscript, the day Nick had returned from Eastern Europe, a young man named Richard Slater had called him at the *Courier,* saying he had information he wanted to share, but their meeting would have to be secret. Intrigued by the air of secrecy and always on the lookout for an interesting story, Nick had agreed.

When Nick had met Slater in an obscure bar and grill off Central Avenue in downtown St. Petersburg, he'd discovered Richard Slater was just a kid, barely eighteen, and frightened for his life.

"He sat at the back of the room, watching the door," Nick had written, "and every time it opened, all the color drained from his face, as if he was expecting death itself to walk through.

"After I had shown him my identification and assured him our conversation was off the record, he relaxed slightly and began to tell me about himself. His parents had divorced when he was small, and after that Richard had lived in Cleveland with his mother. His father, however, had returned home on a regular basis, beating and terrorizing his ex-wife and child.

"In desperation, Richard's mother had fled south to Jacksonville, but a succession of live-in boyfriends had taken up the abuse where Richard's father had left off, making his life such hell that he dropped out of school at sixteen and ran away from home. He ended up in Tampa, working for a lawn service.

"One night at a local bar where Richard and his coworkers gathered to watch sporting events on the big-screen TV and drink beer, served by an agreeable bartender who never checked I.D., a big man, dressed in military fatigues, approached Richard.

"Richard said he'd first thought the man was an airman from McDill, but as they talked, the man identified himself as a recruiter for the Sword of Gideon."

The Sword of Gideon. I shivered at the name, a Biblical term for an unholy group from hell.

At first, Richard had told Nick, he had been led to believe the Sword of Gideon was a combination religious/survivalist organization, dedicated to building self-esteem in young men by training them for meaningful work. Persuaded by the charismatic recruiter, longing for a feeling of belonging and a sense of purpose in his life, Richard had eagerly joined the organization.

Along with a group of about thirty other young activists, Richard was taken by bus to a secret camp in the northern part of the state, where they bivouacked in tents in a pine forest and underwent grueling training in wilderness survival and paramilitary activities, including hand-to-hand combat, weaponry, communications, and explosives.

Richard had told Nick they'd also received religious instruction, an indoctrination into a bizarre Christian fundamentalism. They were taught that the peoples of Northern European origin were the Lost Tribes of Israel, Jews were the spawn of Satan out to take over the world through its financial institutions, and all other races, including Hispanics, Asians, and Arabs, were subhuman, what they called "mud people."

At first, Richard had said, he'd enjoyed the fellowship of the group, the feeling of being part of a group, the boost the philosophy of white supremacy gave to his own low self-image, but his attitude toward the Gideons changed when he was given a clerk's position in the organization's camp headquarters.

Although a high school dropout, Richard Slater, unlike many other of his fellow recruits, Nick wrote, was an intelligent young man with well-developed skills in reading and writing. These skills had come to the attention of the group's commander, who'd given Richard the coveted office job.

While working in the office, Richard had had access to a top secret file that outlined the goals of the Sword of Gideon. He had read the detailed list of terrorist activities in Florida and throughout the Southeast, acts designed to paralyze the infrastructure of the region, from highways and bridges to airports and water treatment plants, even nuclear power facilities.

The Gideons had designed their plot, not only to maim, kill, and disrupt but also to cast suspicion and blame on Hispanic and African-American groups. Their ultimate goal was to create a climate, and ultimately a call, for the uprising of the "downtrodden" white race and the overthrow of the United States government.

Gideon leaders referenced the government's "murders" of David Koresh and his followers at Waco as proof that drastic measures were needed. They planned to incite young recruits to action with the threat of being killed by FBI, ATF, or even United Nations troops.

When Richard saw those plans, his enchantment with the Sword of Gideon tarnished and he wanted out, but he had learned in their indoctrination program that no one ever left the group and lived. That was why he had come to Nick. He hoped that if the two of them could gather enough information, publish it as both a newspaper series and in book form, the Sword of Gideon, with its goals thwarted, would disband, its leaders would be arrested, and Richard, shielded by the glaring light of national publicity, would be safe.

To carry out his plan, Richard had made copies of the Gideons' schemes and timetables for the terrorist attacks. He'd also secured a roster of the membership, and he'd given all those documents to Nick.

At that point, Nick's manuscript ended.

I had studied the Gideons' tactics included in the file. If carried out, such plans might not automatically activate an uprising among what the Gideons referred to as "the oppressed white race" of the country, but their actions would, without doubt, sow death, destruction, and chaos. The bombing of one building in Oklahoma City had shaken the country. I shuddered to think what such horror, multiplied a hundredfold, would create.

With the existence of disgruntled pockets of self-styled militias throughout the country, inherent in those plans was the distinct possibility that the disasters the Gideons precipitated could incite the civil war I had spoken of to Mitch.

I had scanned the membership roster, a chilling list, which included some municipal and state officials, a few local and state police, including Detective Dillard, and even a United States congressman.

A note in Nick's handwriting at the bottom of the roster warned that not all recently recruited members were included, and that the attached supplemental list identified a special cadre of commanders in key positions by code name only.

Using the information from the file, I was able to piece together all that had happened. The Gideons must have discovered Richard Slater's defection and killed him. His disappearance would explain Nick's search for a person who had worn a military-style camouflage cap. His disappearance would also explain Bella's insistence that the man was dead.

Somehow the Gideons had discovered that Slater had given Nick the file. Pain stabbed through me at the thought of what Slater must have suffered at the hands of the Gideons when they'd forced the file's whereabouts from him before killing him. When Nick was run off the interstate, the Gideons must have been in pursuit, hoping to retrieve their missing file.

But their plans had gone awry. Nick's car had flipped and Nick had died before they could question him. Those bastards—what would they have done to Nick if he had lived?

Nick had left the file with Finley. The Gideons must have panicked when they didn't find it in his car. So they had searched Nick's condo and my house and office. I figured the other offices had been searched either as a cover to divert attention from me or because the Gideons thought I might have given the file to a colleague to hide.

When they hadn't found the file, and I hadn't helped them, they had blown up Kristin Montgomery's car, the one exactly like mine, as a warning of how serious they were.

They believed I either had the file or would somehow find it for them—and they were right. How much they appeared to know about me terrified me.

But as hard as I tried, I couldn't fit Moira's death into the puzzle. If killing her had been another attempt by the Gideons to force me to find the file, they'd been awfully quiet about it. I'd received no more calls or threats, but then I hadn't been at home yesterday or last night either.

I was locked in a terrible dilemma. I couldn't give them the file. Once they had it, I had no doubt they would kill me with as little hesitation as they had killed Nick, Kristin and Chad, and Richard Slater. I knew too much for them to allow me to survive.

I couldn't go to the police because I had no way of knowing who might be a secret commander, listed only by code name on Slater's roster. The fact that Dillard was a member made me fear there might be other Gideons hidden in our local police force.

I put myself in the Gideons' place to imagine what they might do next, but I couldn't comprehend minds with so little regard for human life. Although I longed to share my dilemma with someone, I realized whomever I told would be in as much danger as I was.

A thought more frightening than anything else seized me. The Gideons knew a great deal about me, my habits, my friends, my work. Someone close to me had to be providing them with information, or worse yet, someone close to me *was* a Gideon!

I returned to my bedroom, gathered Nick's papers strewn across my bed, stuffed them back into the envelope, and, because I could think of no other place they would be safe, hid them once more in the bottom of the clock case. I considered taking them to the bank Monday to lock in my safety deposit box, then remembered the car that had followed me the day before. Such a move might alert the Gideons that I had the file.

I tried to contrive some clever way of guaranteeing my safety, like a sealed letter to be opened upon the writer's death, a favorite movie ploy, but my body ached with exhaustion and fatigue clouded my mind until I couldn't think. I crawled into bed for a few hours' sleep before my meeting with Carol. After that, I had no idea what I would do.

I had just finished dressing when the doorbell rang. The sound startled me, and I panicked, believing the Gideons had traced my journey to Okeechobee, talked with Daniel Finley, and now had come for the file—and me.

Nick's gun still lay in the foyer table, and I raced to get it. The person at the door continued to push the bell as I fumbled awkwardly, attempting to reload the bullets Major Lowery had so helpfully removed. I had inserted all but the last bullet when I heard Kevin's voice.

"Dr. Garrison? Alex? Are you all right?"

Weak with relief and feeling very foolish, I slid the gun back into the drawer and opened the door.

"I'm sorry I took so long. I was getting dressed." My body hadn't received the message that imminent danger had passed. My voice trembled and my hands shook.

"Alex, you're white as a ghost and shaking all over." He pulled my quivering body to his, smoothing my hair as he'd done the day I'd gone to pieces in my office.

"I'm sorry about Moira," he said. "I came as soon as I heard. I know she was your friend."

He released me, and gratitude for his presence surged through me. I didn't want to be alone.

"Come into the kitchen," I said. "I'll make a fresh pot of coffee."

I started coffee brewing and defrosted cinnamon buns in the microwave, while Kevin sat at the table, looking at the headlines of my morning paper.

"I didn't know anything about this until I saw it in the paper this morning," he said. "I worked on my dissertation in the library yesterday until it closed. By then, the police vehicles had left, and everything seemed normal."

Normal. I had forgotten what normal was.

He stopped talking long enough to devour one cinnamon bun and start on another. As when Nick died, I had no appetite.

"I didn't know about it myself," I said, "until I returned from a concert last night. Carol left a note on my door. She'll be here in a few minutes. We're going to visit Jawole."

He stopped eating. "Jawole's husband murders your good friend in cold blood, and you're going to visit her? I don't get it."

"You can't believe Emmett killed Moira?"

He shrugged. "I've seen them arguing, going at it as if they hated each other's guts. And you know how sarcastic Moira could be. Maybe she pushed him too hard and he snapped."

I sat at the table with my head in my hands. "I'm afraid that's what the police think, too. But I've known both of them a long time. Beneath that surface animosity, they had great respect for each other."

"If Emmett didn't kill her, who did?" He repeated Mitch's question of the night before.

The Gideons. I was trying to decide whether to tell him what

I'd discovered when Carol breezed in the unlocked front door and into the kitchen.

"Good morning, duck—"

She stopped when she saw Kevin sitting with me at breakfast, a cozy domestic scene, and the look on her face told me she'd jumped to all the wrong conclusions. She grinned widely, hoping for the worst.

"Kevin stopped by," I said, ruining her fun, "when he read about Moira in this morning's paper."

Carol's grin faded as the knowledge that he hadn't spent the night dashed her hopes of my finally adding some sexual spice to my life.

"And I've got to be going." He swallowed the last of his coffee and got up from the table. "You'll let me know about the services?"

"As soon as we know anything," I promised.

When he left, Carol's grin returned. "I'd say he has an unscholarly interest in you."

I blushed, recalling the fervor of his kiss on the beach. She had hit too near the mark, but Carol had always been perceptive where I was concerned. Because of that perception, I'd have to be careful and not give away what I'd learned about the Sword of Gideon. I was under sentence of death myself. I didn't want to pass that sentence on to her.

The best defense is a good offense. "My relationship with Kevin is strictly professional. Don't go projecting your own lusts onto me. I saw how you looked at him."

It worked. Carol quickly changed the subject. "We'd better go now. Jawole wanted us to come while her aunt has the children at church. We can talk more freely without them there."

Jawole opened the door of their attractive Tudor-style home in Belleair. Her posture and expression were serene as always, but the constant movement of her slender hands, adjusting her hair and clothes and playing with her earrings, exposed her distress.

"Thank you for coming. No one else, except our family and a few close friends from church, has called. I feel like a leper ... or should I say a leper's wife?"

Tears formed in her large, expressive eyes, and she brushed them away quickly and led us into a formal living room, decorated with natural woods and fabrics and several pieces of African art.

"Jawole," Carol said, "Alex and I know Emmett didn't kill Moira. It's only a matter of time until the police come to the same conclusion and go after the real murderer."

Jawole smiled sadly. "You are living in a white man's world. You don't know what the legal system is like for people of color."

"White or black, justice is justice and truth is truth," Carol said.

"Not always." Bitterness laced Jawole's voice. "Moira was a white woman, and it appears to the police my Emmett, a black man, has murdered her. They are ready to believe Emmett's disagreement with her over the curriculum issue was sufficient reason for him to kill her."

"I told them he couldn't have killed her," Carol said, "but they didn't want to hear it."

"No." Jawole's long, slender fingers pleated the folds of her skirt. "They want to believe he's guilty. If only they knew how often he was provoked by issues and epithets much worse than anything Moira ever said to him. Each time, he turned the other cheek, refusing to stoop to violence."

I reached out and covered her nervous hand with my own. "Everyone at the university knows Emmett believes in nonviolent methods to resolve conflicts. The police investigation will prove that."

Tears spilled over and ran down her high cheekbones across the rich mahogany of her face. "According to statistics of conviction of black men in similar cases, the outlook for my Emmett is very bad."

"No," I said, "their evidence is circumstantial. They can't hope to convict him on it."

"You are very kind, but don't you see? They want him to be guilty. His attorney said the judge has remanded Emmett to prison without bail. I don't know if Emmett will ever be a free man again."

In view of those facts, I could think of nothing comforting to say, and I knew too well the feeling of being trapped in a personal hell.

"What happened yesterday?" Carol asked.

"We had promised the children we would take them to the new Disney movie. Security called from the university and said there had been a problem at Emmett's office. I took the children on to the theater, and Emmett went by the school, then met us later."

"And the problem at his office?" I asked.

"There was no problem. When Emmett arrived at the university, everything was in order. He spent about fifteen minutes looking for a security guard. When he finally found one, the guard checked with the security office and said no one there had called Emmett, so Emmett left campus and joined us at the movies."

"Emmett didn't see Moira?" Carol asked.

Jawole's dark eyes flashed with anger through her tears. "The only person Emmett saw was the security guard, who later identified Emmett as the only other person in the building that afternoon."

"Sounds like someone wanted to make certain Emmett was seen," I said. "Did you tell the police about the call?"

Jawole nodded. "Emmett and I both told them, but they just looked right through us, as if we were invisible." Her tears had washed away the anger. "They arrested him anyway, in front of his own children."

Helpless and frustrated, I could think of nothing to assist

Jawole and Emmett. Emmett had been set up, but I had no reason so far, except a terrible premonition, to suggest the Gideons were responsible.

We stayed with Jawole until the children came home from church. The two, chubby bright-eyed toddlers didn't know yet how cruel the world could be. They showed us colorful drawings they had made in Sunday school and sang to their mother a song they had learned.

I ached for the family, but I didn't know what to do. Emmett, at least, would have a trial. Circumstances had already sentenced me, unless some miracle occurred to save me.

I had long ago stopped believing in miracles.

When Carol dropped me off, I found the connection I'd been expecting between Moira's death and the Sword of Gideon. Propped against my doorstep, wilting in the noon sun, stood an arrangement of blood-red carnations and scarlet roses.

The attached sympathy card was signed simply *G*.

Twenty-one

I didn't want that tainted bouquet in my house.

After throwing the flowers in the trash, I went to bed and slept straight through the afternoon and night. I awakened Monday morning with the heightened sensory perception the death of someone close, or the awareness of one's own mortality, brings.

As I walked from my car to the Arts and Letters Building, the sky seemed a deeper blue, the grass more verdant, the fresh young faces of students more poignant, and the salt air more bracing. I reveled in the sensations, keenly aware that Moira would never experience them again.

Monday was a somber day at the university. Three deaths in one week and the arrest of one of the most popular professors on campus had touched everyone in some way, leaving in the wake of such sadness a nagging fear that the worst might not be over.

A small group of students, many in tears, gathered before Moira's office as I passed. Several had left flowers in front of the door, which was sealed with special tape by the police. The hall in front of Emmett's office was empty, and I promised myself that when my afternoon classes were over I would visit him.

My uncharacteristic resignation toward my own predicament persisted, allowing me to contemplate my own death, if not without fear, at least without panic. I experienced, too, an urgency to accomplish what I could to help Emmett and expose the Gideons before they discovered I had the file and came for me.

I had decided upon waking to tell no one about Nick's file. Although I longed for the wisdom and protection of both Kevin and Mitch, especially Mitch, I would be selfish to place them in jeopardy for my sake.

The students in my morning class were subdued, and they asked no questions about Saturday's murder. Mid-morning notices appeared on bulletin boards of a requiem mass for Moira at St. Cecilia's on Thursday.

After my first class, Priscilla, who had taken over Emmett's classes, walked into the faculty lounge like a victim in shock. It took her a moment to realize I was there.

"I'm almost afraid to get up in the mornings," she said, "for fear of what tragedy will strike next."

"I know the feeling." All too well.

"How can the police be so stupid to believe Emmett Nyagwa capable of killing Moira? The longer he sits in jail, the colder the killer's trail becomes."

She threw her books on the table with a sigh of disgust and poured coffee. "And poor Moira. What a horrible way to die."

I nodded, afraid to say anything for fear of saying too much.

Her eyes widened and her cup trembled in her hand. "It could have been any one of us. I can't count the number of Saturdays I've worked here alone, thinking I was safe because the building was locked and security on guard."

"How are Emmett's students taking this?" I asked.

"It's hard to tell. They're still in shock over Kristin and Chad. But none of them believes Emmett did it."

"Pris—" I wanted to assure her everything would be all right, but I wasn't so sure of that myself. "Be careful. Don't work here alone until all this is cleared up, okay?"

She appraised me with curious eyes. "Sure, Alex, and you take care, too."

As I left for my next class, I knew that all the care in the world wouldn't save me.

The students of my ten o'clock American history class followed my lecture like sleepwalkers, all except Paul Stephanos, whose piercing eyes never left my face. He was not a degree-seeking student but, like many older citizens in our retirement community, was probably taking the course to pass the time. His interest so far had centered on me, not history.

At the beginning of the session, when I had first noticed his disturbing concentration on me, I had tried to intimidate him, to stare him down, but his scrutiny remained so intense that I was always the first to look away.

He followed me to my office after class, a habit of his. He never took notes but made a point of seeking me out after class to ask about the lecture or assignments.

"I need to talk to you," he said.

I motioned to the overstuffed chair and sat behind my desk, placing the security of its wide expanse between us. I had also left my office door open. I knew nothing about him or why he was so interested in me, but considering all that had happened the past two weeks, my previous uneasiness over him blossomed into a virulent distrust.

"How can I help you, Mr. Stephanos?"

"I need to talk to you," he repeated.

I forced a smile. "That's what you're doing, isn't it?"

He shook his white, shaggy mane, and his ice-blue eyes narrowed. "I need to talk to you somewhere else, away from school."

"If you have a problem with the course, we can discuss it here, now. That's why I hold office hours."

He slammed his fist against the top of my desk, making me jump. His rudeness angered me, and I struggled to keep my temper. Before I could ask him to leave, he struck the desk again.

"What I need to talk about has nothing to do with school. It's a personal matter."

I had no idea what he wanted, nor by that time did I care.

"We have a faculty policy against socializing with students outside of campus activities. It's a hard and fast rule I never break."

"But—"

"If you have a personal problem, one of our counselors will help you. Their offices are in the Administration Building. Would you like me to set up an appointment for you?"

He shook his head from side to side, looking as angry and as dangerous as a wounded bear, but I could think of no way to get him out of my office.

The phone on my desk buzzed. Grateful for its intrusion, I picked it up.

"Dr. Garrison, Dean Koenig wants to see you right away in his office," the dean's secretary said.

"I'll be right there."

Stephanos still glowered at me across my desk.

"You'll have to excuse me. I'm wanted in the dean's office."

He went out grudgingly, and I locked the door and hurried away, leaving Stephanos staring holes in my back as I walked down the hall.

When Shirley ushered me into Dean Koenig's office, two men in business suits were with him.

"Dr. Garrison," Dean Koenig introduced me, "this is Detective McCordle and Detective Slane. They have a few questions for you about Dr. Rafferty's death."

McCordle, a big man with a thatch of red hair and a ruddy complexion, reminded me of Major Lowery of the highway patrol. Slane was tall and slim, narrow-faced and small-featured, with an unfortunate resemblance to a weasel. Slane wielded pencil and paper, but McCordle asked the questions.

"How long had you known Dr. Rafferty?"

I cast about in my memory, trying to recall if either man's name had been on Slater's roster in Nick's file. Both names seemed unfamiliar, but hundreds had been listed and I couldn't remember them all. I took too long to answer.

"Please, Alex." Dean Koenig's voice was terse. "I promised

these gentlemen our faculty would give them the utmost cooperation in their investigation."

"Sorry," I said. I'd forgotten the question and asked McCordle to repeat it.

"How long had you known Dr. Rafferty?"

"Five years. She came to Suncoast the same year I took over as head of the American Studies Department."

"So Dr. Nyagwa was in your department?" he asked.

"Yes, he is in my department, and I don't believe there's any way he killed—"

"Tell us about the recent disagreements between Dr. Nyagwa and the deceased."

Jawole was right. They did not want to hear what I had to say unless it supported their conclusions. I told them, much as Carol had, about the recent arguments.

Slane nodded happily, scribbling my answers as swiftly as I gave them. McCordle's next question caught me totally off guard.

"Where were you Saturday afternoon at the time of Dr. Rafferty's death?"

"Am I a suspect?"

I was stalling with the question. In spite of McCordle's benign appearance, I couldn't risk trusting him, nor did I trust Slane. If I told the truth, would Dillard or someone like him have access to their report and put two and two together to discover I had found the file?

Dean Koenig cleared his throat and stared at me with a fierce look. I sensed an inevitability in the movement of events.

I told the truth, not because of any superior moral fabric on my part, but because my mind wouldn't function fast enough to construct a convincing lie. "I drove to Okeechobee Saturday morning and was there until three o'clock Saturday afternoon, when I left to drive home."

"Anyone there who can vouch for that?" McCordle asked.

"Yes, Daniel Finley, the manager of Royal Palm Court, and a waitress at Jake's Cafe across the street."

The weasel-faced Slane smirked as he wrote my answer, but McCordle had the decency to look embarrassed as he asked his next question.

"Were you alone?"

"Yes."

I grew suddenly weary, tired of struggling with the terror of the last few weeks, and I longed to lay the entire burden of the Sword of Gideon on McCordle's wide shoulders and have done with it, whatever the consequences.

"Detective—"

"Just a few more questions, please."

Slane stared at me. His hooded eyes and the darting tongue that licked his thin lips unnerved me, and somehow I dared not share the secret of the Gideons with him.

"Ask as many questions as you wish, Detective McCordle," I said. "As Dean Koenig indicated, you have my full cooperation."

His other questions requested routine information, my address and phone number. Dean Koenig thanked me when McCordle finished and dismissed me.

I stood in the hallway outside my office, where gray duct tape covered the fracture that split the exterior glass wall from top to bottom, just as the Gideons had rent the fabric of my life.

Bella was right. Now it was only a matter of time before they came for me, too.

But as I thought of Bella with her tattooed identification number from the Nazi death camp, I remembered also the millions of Jews of Europe who'd waited docilely until the soldiers of the Third Reich had come for them. For the first time, I understood their resignation to their fate, and in understanding it, I refused to allow myself to go as gently as they had.

Instead of eating lunch, I spent the next hour in the library, where I located what I needed to know.

In an *Editorial Research Reports* article on the growing danger of hate groups, I learned that the Federal Bureau of Investigation had a civil rights and special inquiry section to deal with cases of violence by hate groups.

No longer willing to wait until the Gideons came for me, I would study the roster in Nick's file to see if any FBI agents were listed. If not, I would deliver the file to the local special agent of the FBI. The Gideons would have to deal with them, and perhaps the FBI could provide some sort of protection for me until the members of the Sword of Gideon had been arrested.

Mitch was waiting when I returned to my office. "I came to take you to lunch. From past experience, I'll bet you haven't eaten anything for the past two days."

He leaned against the wall by my door in khaki slacks, a polo shirt, and top-siders, with his hands in his pockets and his face lighted by a crooked smile.

At that moment, I knew I loved him. There could be no turning back.

"You're right," I said, "but I have a class in five minutes."

"How about after that, a late lunch?"

I shook my head. "I'd love to, but I promised myself I'd visit Emmett this afternoon."

He didn't give up. "The county jail is almost to St. Petersburg. Let me drive you down, and we'll stop somewhere for a quick lunch on the way."

I had dreaded going to the jail alone. Mitch would be familiar with procedures and make it easier. He might be helpful in asking Emmett the right questions, too.

"Agreed, but on one condition."

"What's that?"

"While I'm in class, you'll use the phone in my office to check the visiting hours. I don't want to miss seeing him today."

"That's simple enough. I'll be waiting here when your class is over. Just try not to pass out from hunger before I can feed you this time, okay?"

His tone was teasing, but the concern in his eyes was real.

Having someone to look after me felt good. I could get used to it on a permanent basis.

I left him seated at my desk with the phone book and went reluctantly to class.

Twenty-two

Emmett Nyagwa was a broken man when we saw him that afternoon. His proud posture had shriveled to defeat under the shapeless orange coverall of a county jail inmate.

"You should not have come, Alex. I am ashamed for anyone to see me like this."

"You're the same person you've always been," I said, "and I had to tell you I don't believe for one minute you had anything to do with Moira's death."

"You are very kind, but your opinion will not carry much weight in this place, or in a courtroom, I'm afraid."

"Emmett," Mitch said, "Jawole told Alex you were called to the campus under false pretenses on Saturday. Can you remember anything else unusual about that day?"

Emmett shook his head, and I noticed for the first time streaks of gray in his dark hair. Then he smiled and shrugged, "Unless you call being arrested unusual—"

He stopped in mid-sentence, as if remembering.

"What is it?" Mitch asked. "Even the smallest thing may be significant."

"The police asked me over and over what I had been doing on campus that afternoon, and even though Jawole and I each told them the same story of my being called to campus by someone claiming to be security, they paid little attention to that fact."

"Then what?" Mitch prodded him gently.

"A Detective McCordle brought in an African ceremonial spear and asked me if I recognized it."

"Did you?" I was not as patient as Mitch in letting Emmett's story unfold.

"Yes." His smile was a mixture of humor and chagrin. "It was mine. It must have been stolen from my office the night of the break-in."

The events from that night were burned in my memory. "But you said that night that nothing was missing."

"That is what I thought at the time," Emmett said. "Several art objects were smashed beyond repair. I had simply gathered the pieces, including the broken shafts of several spears, and thrown them away. I was too upset to notice if one was missing."

"So there could be some connection between the campus break-in and Moira's murder?" Mitch said.

"That connection will do me little good since the police have come up with nothing on the break-in," Emmett said.

"I've been in police work a long time. Believe me, it's a good start. If nothing else, the spear stolen in the break-in and the fake call from security could be enough to plant reasonable doubt in a jury's minds."

"Thank you for giving Emmett hope," I told Mitch as we left the prison complex parking lot.

Mitch kept his eyes on the traffic as he drove. "I'm afraid any hope I gave him is pretty hollow. In the murder of a white woman by a black man, the conviction statistics are against him."

"That's what Jawole said."

"Unfortunately, she's right. Emmett is in serious trouble unless the police find Gideon."

"Gideon?" I couldn't bring myself to tell him Gideon wasn't one man but a small army.

"Didn't you say he left a note on your desk the night of the break-in?" Mitch asked.

"Yes, but as Emmett said, the police haven't been able to locate this Gideon."

"Give it time. Police work requires lots of patience. Sometimes it's just a matter of waiting until the one you're searching for calls attention to himself."

"How many more have to die before Gideon draws enough attention?" Frustration gave an edge to my voice. "I'm sorry. I didn't mean to take out my fears on you."

He reached over and massaged the back of my neck with one hand, smoothing my tension away.

"That's why I'm here," he said.

I closed my eyes, yielding to the comforting manipulation of his fingers. The Gideons were the key. If the FBI could find them, not only would I be safe but Emmett would be free. I would check the roster in Nick's file for the names of agents as soon as I got home. If no names were listed, I'd call the FBI right away.

Mitch dropped me off at the Arts and Letters Building, and I went in to pick up my briefcase before returning home.

When I stopped to check my mail in the faculty lounge, Dean Koenig was pouring himself a cup of coffee. He eased himself onto a chair at the table. Weariness permeated his every movement.

"Ah, Alex, I was getting ready to drop a note in your mailbox." He took a sip of coffee, made a face, and set the mug aside. "Do you have a minute?"

"Sure." I placed my briefcase on the table and sat across from him.

"First, I want to thank you for your cooperation with the police today. I know how you feel about Emmett, but it's very important the university maintain good relations with the local authorities."

He closed his eyes and pinched the bridge of his nose, a gesture of exhaustion he had used often lately. "God knows, we've needed them in the last week."

I couldn't share the dean's appreciation of the local police force. "I wish they'd be more open-minded in their investigation. Emmett didn't kill Moira, but they'll never find who did if they don't consider other suspects."

Dean Koenig looked surprised. "Such as?"

"I don't know," I lied. "But I know it wasn't Emmett, so it had to be someone else."

I didn't want to broach the issue of Gideon. I wanted to attract as little attention as possible until I'd turned Nick's file over to the FBI.

"I find Emmett's guilt hard to take myself," he said, "but the evidence is stacked against him."

He shook his head and his shoulders slumped with fatigue. I felt sorry for him, having to deal with break-ins, the death and injury of students, and the murder of a faculty member all within such a short space of time. Many administrators did not face such an accumulation of disasters in a lifetime. The stress of the past weeks had drawn new lines across his forehead and created a more pronounced sag to his jowls.

"Was there anything else?" I asked.

"Yes, but I can't remember. Hold on—" He fumbled in his coat pocket for a small notebook and flipped hurriedly through its pages. "Ah, here it is. I want you to say a few words of remembrance at Moira's requiem mass Thursday."

"Me?"

"You were her closest friend on the faculty, so I think it would be appropriate."

The thought of speaking in public made my throat dry and my hands sweat. "I'm flattered, but I'm really not very good at that sort of thing—speaking before large crowds. There must be others on the faculty better qualified."

"Don't be silly, you do it every day." For a moment his tired eyes twinkled. "Only you call it teaching. Moira would have wanted you, not someone more qualified or more comfortable with speaking."

It was the least I could do for Moira. I wished I had been a better friend. I hated the finality of death, with no second chance to correct past deficiencies and mistakes or to carry through on all those good intentions left undone.

"I'll be happy to speak at the mass." I'd have Carol, who was good with words, help choose something appropriate to say.

"Excellent, I knew you'd rise to the occasion." He stood and picked up his coffee mug. "I'll see you tonight at the wake, then?"

"Wake?"

"Sorry, I thought you knew. The details are in your mailbox. Moira left instructions that upon her death, she would foot the bill for the entire faculty to hold a wake at her house, a real Irish send-off."

He left the lounge, and not a moment too soon. For the first time since Moira died, I broke down and cried for my friend.

"To Moira."

Reginald Hartwick raised his glass and the rest of us followed.

"May you arrive in heaven before the devil knows you're dead," he said.

"My God," Carol said quietly to Mitch and me, "what wretched taste the man has."

"It's appropriate," Mitch assured her. "It's an old Irish toast. Many of the men on the New York police force are of Irish descent, just like Moira. I've heard that toast many times."

"I keep expecting to see Moira." I glanced around her spacious townhouse, where we'd gathered at her posthumous invitation.

The buffet table was heaped with more food than even that voracious crowd could consume, and the caterers were doing a booming business at the bar.

In addition to mourning a lost colleague and friend, we all were too aware it could have been any one of us murdered instead of Moira. No one, except the police, was buying the idea that Emmett Nyagwa was a murderer, and if he hadn't killed her, whoever did was still free somewhere, maybe even there among us.

Reginald and Mitch sat at a table on the patio, their heads together over large glasses of beer. I couldn't hear what they were saying but assumed Reginald had finally seen his chance to discuss New York art museums.

"Who's your friend?" Kevin joined me on the deep sofa in the living room and nodded toward Mitch on the patio.

"Mitchell Lawton, my neighbor. Didn't you meet him at the Koenigs' party?"

"I escaped the madding crowds by hiding in the garden, remember?"

"Ah, yes." Looking back, it was hard to reconcile the self-assured Kevin McDermott beside me with the shy young man of just over a week ago. He was a man of many faces. The one he turned on me now was almost overbearing.

"What do you know about this guy?"

Good grief, I thought. He sounded like Burke.

"He's on leave from the New York City Police Department, and he's a good friend of Herman and Rosa Myers, who are like family to me. Why do you ask?"

"Because he's a stranger, because he's with you, and because I worry about you. Things haven't been exactly calm around here." He placed his arm along the back of the sofa and slid closer. "I couldn't stand it if anything happened to you, Alex. You—"

"Hello." Mitch had broken away from Reginald and stood looking down at us.

Kevin's arm dropped around me possessively. He smelled of bourbon, and his aggressive behavior must have been the result of too much drink.

"You must be Kevin," Mitch said.

I tried to wriggle out of Kevin's grasp, but he only gripped me tighter. Mitch smiled at my dilemma, and I resisted the urge to kick him. I felt like a piece of candy at a taffy pull.

"How did you know?" Kevin's tone was hostile, and his words were slightly slurred.

I sat still to humor him.

"It's my business to know things. Alex, can I get you another drink?"

I peered down at my glass, which was full, and back to Mitch. "No, but I'd love some fresh air. Excuse me, Kevin."

I pried his fingers from my shoulder and got up from the sofa. Mitch took my arm and guided me through the crowd to the empty patio.

I glanced back at Kevin, slumped on the sofa, fast asleep. I had never known him to be a drinker. The stress of the last week was taking its toll on all of us, and Kevin was no exception.

The night air was cool, a welcome change from the hot, smoky atmosphere inside. I inhaled deeply.

"How much do you know about Kevin?" Mitch asked.

If the situation hadn't been born of tragedy, it would have been funny—three men in my life, each distrustful of one another.

"As much as I know about you," I said.

He stood behind me with his arms around me to warm me against the night chill and spoke softly in my ear. "Don't try to be cute, Alex. There's a killer loose, and I want to make damn sure he doesn't get his hands on you."

I giggled as always when I'd had more than one drink. Kevin suspected Mitch, Mitch suspected Kevin, and Burke probably suspected them both. If either of them was a killer, they'd both had their hands on me that night.

Forty-eight hours later, the situation would no longer be amusing.

Twenty-three

I'd had no time to check for names of FBI agents on the roster in Nick's file Monday. Carol had called to ask my help with some last-minute details for Moira's wake, and I had fallen into bed after the gathering that night, physically and emotionally exhausted and slightly inebriated.

Tuesday I had even less time. Moira's brothers and sisters and their families began to arrive, and Carol and I took turns between classes meeting them at the airport in Tampa to drive them to Moira's townhouse.

Tuesday evening I labored over Moira's eulogy, choosing T. S. Eliot's "Little Gidding" from *The Four Quartets,* the poem Carol had read at Nick's memorial service, as part of my remarks. I found its hopeful message more comforting than the traditional Bible passages, which always reminded me of my mother's suffocating fundamentalism.

Wednesday morning classes were canceled so students and faculty could attend the memorial service for Kristin and Chad in the university chapel.

As I crossed the campus toward the chapel, I realized that cancellation had spared me from facing Paul Stephanos and his problems until Friday, a welcome delay. By then Nick's file would be in the hands of the FBI and I could concentrate on my work once more.

The memorial service was an emotional event. The chapel, with its tall, clear windows overlooking the bay, was filled to capacity with students, faculty, and members of the community.

Amidst a bank of floral arrangements, a small draped table before the chancel displayed framed photographs of Kristin Montgomery and Chad Devereux. The youthful exuberance and attractiveness captured in the pictures magnified the horror of their senseless, untimely deaths.

I blocked out the messages, spoken by ministers, family, and friends. Listening to their thoughts and feelings, so much like what I was experiencing over the loss of Nick, was more than I could bear.

When the tributes ended and the university choir began to sing, I sighed with relief. I had taken a seat at the back of the chapel, and when the congregation rose to join the choir in "Amazing Grace," I spotted Detective McCordle standing at the rear of the room, studying the crowd.

When the service ended, McCordle caught Kevin as he passed and pulled him aside, engaging him in conversation. The two left the building together, and when I worked my way through the crowded aisle to the doorway, they were nowhere in sight.

I returned to my office to find a message from Burke to call immediately on "a matter of great urgency," according to the student assistant who had taken the call. Thinking it only some difficulty in Nick's estate and knowing Burke's tendency to grandstand, I threw the paper on my desk, planning to deal with it later.

Before I could take my jacket off, my phone buzzed.

"Why haven't you returned my call?" Burke roared.

I could measure his impatience by the decibel level of his voice.

I attempted to curb my irritation and answered in what I hoped was a reasonable tone. "I just walked in and only finished reading your message a moment ago."

"You have to come down here right away, Alex. I have to talk to you."

"If it's that urgent, just tell me now and save me a trip." I assumed "here" meant his downtown office.

"It's not something I can say over the telephone. I need to talk to you face-to-face."

He was beginning to sound like Paul Stephanos.

"Look, Burke, can't it wait until afternoon? I'm going to lunch in a few minutes, and then I have an afternoon class."

"Forget lunch." His voice, deadly and low, frightened me as his yelling had not. "You won't feel like eating after you hear what I have to say."

I seldom liked what Burke said, but I wasn't in the mood for lunch. Better to get it over with. "I'll be there in fifteen minutes."

The drive downtown took only ten minutes, and a few minutes later Burke's personal secretary, Miss Swenson, a statuesque blonde with a plunging neckline and the personality of an iceberg, showed me into his inner office.

My feet sank into the deep plush of the pale silver carpet. Without looking up, Burke motioned for me to sit down. I perched impatiently on the edge of a skeletal chair of chrome and soft black leather.

Burke did not move or glance up from behind the massive slab of black marble on chrome pillars that served as his desk.

For several long minutes, I stared at the brilliant Jackson Pollack painting that almost covered one wall, its writhing primary hues the only color in the room, and waited for Burke to finish the notes he was making in a file.

Burke had chosen two famous minimalists to design and decorate his office, and while it had won awards for artistic merit, it was as cold and unappealing as the man I had almost married.

I waited until I could stand it no longer, realizing the delay was Burke's way of exercising control.

"Tell me what you want now or I leave," I said. "I have a class to teach in forty-five minutes. I can't wait around while you play mind games with me."

Burke closed the file and set it aside. "When I tell you what I've discovered, you won't be in such a hurry."

"Then tell me!"

I could raise a few decibel levels on my own, if provoked, and Burke could provoke me better than anyone.

"Alex, Alex." He shook his head condescendingly. "I told you to check things out for yourself, but you refused, stubborn and hardheaded as ever. You think you don't need a man to take care of you, but you're wrong. If left on your own, you'd soon find yourself in great difficulty."

"What in heaven's name are you rambling about? Spit it out now and make your point, or I'm outta here." I stood to make good my threat.

"Mitchell Lawton is a fraud." His words fell like bricks in the stillness of the room.

"What are you talking about?"

"Remember me asking what you knew about him?"

"Yes, and I believed it was none of your business. If Rosa and Herman thought enough of him to rent him their house and introduce him, that was good enough for me."

"Exactly what did Rosa tell you about him?"

"This is still none of your business, but if you insist, she said he was on medical leave from the New York Police Department because he'd had an emotional breakdown after the death of his partner."

Burke shook his head again. "So he lied to them, too."

"What do you mean?"

"I think you'd better sit down, Alex."

"If you're concocting some story out of jealousy, it won't work. No matter who or what you say Mitchell Lawton is, you and I are finished."

He spread his palms against the surface of his desk and leaned toward me. "You and I will never be finished as far as I'm concerned. I've waited six years for you to come to your senses. I'll wait as many more as needed. In the meantime, I won't have you endangering yourself by consorting with a cold-blooded killer."

I looked at him in amazement. "You've gone too far this time, Burke."

I started for the door.

"I have the documentation from the New York City Police Department to prove it."

I remembered the day the highway patrolman had told me Nick was dead. The same feeling of disbelief and disorientation I had felt then returned. I moved across the room like a sleepwalker and sat down in the chair facing his desk.

"I'm listening," I said.

"I was curious about this man who had appeared so suddenly after Nick died and took such a vital interest in you, so I called the NYPD."

"Why would they give out information to you?"

"As an officer of the court, I have a certain *quid pro quo* relationship with the police. They're usually happy to help me out."

He rose from behind his mammoth desk and took the chair beside me. "I told the public relations officer we had a man who had recently come to our community, claiming to be an NYPD detective on medical leave, and I simply wanted to verify his claim."

Burke reached over and clasped my hands in his. I was too deep in shock to mind.

"Lawton was an NYPD detective, but he was dismissed last September for shooting a thirteen-year-old black youth to death . . . in the back. He goes on trial in January. The shooting was not the first time Lawton has been in trouble. His personnel file cites several reprimands for use of excessive force, all against minorities."

My head whirled and for a moment I feared I would throw up on the pristine pearl gray of Burke's plush carpet.

He crossed to a file cabinet hidden behind a panel, extracted a folder, and handed it to me. "The official I spoke with faxed me these documents. I requested them because I knew you wouldn't believe me without them."

I opened the folder with reluctance and began to read. If anything, Burke had soft-pedaled reality. According to the reports, Mitchell Lawton was a violent, bigoted child killer.

I returned the folder to Burke and yearned to kill the messenger. I took several deep breaths, waiting for my anger toward him to dissipate. It wasn't his fault Mitch was no good. He'd only discovered the fact.

"I'm sorry about all this, Alex. Promise me you'll be careful. The man is very dangerous."

I nodded and, moving as if in a dream, left without speaking.

By the time I reached the campus, the numbness of shock had worn off, and I began to shake. I pulled into my parking space and spotted Detective McCordle again. This time he was huddled in conversation with Mitch outside the front entrance of the Arts and Letters Building.

Fearing Mitch had come to take me to lunch, I scrunched down in the seat, praying he wouldn't look my way. After a few minutes, he walked away with McCordle, deep in discussion.

Somehow I managed to get through my afternoon class, then hurried back to my office and locked the door. I needed time to myself as I tried to reconcile the violent person portrayed in the police reports with the Mitch I knew. The effort was futile, forcing me to face the fact that I had fallen in love with a man who didn't exist.

In the midst of my grief was anger, anger at myself for being such a rotten judge of men. In retrospect, my misjudgment of Mitch was not so unlikely. Only seven years before I had fallen blindly in love with an arrogant, hedonistic, egotistical male chauvinist. Obviously my perception, as far as men were concerned, hadn't improved.

The magnitude of the situation in which I found myself suddenly struck me as I searched for a way to break off from seeing Mitch without angering him. I could claim migraines for only so long before I'd have to tell him I knew about his past. Then

I'd be faced with the possibility of igniting the latent violence of his personality.

Slowly my numbed brain began to draw connections. Mitch had arrived shortly after Nick had died. He had appeared the day my office was vandalized, and he was next door the day my house had been searched. He knew my comings and goings, and most damning of all, the time he had spent with me on Longboat Key had been the longest span of time without a call or threat from the Gideons.

I faced the frightening probability that Mitch was a Gideon himself.

It all fit: the violence, the racism. How he must have laughed at me when I told him my hopes for a world united in racial harmony.

Burke was right. Mitch was dangerous, and I must do anything I could to avoid him. My phone rang, and I reached for it with reluctance.

"Hi, I missed you at lunchtime."

Mitch sounded the same, but knowledge of his past had changed me forever. "Yes, I had to meet Burke to go over some details about Nick's estate."

"How about dinner tonight?"

I felt torn in two, part of me yearning for the Mitch I loved, the other terrified of what he was. "No, I don't think so—"

"Alex, are you okay? You sound strange."

The caring in his voice made my heart ache for what I'd lost. "I'm all right, just a migraine. I'm on my way home. I plan to take my medicine and sleep until time for Moira's service in the morning."

"Can I pick you up then?"

He was nothing if not persistent.

"Thanks, but I promised Carol and Sam I'd go with them . . . faculty solidarity."

He was silent for an instant. "Better get home and take care of that headache. I'll talk to you tomorrow."

The receiver clicked, and I sat and stared at the phone before rousing myself from the daze I'd been in since my visit to Burke's office.

If Mitch was a Gideon, getting Nick's file into the hands of the FBI became more important than ever. I hurried down the hall, heading for home to check the roster before going to the FBI, but Kevin stopped me.

"Hi, Alex, got a minute?"

"Not really. Can it wait until tomorrow?"

"It won't take long. I wanted to talk to you about this McCordle guy."

"The detective?"

"Yeah. He grabbed me when I left the memorial service this morning and grilled me for almost an hour. Do you know what's going on?"

I set down my briefcase and purse and pulled on my jacket, hoping Kevin would take the hint. "I'm afraid I do. They questioned me Monday. I think all they're really trying to do is build their case against Emmett. They'll probably question everyone who had access to the building."

"Whew, that's a relief. I thought they'd singled me out for some reason, and it was making me plenty nervous. Knowing they're talking to everybody puts a different light on things."

I opened my purse, took out my car keys, and jangled them suggestively.

Kevin didn't seem to notice. "I wasn't much help. As I told them, I was in the library from noon till ten o'clock that night, and with witnesses to prove it."

A convincing alibi, something Emmett didn't have. I wondered where Mitch had been on Saturday afternoon.

A stab of blinding light pierced my vision in self-fulfilling prophecy. I was in for the mother of all migraines.

"I can't talk now, Kevin. I'll see you tomorrow afternoon. But don't worry about McCordle. He's questioning everyone."

Including Mitch. I remembered seeing McCordle with Mitch after lunch and wondered if he'd been questioning Mitch, too. Or had they been conferring on how to make the case against

Emmett even more airtight? Was McCordle, like Dillard, a Gideon?

I hurried home, anxious to reach my bed before my headache incapacitated me. I threw my bag and briefcase on the foyer table, gave a fleeting check of the clock case to make certain the file was still there, and took the maximum dose of my medication. As much as I wanted to contact the FBI immediately, I'd have to wait until tomorrow.

Hours later, I was awakened from my drugged sleep by the ringing of the phone beside my bed. The red numerals of the digital clock told me it was two A.M., and my heart raced with anxiety. A telephone call in the middle of the night always meant bad news.

The news was worse than any I could have imagined. The distorted voice, the one I had come to call Gideon, snarled at me. "I know you've got the file. You picked it up in Okeechobee, didn't you?"

His question brought me fully awake, but he didn't give me time to answer.

"If you don't bring the file tomorrow night to the west entrance of Seaview Mall, your friend Carol will die, just like Moira Rafferty did. I'm through being patient with you, Dr. Garrison. If that file isn't in my hands by eleven o'clock Thursday night, Carol Donahue is a dead woman."

Twenty-four

Although it was two o'clock in the morning, I had no hope of getting back to sleep after receiving the Gideons' threat. My headache had eased only slightly and the sedative effects of my medication had worn off, but I dared not take any more pills. I had to keep my mind clear.

I reached to turn on the light beside my bed but remembered my bedroom was on the side of the house next to Rosa's and feared Mitch might see the light on and come over to check on me. I groped in the dark for my robe and slippers and made my way through the unlighted hallway into the kitchen.

Moonlight streamed into the kitchen windows, enough to see to make coffee. While the pot brewed, I went to the clock and removed the file from its hiding place.

After I'd also retrieved a small reading light from my bedroom nightstand, I poured myself a mug of coffee and retreated to the dining room to study the roster in Nick's file once more.

Two hours and several cups of coffee later, I rose and stretched. I had been over every document taken from the Gideons but had not found a single reference to any Gideon infiltration of the FBI. Several code names of secret commanders were listed, but none of their affiliations were given. I'd have to take a chance.

At that point, I had no choice. If I did not go to the FBI, I had only two other options: turn the file over to the Gideons, at which time they would kill me to keep me silent, or wait to see if they carried out their threat to murder Carol. I had no doubt they would.

I decided to drive to the mid-county location of the nearest FBI office as soon as Moira's service ended and tell them everything. That decision made, I folded my arms on the table, laid my head down, and fell asleep.

When the ringing telephone awakened me, sunlight was streaming through the dining room doorway from the kitchen. I had no idea how late it was.

"Good morning, ducky." Carol's cheerful voice greeted me when I picked up the phone. "Just checking to see if you're going to the church today with your gorgeous hunk or if you want to ride with Sam and—just a minute."

She had placed her hand over the receiver, but I could still hear her slightly muffled voice.

"Jillian Donahue, you are not going to school without a bra. I can see your nipples through that blouse. March right back to your room and dress properly."

It was early yet, I thought. The children hadn't left for school.

Carol came back on the line. "Now, where was I?"

"You were offering me a ride to the church. I'll take you up on that."

"Good. We'll pick you up just after ten."

As she hung up, I could hear her issuing instructions to Trevor, something about chocolate milk on his cereal, and the possibility of the Gideons' harming my wacky friend terrified me.

Hours later, I sat in a front pew at St. Cecilia's Cathedral. Ethereal strains of Mozart's "Ave Verum Corpus" and the haunting Irish melody of "The King of Love My Shepherd Is" registered only slightly on my tortured mind.

Guilt consumed me. I could have done nothing to prevent Nick's death, but if I had found the Sword of Gideon file sooner and taken it to the authorities, Kristin, Chad, and Moira might still be alive, Emmett out of jail, and Carol out of danger.

I stared at the brass-bound casket beneath a massive spray of rubrum lilies, pink roses, and Queen Anne's lace. Nothing could bring back the dead, but I had to do everything I could to make certain no one else died.

Carol's elbow jabbed my ribs, and I came out of my guilt-ridden reverie. The choir had finished, and the priest was looking my way and gesturing. I gathered my notes and climbed to the lectern to pay a last tribute to my friend.

My gaze swept over the crowded church. Moira's brothers and sisters, their families, and the faculty of Suncoast University filled the front pews. Hundreds of students, many of them weeping openly, sat behind them, and in the back of the nave stood reporters, photographers, and television camera crews.

The acrid smell of burning candles and cloying incense saturated the air. Beside me, the priests' vestments reeked of camphor. A wave of giddiness washed over me, and I took a deep breath, praying not to faint.

My voice faltered only once, when I caught sight of Mitch, standing between Dillard and McCordle at the rear of the church. I could not read his expression so far away, but at a distance, he still looked like the Mitch I loved. I had to remind myself he was a fraud and, even worse, a danger.

I managed to finish my remarks and return to my seat before breaking down. I'd lost too much—my brother, my friend, and the man I'd grown to trust and love. As much as I abhorred public displays of emotion—the result of early conditioning by my repressed mother—I sobbed uncontrollably.

When the mass ended, Sam and Carol flanked me and helped me out a side door, away from the press of the crowd.

"You're in no shape to go to the cemetery," Carol said. "Come home and have lunch with us."

"It wouldn't be respectful not to go," I said.

As much as I wanted to get away, I knew what a stickler

Moira had been for tradition. Going to the graveside was the least I could do for her.

I blew my nose and forced a smile. "I'll be okay, really."

"Whatever you say, ducky."

We joined the procession of cars that followed the hearse to the shaded lawns of Sylvan Abbey and watched as the casket was lowered into the sandy soil beneath the moss-laden branches of spreading oaks.

Detective McCordle remained at the roadside, observing the mourners, his presence a grim reminder of the violence of Moira's death.

How much hate did it take, I wondered, to plunge a weapon through a woman's heart while she looked you in the face?

I still couldn't grasp that Moira was really dead. I hadn't even come to terms with Nick's death yet. Everything was moving too fast. I prayed I could intervene in time to save Carol.

"Thanks, both of you," I said.

Sam and Carol had dropped me off at my door. I planned to drive straight to the FBI.

"Carol, would you tell Kevin I'm not feeling well and ask him to take my three o'clock class?"

"Sure, ducky."

Sam drove away with Carol watching from the window with her worried mother look.

I washed the tears from my face, hastily repaired my ravaged makeup, and retrieved the file from the bottom of the clock case. Then common sense pulled me up short. If the Gideons followed me, they could grab the file, and I'd be a dead woman.

I jammed the file back into its hiding place. As long as it remained hidden, my life was safe. I left without it.

The unimpressive appearance of the small mid-county FBI office did little to inspire confidence. I pulled into one of several empty parking spaces and tried to bolster my sagging courage. This was my last hope.

I opened the glass outer door and stepped into a small anteroom, where a very pregnant woman was giving instruction to a younger woman seated behind the reception desk.

"It's not as complicated as it looks," the pregnant woman said. "Reports to Tampa go here, to Washington—"

She stopped and looked at me. "May I help you?"

"I'd like to speak with an agent, please."

The pregnant woman glanced at her coworker, obviously a trainee, with a you-handle-this expression and moved away.

"Can you tell me what this is about?" the younger woman asked.

"It's—no." I couldn't explain the Gideons in just a few words.

She must have heard the panic in my voice. "Is it an emergency?"

"I have to see someone now."

She motioned to a chair in the tiny waiting area. "If you'll have a seat, I'll see if someone is available. Your name?"

"Garrison, Alexandra Garrison."

At the sound of my name, the pregnant woman stopped sorting her papers and returned to the front desk. Flipping the pages on a notepad, she pointed to a memorandum. Even though she spoke in low tones to her trainee, I could hear every word.

"Special Agent Winslow left instructions that if Dr. Garrison came in, he wants to see her immediately."

I sprang to my feet. "Never mind, I'll come back later."

"But Agent Winslow's here. He can see you now." The trainee had picked up her phone and was buzzing the intercom.

I jerked open the door and fled to my car. Winslow had to be a Gideon. How else would he know to expect me?

I was trapped, unable to find help because every law enforcement agency I turned to was infiltrated by Gideons.

The answer came in a flash of insight. If the Gideons' involvement extended only throughout the Southeast, I had a chance if I contacted the FBI in another section of the country, perhaps Detroit or even their Washington headquarters. I would specify an African-American agent, but I had to move fast if I was to save Carol.

The sky had darkened, rain was beginning to fall, and a strong wind was gusting by the time I reached home. I hated flying, especially during a storm, but I had no choice. I called the airlines and made a reservation on the evening flight to Washington.

Hurriedly, I packed a bag with the few things I would need, then called Sam, catching him at his office right before quitting time.

"Sam, please don't ask me any questions, just listen. Carol—maybe all of you are in danger from the same people who killed Nick and Moira."

"Alex, are you—"

"Just listen!" I screamed into the phone. "I haven't much time. Get your family home, lock the doors, and don't let anybody in—especially the police—until you hear from me again."

There was quiet on the other end of the line.

"Sam?"

"Yes."

"I know this sounds crazy, but, believe me, I know what I'm doing. I'm flying to Washington to contact the FBI."

"Why go to Washington—"

"I have dangerous information, and the killers have threatened to kill Carol if I don't turn that information over to them tonight. Nick found out these people have infiltrated every major law enforcement agency in the Southeast, so *don't* call the local police or FBI office. Do you understand?"

"I don't understand, Alex," he said, "but it won't hurt for us to stay put tonight. Will you call us from Washington?"

"As soon as I've talked with someone at FBI headquarters—and Sam!"

"I'm still here, Alex."

"Don't trust Mitch Lawton, either."

I hung up, gathered my overnight bag and purse, and checked the clock case to make certain the file was still there. The storm had gathered intensity, and the roar of the wind and the spatter of driving rain against the windows drowned out all other sounds.

I double-checked my purse for my credit cards, pulled on my raincoat, and opened the front door.

A large man with water running off the brim of his hat confronted me. He flashed a badge and smiled. Behind him in the driveway, stood a gray sedan with tinted windows.

Twenty-five

"I'm Special Agent Winslow, FBI. May I come in?"

Fear turned my mouth dry. "I'm sorry, but I was just leaving. I have a plane to catch."

"This won't take long," Winslow said.

He pushed past me and entered the foyer, standing in front of the grandfather clock with rain dripping from his coat. "Whew, it's really beginning to blow out there."

He removed his hat and began shucking his raincoat. I remained where he had brushed by me, one hand still on the door, the other grasping my overnight bag.

He tossed his wet garments across a chair. "This will be a lot easier and a lot quicker if we sit down."

I set down my bag and purse, followed Winslow into the living room, and sat on the sofa opposite him. I felt deadly calm. Events had been taken out of my hands, and I could do nothing now but follow where they led me. Grim resignation erased all other emotion. I felt as if I were already dead.

"I don't blame you for bolting from the office," he was saying. "You must have thought I was one of the Gideons when you heard I asked to see you."

My head snapped up. That wasn't what I'd expected him to say, and a tiny flicker of hope flared deep within me. It burst into flames at his next words.

"The Bureau has had the Sword of Gideon under surveillance for the past few weeks. I've been assigned to that case here in the Tampa Bay area."

"I see."

I was hopeful, but wary. I would let him continue before deciding whether he was friend or Gideon.

"We know you've got a file one of their defectors gave your brother, so if you'll just hand that over to me, you can catch your plane."

Alarm signals clamored in my brain, drowning out my hope. He was too slick, he moved too fast, and he hadn't asked any questions.

"What makes you believe I have a file?" I asked.

"What?"

I could tell he had expected no opposition, but I wasn't going to make things easy for him. "Why do you think a defector gave my brother a file and that I now have it?"

He paused just a fraction of a second too long. "Because we have operatives within their organization whose job is to report such things to us."

I couldn't be certain. Maybe he was telling the truth, but if he wasn't and I trusted him, I would be killed. I stalled for time, hoping to think of some way to save myself.

"Look, Agent Winslow, I do have a plane to catch, and it's going to be slow driving to the airport in this storm. I need to get going."

I stood and walked toward the door, hoping he would follow. "Besides, I don't have the file here. Why don't I pick it up and bring it to you tomorrow afternoon when I return?"

"We need that file immediately in order to proceed with our investigation." He sat back, entrenching himself more firmly, ignoring my attempt to make him leave.

"If it's so important, why haven't you contacted me before now?"

Any doubts I'd had about his allegiance disappeared when he drew his gun. "Sit back down and stop playing games, Dr. Garrison. We've been real patient with you. You get me that file now or, as we promised, your friend Carol is dead."

His charade was over. Winslow was one of them. It had been

he who had watched my house, followed me to Cassadega, and attempted to follow me to Okeechobee.

I stayed where I was and continued to play for time, trying desperately to think with a mind frozen with fear.

"Don't act like you've been doing me any favors," I said. "You bastards killed my brother. And as for being patient with me, anything you've done has been to avoid calling attention to the Gideons, not out of concern for me."

He leaned toward me with his face contorted with anger. "You're too smart for your own good, but that's also one of the reasons you're still alive. When we couldn't find the documents on your brother or in his apartment, we figured if we put enough pressure on a bright lady like you, you'd find them for us."

The guilt I'd felt at Moira's funeral returned tenfold. If I'd been smarter and found the file sooner, three other people might still be alive, and I wouldn't be staring death in the face.

My anger at what they'd done to Nick gave me courage. I wouldn't make it easy for them. "What makes you so confident I have the file now?"

I clung to the desperate hope that, if I could make him doubt I had the file, he might leave me alone for a time longer, long enough for me to catch that flight to Washington.

"You told the local police you'd been to Okeechobee. One of them who belongs to us interviewed Daniel Finley, using Rafferty's murder and your alibi as cover. Finley fell all over himself trying to be helpful. Told how he'd given you a big manila envelope full of papers your brother had left with him for safekeeping."

He grinned with a cold, terrifying expression and waved his gun at me. "If we'd had any doubt, the fact that you went to the FBI and not the local police indicates you've seen the membership roster."

"But your name's not there." I was still trying to buy time.

His cold smile widened. "It's there all right, but it's in code."

Just as Mitch's must be, I thought. As least Mitch had the grace to leave the dirty work to someone else.

Winslow stood and his expression turned deadly. "The file. Now."

"I told you, I don't have it here."

That file was my life insurance. The longer I kept it hidden, the longer I stayed alive.

"Then we'll have to go get it," he said.

I remembered Nick's gun in the foyer table.

"I'll get my things." I went to the foyer and opened the drawer.

Winslow was right behind me, and the barrel of his gun pressed between my shoulder blades. "Don't try anything. I might not kill you before I get the file, but I could hurt you real bad, bad enough so you'd wish you were dead."

My hand passed over Nick's gun. With Winslow's pistol rammed into my back and my inexperience with weapons, I wouldn't have a chance.

My hand grazed a ring of keys that had belonged to my mother, keys to the public library I had been meaning to return for years, but had never gotten around to. I prayed the locks hadn't been changed.

"Here are the keys."

I turned slowly and held them up. A glance over his shoulder at the clock told me it was after six o'clock, and the downtown branch would be closed by now.

"Keys to what?"

"The public library. My mother used to work there. I figured it was as good a place as any to hide the file."

I could tell from his expression he didn't know whether to believe me.

"I believe what you said about hurting Carol," I said. "I'm not going to do anything to jeopardize her safety."

"You'd better not be jerking me around, lady. I get mean when I'm angry, and you've already stretched my patience."

He shrugged back into his raincoat one arm at a time, shifting the gun from hand to hand, keeping it trained on me. "We'll take your car and you'll drive. And no funny business."

I hadn't removed my coat, so I had only to pick up my purse. When I opened the front door, the wind tore it from my grasp and slammed it back against the wall. I needed Winslow's help to close it behind us.

"There's a tropical storm moving in," Winslow said. "The sooner we get this over with, the better."

I inched the car along the deserted, rain-slick streets. At several intersections, power was out and traffic signals weren't working. Street signs shimmied in the wind, and palm branches cartwheeled across our path. Occasionally a gust of wind slammed into the side of the car, and I fought the steering wheel to keep from being forced off the road by the blasts.

At any other time, the violence of the storm would have terrified me, but I was too busy thinking how to escape the man at my side. I might have only one chance, and I had to make it good. As I drove, I mapped out a plan in my head, knowing it was a long shot, but the only shot I had.

It was after seven by the time we reached the library. I parked in a place near the entrance reserved for the handicapped. When I stepped out of the car, the force of the wind tearing in off the bay almost knocked me down. Winslow came around and gripped my arm, and together we struggled up the wet stairs to the front doors.

I selected a key that I hoped still worked and disengaged the security system. I had considered leaving it on and setting off the alarm as we entered, but if someone like Dillard or McCordle responded, I would be worse off than I was already. I decided to stick with my original plan.

I chose a second key and unlocked the wide, glass-paneled door, breathing a sigh of relief when the lock yielded and the door opened without the sound of an alarm.

I stepped into the darkened room and reached for a light switch, but Winslow knocked my arm away.

"Light up this place and any patrolman who passes by will know we're here. Where's the office? There's got to be a flashlight around somewhere."

I groped past the circulation desk and into the workroom behind it, feeling my way toward a large cabinet at the back of the room where flashlights were kept in readiness for the frequent power blackouts from our famous Florida lightning storms. I found two flashlights and gave one to Winslow.

"It's downstairs in a file cabinet in the storage closet," I said. "Follow me."

Even with both flashlights, we had to pick our way slowly through the maze of shelves to the stairway that led downstairs to the children's section. At one point, Winslow stumbled behind me, knocking me forward. As I fell to one knee, my stocking ripped and pain radiated up my leg. When he jerked me to my feet, blood trickled down my shin.

Downstairs, we worked our way through the low shelves, easels, tables, and chairs of the children's section and into an unused interior hallway. I paused before the door of a large storage closet, the closet where my mother had locked Nick away so many years ago. A glancing beam from my flashlight revealed the key in the lock, just as it had been for over twenty-five years.

It might be the last thing I live to do, I vowed to Nick in the darkness of the library basement, but somehow I would see the Gideons pay for what they had done to him.

I opened the door and shined my light onto the fluorescent light fixture with its short cord.

"There are no windows in this room," I said, "so no one can see us from outside. If you can reach that light for me, I can see which file cabinet I'm looking for."

I hung back in the hallway as Winslow stepped into the narrow confines of the closet. He set his flashlight on the nearest cabinet and reached for the light.

At that instant, I slammed the door, turned the key in the lock, and pulled it free. I ran, scattering chairs and easels as I crossed the room. Behind me, Winslow shouted and hammered on the door as I climbed the stairs, stumbling in the dark and banging my knees and shins.

I fled through the front doors, stopping only long enough to reset the security system. If he escaped from the closet and left the building, the police would be alerted.

I leaned into the wind and rain and fought my way to my car. The strength of the gale slowed my progress to a crawl. I was soaked to the skin by the time I slid inside my car, and my shins ached with bruises, but the exhilaration of being alive and free outweighed my discomfort. I locked the doors and started the motor.

My first inclination was to head for Tampa and the airport to catch a plane to Washington after the storm passed, but I realized I had only slowed Winslow down, not stopped him. The airport would be the first place he or his fellow Gideons would search for me.

I could barely see ahead of me through the sheets of wind-driven rain pouring over the windshield, but I decided to attempt the drive to Longboat Key. I had dry clothes at the cottage, and when the storm cleared, I could fly to Washington from the Sarasota airport. The one place I could not go was home.

I turned on the car's heating system, but I shivered as much from fear as from cold as I headed south toward St. Petersburg and the interstate bypass. Few other travelers braved the weather, but even though traffic was sparse, wind and rain slowed my progress.

In between tunes on the radio, the announcer described a tropical storm with gale force winds that was pounding the Bay area. I drove as fast as I could on the rain-slick highway, desperate to reach the Skyway Bridge before high winds shut it down. If I didn't reach it in time, I'd have to drive across the bay to Tampa, then around its eastern shore to reach Longboat Key. The sooner I was off the road, the less likely I was to be spotted by officers loyal to the Gideons. I trusted no one.

When I opened the window to pay the Skyway toll, rain drenched me once more. I inched onto the causeway leading to the bridge, and suddenly I was driving through my recurring nightmare. I couldn't make out the lights of the bridge ahead through the fury of the storm, and I drove into nothingness, hugging the white line that edged the road for guidance.

I moved at a snail's pace, with no idea of what progress I was making. I couldn't even be sure I was still on the road that led to the bridge. Only the green glow of the dashboard lights lit the black cocoon in which I hurtled through the storm. My headlights could not pierce the gloom ahead.

Tears of rage and fear poured down my face like the rain sheeting off the windshield. Somewhere ahead was an exit to a rest area on the bridge's north side. If I took that by mistake, it would be impossible to regain my bearings in the storm. The rest area itself might be underwater from the storm surge.

Suddenly, flashing red lights loomed above, spelling out: *Danger—High Winds*. I had begun the ascent of the main span. The winds blasted stronger there, buffeting my car as if it were paper. My fear of falling bridges and plunging into endless blackness almost paralyzed me.

I screamed when a mighty blast pummeled the car, and I gripped the wheel even tighter, trying to hold the Toyota on the bridge by the strength of my will. The punishing winds seemed to come from all directions, threatening to yank control of the car from my hands. Unexpected spears of light pierced the darkness, illuminating the car and bridge in a gray glow, and a roaring, thwacking sound drowned the screams of the storm. Above hovered a helicopter, tracking my course across the main span.

Time seemed to stand still as the bulky chopper treaded air directly above me. With my nerves strung tight and raw with terror and my reason poisoned with fear, I knew the Gideons had found me.

Light stabbed through the windshield, blinding me, and I slowed to a stop, afraid I would crash into the side of the bridge or, worse, over the edge if I continued. Still the giant bird hovered, pounding the car with the violent beat of its rotors, and I wondered if they would land to capture me or try to force the Toyota over the side.

For a moment the onslaught of the rain lessened, and in the

darkness to the west of the bridge, almost directly beside me, a hot white flare blossomed and grew. The search beams of the helicopter tracked toward the flare's source, where a small boat rode the towering waves beyond the base of the bridge. As the chopper moved toward the disabled vessel, I picked up the red and white markings of the United States Coast Guard and realized that paranoia had me in its grasp. Not I, but endangered boaters were the object of the chopper's search.

My relief and chagrin were fleeting, and fear prompted me to start the car and move forward once more. Only the prospect of remaining on the bridge terrified me more than crossing it. After an eternity of driving into blackness, lights flickered ahead at the Skyway's southern end. A few cars were backed up at the toll plaza, where a highway patrol car with flashing lights blocked the way. The bridge had been closed.

After the terror of the treacherous Skyway crossing, the rest of my trip, although slow and awkward in the driving rain and gale winds, seemed relatively easy. As I worked my way slowly toward the islands, my crying ceased and the warmth from the car's heater eased my trembling. Shortly before midnight, I parked next to Aunt Bibi's cottage. My body had stiffened rigidly into driving position, and I had to pry my clenched fingers from the steering wheel.

When I turned the light switch in the living room, nothing happened. The power was out, probably from lines downed by the wind. Waves crashed against the deck, dangerously close to the house, but I was too wet, cold, and exhausted to care.

Using the flashlight I'd brought from the library, I found an old warm-up suit in my closet. I stripped off my wet clothes and shoes, pulled on the soft pants and jacket, wrapped a blanket around myself, and lay down. I planned to rest only until the storm had blown over, but my terror had drained me and I fell into a deep sleep.

Sometime later the sweep of headlights across the bedroom walls awakened me. A car had turned in the driveway and was making its way toward the cottage.

The Gideons had come for me, as Bella had predicted, but I had not expected them so soon.

I scrambled to my feet, crouching below the level of the windows, and rummaged on the closet floor until I found an old pair of sneakers. I slipped them on hurriedly, then crawled into the living room toward the door that opened onto the deck above the beach.

As I eased the door open, a car door slammed. They knew I was there—they had seen my car. My only hope was to find a neighbor to take me in. I closed the door behind me and crept on my hands and knees across the wave-washed deck toward the beach.

The roar of wind and waves drowned out all other sounds, and the rain fell in torrents, drenching my dry clothes. Once I had crossed the deck, I clambered to my feet and ran south along the beach to my nearest neighbors. My feet sank in the deep sand, and I ran against the wind, making slow progress.

Dear God, I prayed, please let them be at home.

When I reached their door, I tried the bell, but no one answered. Remembering that the electricity was out and the bell wouldn't work, I banged on the door with my fists. When there was still no answer, I stumbled around the house to their back entrance and pounded on that door, again with no results.

Rage gave me strength. I could not allow the Gideons to silence me. I had to live—for Nick and Moira, Chad and Kristin, and Richard Slater, and however many other innocent victims. I had to live long enough to get that file to the FBI.

And I had to live for myself.

Banging on the door, feeling the needles of rain driven into my face by the gale, I did not want to die.

By now I admitted that my neighbors were not home. The next house was too far down the open beach. If I tried to reach it, the Gideons would see me.

I cast about for a place to hide. Beside me, a zigzagging staircase rose to a widow's walk atop the house. If I climbed to the top, I could lie down and hide until whoever was chasing me had passed. Then when the rain cleared, I could see from my lofty hiding place whether they had given up and left the cottage. When they had, I could return to my car.

I started up the slippery stairs, hugging the banister to keep from being blown off onto the patio below. I had ascended only a few feet when a hand grabbed my ankle with such force its nails dug into my flesh.

Over the roar of the wind, a familiar voice shouted, "You didn't really expect to get away, did you?"

The hands pulled me from the staircase, grabbed my shoulders, and turned me to face my captor.

"Not you!" I screamed the words over the wind.

His hair, matted and wet, hung in his eyes, but I recognized the lines of his face and the set of his mouth.

It was Mitch Lawton.

Twenty-six

Mitch dragged me back toward the cottage.

His fingers bit into the flesh of my upper arm with bruising force, but I had no will to resist. Oblivious to the wind and rain pounding the beach, I succumbed again to the recurring numbness I'd experienced so often since Nick's death.

Mitch was silent, his face set and grim. I wondered if he felt anything for me, or if all his caring had been an act so I would confide in him the whereabouts of the file.

I stumbled up the deck and into the dark kitchen, where he left me while he went into the bathroom for towels. I wished he would kill me and get it over with. Some things were worse than death, like watching the man I'd loved turn into a monster before my eyes.

"Dry yourself off, and if you have any dry clothes, get into them." He tossed me the towels.

I wrapped one around my streaming hair and went into the bedroom. The flashlight from the library was where I had left it on the bedside table, and I used its light to find a robe in the closet. I stripped off wet clothes for the second time that night, wrapped the terry robe around myself and tied it tightly at my waist.

When I returned to the living room, Mitch had lighted several hurricane lamps and was boiling water over a can of Sterno. The lamplight threw eerie shadows that danced on the ceiling, and Mitch's face, half in darkness, wore an expression I couldn't read.

He used the boiling water to make tea, moving with ironic efficiency in my kitchen.

"Drink this down. You'll be lucky if you don't catch pneumonia," he said.

With a brusque angry movement unfamiliar to the Mitch I had known, he thrust the steaming mug into my hands and pushed me into a chair at the table.

I vented an unladylike snort. "If I live long enough."

He stared at me for a moment, then disappeared into my bedroom. When I realized that he hadn't had a gun, I calculated the distance to my car keys and from there to the door. I'd never make it.

In a matter of seconds, he was back with the flashlight. He reached with his other hand into his jacket.

Now the gun, I thought with a tremor, hoping he would kill me quickly.

But instead of a gun, he withdrew what looked like a thin leather wallet, flipped it open, laid it on the table before me, and shined the bright beam of the flashlight on it.

A picture of his unsmiling face stared back at me from beneath a clear laminated cover. The photo was attached to an identification card that read Federal Bureau of Investigation, and the name beside the photo was Michael Antonelli. On the other side of the open leather folder gleamed the brass badge of the FBI, topped with the federal eagle.

"You have to trust me. I'm not one of them." His voice softened with persuasion.

I sensed I was moving through one of those crazy, disjointed dreams, where nothing makes sense and everyday people and events become bizarre, convoluted images of reality.

"You must trust me," he said again.

In the glow of the flashlight, I could read the pleading in his eyes, dark eyes like Nick's, but I had experienced too much deception to trust easily ever again.

"If you're not Mitchell Lawton and you're not a Gideon, who are you? What are you?"

My anger had dissolved, replaced by a consuming weariness. I didn't know why I bothered to ask. I doubted I'd believe anything he told me.

"Michael Antonelli is my real name. I've been working undercover since skinheads murdered my partner, Dexter Harris." He shrugged with an embarrassed smile. "That much of what I told you is true."

He stripped off his wet jacket, and as he toweled his dripping hair, I spotted his gun in a holster at his back. When he'd finished, he sat across the table from me, his hands cradling his cup of tea.

"I didn't tell you the whole story about Dexter. Maybe I'd better start there." He gulped the steaming tea, and I glimpsed a momentary trembling in his hands. "Several weeks ago, Dexter got a call from your brother."

"Dexter knew Nick?"

He nodded and his damp hair glistened in the lamplight. "Dexter had been Nick's contact for a few stories when Dexter was with the Tampa office of the Bureau in the eighties. Nick called to ask if Dexter knew anything about a group that called themselves the Sword of Gideon."

"My God, you knew who Gideon was all along." I had thought nothing else would surprise me. I was wrong.

"All we knew was what Nick had told us, that the Sword of Gideon was a white supremacist organization more dangerous than the Klan, similar to the Covenant and Sword of the Lord and the Order."

Mitch didn't have to convince me how dangerous they were. "Did Dexter help Nick?"

Mitch shook his head. "No, but Dexter did contact a few agents in the Tampa area to see what he could find out. No one could tell him anything. Shortly after he made those inquiries, Dexter was attacked and murdered by skinheads."

"And you suspected the Gideons were behind it?"

"Not at the time. I considered it a coincidence. But a few days later, when I read that Nick had died in a suspicious car accident, the possibility of the Gideons being involved seemed more likely."

Bitterness welled in my throat. "A *suspicious* accident? Nobody here seemed to think so."

"I knew that Nick had been on the trail of the Gideons, so I decided to follow up. That's when I came to Florida undercover."

"Herman and Rosa, do you really know them?"

"No, and neither does my father, who's an NYPD detective, by the way. My boss at the Bureau is an old friend of Herman's. Together they arranged for me to use the Myers' winter home and told Rosa just enough to pass on to you in hopes you'd trust me."

I felt transparent and used.

He reached across the table and grasped my hand. "We were afraid if Nick had shared any information with you, you might be in danger from the Gideons."

"You didn't come all the way to Florida just to protect me." I still found his story hard to believe.

"We had no idea about the file, but we hoped you'd have information you would share with us. Since we were working in the dark, any information about the Gideons would have been helpful."

I yanked my hand from his as anger built within me. "But when I told you what I knew, you insisted those things were coincidences, crank calls, or jumping to conclusions. Why didn't you tell me?"

His face broke into the smile I'd fallen in love with, and I ached to know if his interest in me had been only part of his job, and if anything he'd just told me was the truth.

"I didn't want you making too much noise about the Gideons," he said, "calling attention to yourself or to them. That would have been more dangerous for you and sent them running for cover as well."

My anger surged, and I felt not only used but violated. "Where were you when I needed you yesterday? For somebody supposed to protect me, you did a hell of a job. I was nearly killed!"

"You can thank your friend Burke. The NYPD gave him the story we'd made up to portray Mitch Lawton as a violent bigot, a man who would appeal to the Gideons if they checked him out. We'd hoped they'd try to recruit me."

"If you knew what Burke had told me, why didn't you tell me the truth?" I asked.

"I tried, but you refused to see me, remember? I knew you were safe as long as you hadn't found the file."

I was glad he couldn't see my face clearly in the dim light. Between Burke's interference and my own stubbornness, I had almost gotten myself killed.

"Since you flushed Winslow out of the Gideon woodwork," he said, "I assume you have the file now . . . picked it up on your trip to Okeechobee?"

"What did you do, bug my phone, my house?"

Angry at being misled, but relieved to share the burden of the Gideon file, I trusted him again. I couldn't help it. His name might not be Mitch, but the man before me was no racist killer-cop. He was the Mitch Lawton I loved.

"McCordle is my contact in the local police department. He called me as soon as they picked up Winslow, who made quite a racket getting out of that closet you locked him in, set off the sound and motion detectors."

"How do you know I have the file?"

"Elementary, my dear Alexandra. Winslow tried to make us believe you'd gone round the bend. Said you'd asked him to meet you at the library and locked him in. I figured you arranged to give Winslow the file, discovered he was a Gideon, and somehow managed to lock him up and escape."

His eyes narrowed in the feeble lamplight, and I witnessed again the expression that had frightened me the night he'd told me of Dexter's death. "If Winslow is the one who arranged for Dexter's murder, I'll move heaven and earth to see he gets the punishment he deserves."

I had my own personal score to settle with Winslow. If my testimony would help, I'd see him locked away for life. I tore my thoughts away from revenge and back to the man before me. "How did you know where to find me?"

"When I called Carol, Sam said you weren't there. I could tell from the tone of his voice you must have told him the cop-killer story."

I shook my head. "I warned him not to trust the police or you and to keep his family locked in. I'd had a call early yesterday morning saying Carol would die, just like Moira, if I didn't turn over the file. The Gideons knew I had it."

He looked thoughtful. "How do you suppose they knew? Even I wasn't sure."

"Dillard's on their membership roster. That's what the file contains, member lists, terrorist plans, all pretty scary stuff." I shuddered, remembering.

"But how did Dillard—"

"He must have read my statement to McCordle telling where I was when Moira was murdered. Winslow said one of the Gideons questioned Finley, the motel manager in Okeechobee, who told him I'd picked up papers belonging to Nick."

I began to shake again, not from cold but in a delayed reaction to the terror. Mitch—he would always be Mitch to me—rose and pulled me into his arms.

"I could kill them for what they've done to you," he said.

"Please," I muttered against his chest, "no more talk of killing."

He led me to the sofa and pulled me down against him. Cradled in the security of his arms, I told the rest of my story—how I'd gone to see Winslow and found him expecting me, how I'd been headed to the airport when Winslow arrived, and finally how I'd managed to trick Winslow and lock him in.

When I finished, the warmth had returned to my body and my shaking had ceased. "How did you know where to find me?"

"Part intuition, part good detective work. If you were too

frightened to go home, especially with me next door, and you weren't at Carol's, here was the logical place."

"So you came all this way on a hunch?"

He tightened his embrace. "That and the report from the highway patrol, who saw your car exit the Skyway Bridge at the height of the storm."

"But the Skyway's closed—"

"I came the long way, round Tampa Bay."

A terrifying thought occurred to me. "If you know I'm here, won't the Gideons know, too?"

"Probably." He didn't seem concerned.

The wind had died and the rain stopped. I relaxed in the comfort of his arms and drifted off to sleep. The sound of a car in the driveway awakened me, and I jerked upright in terror.

"Relax," he said. "Reinforcements are here, agents from the Tampa office."

He opened the door to two men dressed in the suit and tie uniform of the FBI and introduced me to Special Agents Sadowski and Jackson. I could have kissed Jackson on the spot, but I restrained myself. The presence of the tall, ebony-skinned African-American erased any lingering doubts that my nightmare was finally over.

Mitch drove me home, with Jackson leading the way and Sadowski following in Mitch's car.

At my house, the three of them looked amused when I dragged the Gideon file from the bottom of the clock case.

"They'd have found that if they'd searched your house again," Mitch said.

"Maybe." I thought of all the presents Nick had overlooked there. With relief, I handed the file to Jackson.

"We'll get moving on this right away to start picking up the people on this list," Jackson said. "I've also called in a special team to guard Dr. Donahue and her family. They should be in place within the hour."

He shook hands with Mitch, who stood with one arm around my shoulders. "Looks like you're already well protected, Dr. Garrison."

Jackson and Sadowski left with the file, and I closed the door behind them, believing for the first time since Nick had died that I might be able to get on with my life.

"What now?" I asked Mitch.

"The Bureau will put together a special task force to begin making arrests. They'll try to have everyone in place to make the pick-ups at the same time so we don't give any of these scum enough warning to escape."

"Once they're arrested?"

"They'll be tried. There's enough damning evidence in that file to lock most of them away for a long, long time."

"What about their recruits, those poor young kids like Richard Slater, who joined the group looking for a place to belong, not knowing what the Gideons really were?"

"If they haven't engaged in any criminal activity, they'll be released. But the brainwashing that's been done, the hate that's been nurtured in them—I don't know a cure for that."

Exhaustion caught up with me, and my shoulders slumped.

"You could use some sleep," he said. "You've been up all night."

I looked at him, my Mitch/Michael, his face drawn and gray with fatigue. "So could you."

"But I'm supposed to be keeping an eye on you."

"Then you'd better come with me."

He followed me into the bedroom and locked the door.

Twenty-seven

"Did you ever shoot anybody?" Trevor Donahue asked.

He'd been unable to take his eyes off Mitch from the moment we arrived.

"Trevor!" Carol said with an embarrassed smile.

I believed she would have kicked him under the table if her legs had been longer.

"Geez, Mom, I never knew a real live FBI agent before."

"It's all right, Carol," Mitch said. "There've been times, Trevor, when I've had to draw my weapon, but the only thing I've shot is paper targets."

Carol and Sam had invited Mitch and me, Kevin, and Priscilla to Thanksgiving dinner. They had set the table on the lanai next to the pool and served dinner beneath the clear, bright sky in the warmth of a perfect Florida afternoon. The completed FBI roundup of the Sword of Gideon members was the hot topic of conversation.

"Alex and Carol, you two are really slick," Priscilla said. "I had no idea all this was going on until I read it in yesterday's paper." She grinned at me. "I thought it strange your boyfriend hanging around campus so much the past three weeks, but I never guessed he was working undercover."

I choked on a sip of water at her last words, and Trevor whacked me between the shoulder blades.

"Barbara Shannon, the female agent guarding you, Carol," Pris said, "she had us all fooled. She acted every bit the visiting colleague from the University of North Carolina."

"Barbara did her undergraduate work in English there," Carol said. "It wasn't hard for her to play the role."

"Mother, are you sure you're safe now that Barbara's left?" Jillian eyed her anxiously.

"Your mother is perfectly safe," Mitch said. "We wrapped up the investigation when several Gideons plea-bargained and gave us actual names for the coded ones on the roster."

"So you got them all?" Jillian asked.

"There's one code name we haven't been able to connect with anyone, but it could have been on the list simply as a security check of some kind or one ready to be assigned when needed," Mitch said. "Yes, I think we have them all."

"What about Emmett?" Pris asked. "Have you found evidence to clear him?"

"No," Mitch said. "That's the oddest part of this entire investigation. We haven't come up with anything to contradict the evidence against him."

"I know how much you—we all—care about Emmett," Kevin said, "but, painful as it is, we have to face the possibility that he really did kill Moira."

"I'm afraid you're right," Mitch said. "Not even our informants have been able to shed any light on Moira's murder."

"Emmett didn't do it," Pris said. "The proof's out there somewhere, and it's only a matter of time until someone finds it."

"Dessert anyone?" Carol asked.

I groaned, along with everyone else, too stuffed from turkey, dressing, and cranberry sauce to consider more food.

"Then why don't you leave Alex and me to clear up?" Carol said. "We haven't had a minute alone together in weeks. I'll serve dessert and coffee later."

Carol and I began clearing the table while the others tossed frisbees on the back lawn.

"You were sweet to include Kevin and Pris today," I said.

Carol shrugged. "The more the merrier. Besides, Kevin has no family, and Pris's folks are in Oregon, too far for a weekend flight."

She looked at me intently beneath her red-gold bangs. "I notice Mitch hasn't been given a new assignment yet." She smiled knowingly at all her words implied.

"He'll be leaving next week. He only stayed to have Thanksgiving with me."

"Then what?"

I gazed out over the back lawn, where Mitch played with Trevor and Winston, the Donahues' Welsh corgi. "I don't know. We'll just have to wait and see."

"Do you love him?" Carol had never been reticent about asking personal questions.

"Yes, I—"

"Does he love you?"

"He says he does."

"Well, then?"

"We've only known each other six weeks," I said, "probably the most turbulent six weeks of our lives. We're in no position right now to be making long-range commitments."

I snapped the cover on a Tupperware container of gravy and handed it to her.

"Now's as good a time as any, ducky." Her muffled voice carried from inside the refrigerator, where she rearranged leftovers. "Don't let him return to New York without that commitment. You may lose him altogether."

"If he really loves me, he'll be back."

Carol pulled her head from the refrigerator's depths and gave me a long, searching stare. "Well, there's always Burke, waiting in the wings."

I groaned. "He's been a royal pain in the ass. When he thought I was still seeing Mitch, the killer-cop, he said he understood my acting out my feelings over Nick's death, and as soon as I finished playing Bonnie and Clyde, he'd be waiting for me."

"What a self-righteous—" Carol attacked the remainder of the turkey carcass with her electric knife as if it were Burke himself. Sometimes the depth of Carol's feelings frightened me.

"But that's not the end of it," I said. "When the story broke in yesterday's papers, Burke called to ask me out, now that I no longer need Mitch as a bodyguard. Said he'd known all along I wasn't crazy."

"What'd you say to him?"

"What good does it do to tell Burke anything? If I say something that contradicts his image of himself, he just doesn't hear it. His conceit is incredible—and sad. Deep down, Burke is a very lonely man."

"Don't you go feeling sorry for him." Carol waved the electric knife dangerously close to my nose. "The next thing you know, you'll be going out with him again and—blam!—there you'll be, engaged again."

"Not a chance," I said. "I know what real love is all about now."

I searched for Mitch and watched him instruct the awkward Jillian in the art of frisbee tossing. He was good with children. I turned to find Carol appraising me with knowing eyes.

"Real love," I said, "has nothing to do with control. It's letting the ones you love be free to be themselves. You and Sam know that. That's one of the reasons you two are so good for each other. Burke may never learn that lesson."

We had put away the last of the food, and I scraped Carol's rose-covered English china plates and handed them to her as she loaded the dishwasher.

"Tom Stanislaus called yesterday, too," I said. "Asked if he could interview me about the Gideons."

"That would be some story."

"I told him no. It's not something I can talk about right now. I have a lot of thinking to do before I make any statements to the press."

"What's there to think about? The Gideons are a bunch of bigoted hatemongers."

"The leaders, yes, but the teenagers—kids the Gideons would never have had a chance of converting if they were loved and secure like Trevor and Jillian. Whose responsibility is it to take care of those kids—and others like them—so they don't end up like Richard Slater? How do we keep other young people from falling through the cracks?"

Carol's plump face was flushed from leaning into the dishwasher, and her eyes were sad. "Tough questions, ducky. I don't have any answers."

"Me either. That's one reason I refused the interview. I did tell Tom he could have first rights to Nick's manuscript. If the *Courier* runs it as a series, it will be good to see Nick's by-line again, especially on a story he'd want told."

Carol finished wiping the countertops, then put her arm around my shoulders. "What a nightmare this has been for you."

"It will pass." I sounded more positive than I felt. "One more week, then exams and the session's over."

Carol hugged me. "Maybe by then our lives will be back to normal, whatever that is."

I thought of Nicky and how my life would never be normal without him.

"The end of the session will mean I'm finally rid of Paul Stephanos," I said. "He hasn't bothered me with Mitch around, but he still sits in class and glowers at me. I'll be glad to see the last of him."

We returned to the patio and sat beside the pool, watching the others playing tag football.

You should be here, Nick, I thought. You and Mitch could have been such friends.

I hadn't thought of my mother for days, but suddenly I could hear her voice, quoting one of her favorite Bible verses: "The Lord giveth, and the Lord taketh away."

Twenty-eight

I stood and stretched to rid the kinks from my back and neck. I'd been at my desk for hours since giving my last exam that afternoon, but I'd managed to score the last of the papers and average grades. My computer grade sheets, their bubbles marked with a number-two pencil, sat on my desk, ready to be turned in at the Administration Building.

Across the bay, lights twinkled on the beach along the dark horizon, reminding me of the night almost two months before when my office had been ransacked. I had asked Mitch about it before he left for New York.

"Which one of the Gideons broke into my office?" I hoped the FBI had found some connection that would lead to Emmett's release.

"No one will admit to the break-ins," he said, "or to any knowledge of them."

"Because it may tie them to murder?"

"We've got murder charges against a few of them already—the two who killed Slater and ran Nick off the road and the ex-military explosives expert who blew up Kristin's car," he said.

"Maybe one of them did it?"

"They're all already in so deep they'd have nothing to lose by confessing," Mitch said. "No, I honestly don't think any of them did it."

"Then there's a Gideon left you haven't found yet." My old

fear returned, especially since Mitch would be leaving for New York soon.

"That's only a very slim possibility," he said. "It's beginning to look more and more like Emmett actually is Moira's murderer."

I shook my head vehemently. "I'll never believe that. And what about the vandalized offices?"

"If Emmett had planned to kill Moira, what better alibi than to claim the weapon he intended to use had been stolen? Trashing the other offices kept the spotlight off him."

It angered me that Mitch would consider such thoughts. "If it was such a great plan, why is Emmett sitting in prison now?"

He shrugged. "The best laid plans often go awry. Maybe that's what happened here since Emmett doesn't have the heart of a true criminal."

"Suppose Emmett did search my office. Who searched my house?"

"Winslow admitted to that and to making the phone calls."

Mitch pulled me into his arms. "Are we going to spend my last night here talking about Gideons?"

"No." I feigned innocence. "I thought we'd bake cookies."

But there had been no cookies baked that night, and I had driven him to the airport the next morning, anticipating the endless march of days and nights until Christmas vacation, when he would return.

I stretched again and worked my head from side to side to relieve the tension in my neck, then sat down and reached for a word processing form to request copies of my course outline for the spring session, my last task before I headed home to a very late supper.

Someone knocked at my office door.

"Come in," I called.

Harry, the night security guard, had just been by, checking each hour as he made his rounds. I thought it was Harry back again, but the door flew open, banging against the bookshelves behind it.

Paul Stephanos, his shaggy white hair tousled and his pale blue eyes rolling wildly from side to side, charged into my office and slammed the door behind him.

"What is it, Mr. Stephanos?" I attempted to keep my voice calm, hoping to calm him as well. He wore a frantic, crazed look that boded no good, but it would be almost an hour before the security guard returned to my part of the building. The rest of the building, as far as I knew, was deserted.

"The course is over now, isn't it?" His voice boomed loud and petulant.

"Yes, although I haven't turned in the grades to the central office yet, your course is finished."

His question, asking me to state the obvious, seemed as strange as his appearance. I waited for him to speak again, afraid to anger him by saying the wrong thing.

His agitated glance swept my office, and he appeared disoriented, as if he were on medication or had suffered a stroke that affected his reasoning. His eyes focused on me with a belligerent stare.

"Where's your pretty boy?" he asked.

"Who—"

"The man who's been with you every minute for the past few weeks, where is he?"

I didn't know why he was asking about Mitch, so I told him as little as possible. "He's gone."

Stephanos laughed with a high-pitched, nervous sound. "Gone, is he? I could have told you no one would love you like I do."

I stared in disbelief at the man's madness.

"Why did you leave me, Vera?" He drew the question out in a long, thin whine.

"Vera?"

"Don't be coy with me, Vera!" When he shouted, the veins in his face bulged with rage.

I shrank back in my chair. The only thing to do was keep him talking until Harry came around again.

"I'm sorry," I said. "I didn't mean to make you angry."

His expression crumpled, and he slumped into the chair opposite my desk. "I know, darling. I know you didn't mean to die and go off and leave me like that. But you'd been gone almost three years, and then you came back again, looking all young and pretty, like you used to, and you wouldn't even speak to me, your own husband. What was I supposed to think?"

Dear God. The man believed I was his dead wife, come back to life. I'd told Carol he was crazy.

"How did you get into the building?" If I could get him off the subject of his wife, perhaps his reason would return.

He smiled slyly. "I hid in the men's room until the building closed. I know they lock the outside doors at ten o'clock."

"Why are you here?" I asked. "Do you want to know your grade for the course?"

He shook his head like a stubborn child. "I want to see you, Vera. I waited and waited outside by your car, and when you didn't come, I knew I had to get into the building before it was locked."

"But why did you want to see me? I'm Alexandra Garrison, your history professor."

"No, no, no!" He punctuated each word by banging his fist on my desk. Then he leaned across toward me. "You're Vera, my Vera, and if I can't have you, nobody can!"

He yelled at the top of his lungs, but no one was in the building to hear him and come to my aid. I considered briefly the irony of my predicament, to have escaped the violent Gideons only to be threatened by a crazed old man, just a few feet away across my desktop.

Old, yes, but not infirm. His muscles bulged beneath his fitted golf shirt, and his rage gave him added strength. I tried again to calm him. "What is it you want me to do . . . Paul?"

"Just come home, to our home." He appeared to settle down, but then stood suddenly and began pounding my desk again. "You haven't been home in three years. Where have you been? Why did you—"

"Is there a problem here, Alex?" Kevin McDermott opened the door, and I had never been so glad to see anyone in my life.

"Mr. Stephanos is a bit confused." I managed with some effort to keep my tone soft and soothing. "He believes I'm his dead wife, Vera."

Stephanos, bewildered and disoriented, looked to me, then back to Kevin. "Who are you?"

"I'm Dr. Garrison's assistant. It's late, and you should be home in bed. Why don't you let me walk you to your car?"

Deflated and defeated, Stephanos seemed to shrink before my eyes. He peered at me. "You're not Vera?"

"No. I'm sorry."

"Then I better go find her," he said.

"Come." Kevin took him gently by the arm. "I'll be back," he said to me. "Wait here."

Their footsteps echoed down the deserted hallway as I searched my faculty directory for a phone number. Within minutes, I reached Pat Corrigan, one of the university counselors, to tell her about Stephanos.

"I can access university records on my home computer," she said. "I'll check for his next of kin to see if we can get someone to stay with him. If not, I'll call social services."

As I hung up the phone, Kevin returned.

"I seem to be deeper in your debt all the time," I said. "Thanks for the rescue."

I stacked the last of my books and papers into my briefcase, snapped it shut, and tugged on my jacket. "If you wouldn't mind walking me to my car—"

"Sit down, Dr. Garrison. You're not going anywhere." Kevin stood between me and the door, holding a gun.

I sank back into my desk chair, knowing what he was going to say.

"I'm the missing Gideon, code name Lamplighter," he said, "and we're going to have a little talk, before I kill you."

Twenty-nine

Kevin locked the office door, then took the chair across from me. He appeared relaxed, but the gun never wavered. I stared at the round black hole of the barrel.

"I'm listening," I said. "What did you want to say?"

He laughed with a nervous twitch. "I'd hoped to win you over, make you one of us and keep you from handing over the file. You'd begun to confide in me, and if I'd known you had the file, I'd have told you more about our plans. I even hoped that you and I—"

He ran his other hand through his sandy hair, clasped a handful, and yanked in frustration. "Why didn't you trust me, Alex, and tell me about the file?"

His question, so ludicrous with his gun pointed at my face, made me bite my lip to keep from laughing. It didn't deserve an answer.

"Why didn't your partners identify you with the others?" I asked. "How did you manage to stay free when all the others have been caught?"

"Only the commanders within a certain area know each other's identity, a built-in protection against infiltration."

He smiled smugly, and had it not been for the gun, I would have slapped him.

Anger made me bold. "You can't make me believe the others will take their punishment and leave you free, especially when they've already identified everyone else on the roster."

I glanced at the clock. I had to keep him talking until Harry passed on his rounds in forty minutes.

"Winslow and Dillard," he said, "were the other commanders for this area. They aren't about to blow the whistle on me because they're counting on me to kill you for them. Revenge is sweet."

Monsters, I thought. None of them seemed human.

He grinned, an evil expression at odds with the innocence of freckles across his nose. "They also know I can insure that the Sword of Gideon is restored to its former strength."

"You're only one man," I said. "How can you guarantee to accomplish so much?"

"With your help, Dr. Garrison."

"I'll die first." I meant every melodramatic syllable.

"But you've already helped. Thanks to you, in six months I'll have my Ph.D., with which I'll find a job as an associate professor at a major university. Think what a fertile field that will make for recruiting, especially in my position of trust and esteem."

I couldn't understand Kevin's treachery or his delusions of grandeur. "You, of all people, should know the Sword of Gideon and organizations like it are built on lies and prejudices. Haven't you learned anything from the history you've studied?"

He leaned toward me, and I moved back instinctively from the barrel of his gun.

"Don't talk to me about lies and prejudices." He spoke with deadly quiet between clenched teeth. "The federal government is the biggest liar in the world. Look at what they've done in the name of law and order—murdered innocent men, women, and children at Waco, shot down Randy Weaver's family in Idaho like dogs. And they deny they're wrong. They even deny United Nations troops are poised to take over our country to establish a new world order."

The hatred in his eyes shone as cold as death, but I couldn't allow his rantings to go unchallenged. "Where's your proof—"

He ignored me in his fervor. "The Gideons had nothing to

do with bombing the federal building in Oklahoma City, but they ought to give a medal to the man who did. The government is the enemy, and this is war."

"Haven't you learned anything—" I repeated.

His face contorted in a sneer. "That entire library, all those books," he waved the gun toward my shelves, "are full of lies."

"They're not—"

He snorted derisively. "The Holocaust, the biggest lie ever told to mankind, all part of an ongoing international conspiracy by Jews—"

"You can't truly believe that white supremacist drivel—" I snapped with frustration.

"Henry Ford believed it. Thanks to him and his weekly newspaper, the Jews weren't able to keep secret the *Protocols of the Elders of Zion,* their blueprint for taking over the world. If you want documentation, I can give it to you a mile long."

His eyes grew wide and wild as he spoke. He was no longer the Kevin I had known, he no longer reminded me of Nick. The man had become a miserable creature, distorted by hate.

"How reliable are your sources?" I challenged, placing my palms flat on my desk to stop my hands from shaking. "Is there an objective source in all that list that corroborates your views, or is it all neo-Nazi propaganda?"

He slumped back in his chair, and the hand that held the gun fell to his side. "It's no use trying to convince you. I figured that out weeks ago. My only option is to kill you."

He raised the gun again.

I had to keep him talking if I wanted to stay alive, but I feared angering him further.

I locked onto a safe topic. "How did a bright man like you become associated with the Gideons?"

He relaxed and pointed the gun away once more. "My daddy, a poor dirt farmer in the panhandle, was a Klansman. His membership in the KKK was the only thing in his life that gave him any pride in himself."

"So you're just following in daddy's footsteps?" The sins of the fathers, I thought, failing to keep the sarcasm from my voice.

"I hadn't thought much about the Klan one way or the other," he said, "until David Duke made a recruiting trip to our campus when I was an undergraduate. Before that, the Klan had been strictly a workingman's organization, but Duke gave it a respectable image, a new status."

A skunk in a business suit is still a skunk. I studied Kevin as he spoke and realized he'd been like those teens I'd been concerned about earlier, teens whose lives of poverty and abuse, whose lack of self-esteem made them hunger for a sense of dignity, a place to belong. Unfortunately, he had built his own self-esteem by hating and degrading others, and that hatred had grown and festered like an unclean wound, until he'd lost his sense of justice and, even worse, his very humanity.

Kevin McDermott exemplified the teenager, recruited by white supremacists in youth, grown to a man with all his hatreds set in stone. I felt sorry for him, but not so sorry I was willing to let him kill me.

"Why did you leave the Klan?"

"Not enough action. They talked a good talk, held a few rallies, burned a few crosses, but they had no plan to correct the problem. The Sword of Gideon offers a remedy."

"What do you see as 'the problem'?"

"That the white race is fast disappearing from the face of the earth and the United States government is doing everything it can to speed it on its way. It's as simple as that."

Simple? Nick, Slater, Kristin, Chad, Moira, and God knew how many others violently murdered, and he talked of simplicity. I shuddered at his coldbloodedness.

"And the Gideons' plan?" I had studied the plan in the Gideon file and asked the question only to buy time.

"We hope to create massive disruptions in transportation and communications and to incite civil disturbances and blame it all on the subhuman races. Our ultimate goal is that everyone except those of Northern European descent would be banned from the country or imprisoned in specific areas to insure the domestic tranquility."

I swallowed my disgust. "What's your role in the plan?"

He ran his fingers through his hair again. If he was going to kill me, he seemed in no hurry about it.

"My job is recruiting and propaganda. Once I have credentials from this respected university, I can speak with authority on historical issues, like the Holocaust hoax and the international Jewish conspiracy, and help correct lies that have been spread by Jews and their sympathizers."

His ignorance and hatred made me sick to my stomach. The brainwashing had been too thorough in Kevin's case. All the objective scholarship, all the evidence in the world had not, and would not, change his twisted mind. He believed with all the fervor of a prophet, and he was ready to kill for what he believed.

I wondered if he had killed for the Gideons before. I recalled him standing in my office after the break-in, and suddenly all the pieces clicked together in my mind.

I knew who had killed Moira.

"Why did you kill Moira?" The question formed on my lips before I could stop it.

He smiled his slow, shy smile. "I told them you were smart. That's why we kept putting the pressure on you. I knew if anyone could find that file, you could."

He glanced around my office, the one he had so carefully reconstructed after the break-in. "At first, I was just looking for the file. When it wasn't here, I checked the other offices, thinking you may've passed it on to a friend. But when I found Emmett's spears, I realized one might come in handy later if I had to kill one of your friends to tighten the squeeze on you."

He seemed proud of his ingenuity and more of a monster than ever.

"I broke all the spears but one," he said, "then hid that one behind the bookcase in my office. I handled it with a handkerchief to conceal my prints and preserve Emmett's."

I sat very still, with my hands clutched in my lap, exerting every ounce of self-control to keep my mouth shut. If I'd been bigger and stronger, I'd have leapt across the desktop and gone for his throat.

Before, I'd been frightened and had felt a tiny fragment of pity for him, but now the anger built inside me with terrifying intensity.

If he noticed my anger, it didn't faze him. "I knew about Kristin's car being like yours. I found the notes from Chad when I searched your office. When blowing up the car didn't make you produce the file, I figured it was going to take something more personal to get you moving."

Rage blossomed and swelled within me. Kevin was no impoverished, abused teenager. He was a grown man, a supposedly educated man, who had turned his back on decency and reality in order to feed the hatred in his soul. His organization had killed my brother, my students, and my friend, and I hated him for it.

"I was going to kill Carol first," he said, "but she was never on campus when there was no one else around. Moira worked here alone every Saturday afternoon. It was a cinch to retrieve the spear, take it to her office, and on the pretext of showing her what I'd found, ram it through her heart. She never knew what hit her."

The cold, bitter ring of his laughter made me tremble once more.

"Talk about killing two birds with one stone," he said with a laugh. "Not only was Moira's death an incentive for you to get the lead out and find what we wanted, but it also got rid of that black monkey and his unhealthy influence on young white people."

His eyes glittered with a familiar gleam, and I realized with a jolt that Kevin's mental state was even less stable than that of Paul Stephanos.

"You'll never get away with killing me here," I said. "And

if they arrest you, what happens to your precious Sword of Gideon then?"

I knew reasoning was hopeless. I was more interested in playing for time, praying for Harry's return.

"Of course I'm not going to kill you here, Alex. I'm not stupid. In fact, my plans for you are even more brilliant than Moira's murder."

He grinned proudly across the expanse of the desk.

"If your plans are so brilliant, why don't you share them with me? I can't believe you can murder me without casting suspicion on yourself."

" 'O ye of little faith,' " he quoted, reminding me of my mother and how her Christian fundamentalism had been perverted by his cause. "The brilliance of the plan lies in its simplicity. First, I take you home. Then I have you write a long letter about how despondent you've been since your brother's death and how the other deaths on campus have deepened that depression. Then you'll take your brother's gun . . ." he waved the revolver beneath my nose again.

"That's Nick's gun? How did you get it?"

"Use your head, Alex. How many times have you loaned me your keys to pick up papers you left at home? I had a copy made a couple months ago. I've been in and out of your place more times than you could count."

Bile rose in my throat at the thought of him in my home.

"Now," he said, "where was I?"

"Nick's gun—" I had to keep him talking, even though his words scared me senseless.

"Ah, yes. With your brother's gun, you'll shoot yourself in the head. Messy, but really the quickest, most painless way. No one will suspect anything but suicide when they find your body inside your locked house."

"You've planned this out very carefully."

"I had to," he said. "I'm the last Gideon, the only one free to carry on. If I die, the Sword of Gideon dies with me."

He was truly crazy, delusions of grandeur and all. I checked the clock again, and my hopes sank when I realized Harry would not be around for another twenty minutes.

Kevin saw my glance and chuckled. "We'll be out of here long before Harry returns. I have the schedule of the security team in this building down pat. They'd have been a real nuisance otherwise."

I should have been terrified, but I was too angry. I struggled to think clearly. If I had escaped Winslow, I could escape Kevin, too.

"Why should I allow you to take me home?" I asked. "I could refuse to leave, forcing you to kill me right here. That would put a kink in your well-laid plans."

The madness in his eyes shone coldly, but his voice sounded strangely rational and calm. "You don't want to make me do that. Before they caught me, I'd kill Carol and maybe her husband or one of her kids. You wouldn't want me to have to do that because you'd botched my plans, would you?"

"Let's go," I said, "and get it over with."

Determined to do what I had to do, I rose, slung my purse over my shoulder, and picked up my briefcase.

"Why take that?" he asked.

"Don't you want everything to look normal, in case we run into someone?"

"Okay." He waved me toward the door. "Just get moving."

He pushed me ahead of him, and I preceded him out the door, turning out the lights as I went. In the hall, I set down my briefcase and reached into my bag for my keys.

"Easy," he warned as I slipped my hand in my purse. "Don't try anything funny."

"Kevin," I spoke with patient exasperation, "I always lock my office. It would seem funny if I didn't."

He relaxed, trusting me then. I locked the door and dropped the keys back into my purse.

When I stooped to pick up my briefcase, I bent my knees slightly, grasped the handle tightly, and swung the case up into

Kevin's face, placing all the force of my pent-up rage behind it.

The gun skittered down the tiled hallway as Kevin staggered backward toward the glass outer wall of the hallway.

Bending my head and shoulder like a linebacker, I ran, ramming my body as hard as I could into Kevin's off-balance form.

The window cracked like a rifle shot when he fell against the glass, where duct tape sealed the fissure created by the explosion of Kristin's car. The glass shattered into a multitude of small fragments, falling with Kevin into the courtyard below.

His scream echoed in my ears as the sound of running feet below drifted up to where I leaned against the wall, gasping for breath.

Terrified that he might have survived the fall and be coming after me, I peered through the broken panel into the courtyard.

Harry and another security guard stood over Kevin's body, draped limp and still across a concrete bench. Harry touched his hand to Kevin's neck and shook his head. He flipped on his flashlight and shined it on the spot where I stood, exposed by missing glass.

"That you, Dr. Garrison?" he called.

"Yes, Harry, it's me." My voice wavered in the night air.

"You okay?"

I leaned weakly against the window frame. "I'm all right. What about Kevin?"

"Sorry, ma'am. He's dead."

Thirty

Above, on the flying bridge, Mitch swung the cabin cruiser in a wide arc to pass beneath the bridge connecting Coquina Beach with Longboat Key, and we headed into the Gulf of Mexico.

I reclined in a chair on deck, soaking up the warm December sunshine. Although it had been over a week since Kevin's death, I still shivered constantly and unexpectedly burst into tears. My doctor had assured me that such behavior was a normal reaction to the stress I'd been under and would eventually go away.

I wasn't so sure. I didn't know if I'd ever be able to live peacefully with the fact that I'd sent a man plunging to his death, even though the police had ruled it self-defense.

I tilted my face toward the sky, where frigate birds floated on the air currents so far above they seemed as tiny as sparrows. I remembered Aunt Bibi's advice: "Don't ever let yourself sink so low you find it hard to get up again."

I tried to reason myself out of the pit of depression. I'd had no choice in what I'd done. If there had been any way for me to escape and Kevin to be captured, I would have taken it. And I reminded myself that, had I died and Kevin gone free, others would have eventually died as well.

If there was comfort to be found, I looked for it in the profound impact Kevin's death had on me. John Donne wrote that one man's death diminishes us all, but I believed we felt that loss only so long as we retained our humanity. I could have wished for less pain from killing Kevin, but only those who had become like the Gideons suffered no pain at the deaths of others.

I was comforted, too, knowing that Emmett was free and home with his family. When the police had searched Kevin's dorm room, they had discovered a detailed journal of everything he'd done since joining the Gideons, including his account of the brutal murder of Moira.

When classes reconvened in January, the trauma our campus had suffered at the hands of the Gideons would raise the sensitivities of faculty and students alike to the issues of racism and its corrosive effects. Perhaps then we could adopt a multicultural curriculum to address those issues.

Mitch cut the engines and threw the anchor over.

"Is this spot okay?" he called.

Sunglasses hid his eyes, but I could hear the caring in his voice. He had been my strength through the past week, returning immediately from New York when I'd called him after Kevin's death.

I looked west toward endless water, then east, where the green blur of land marked the horizon.

"Perfect," I said.

I dug into the bag at my feet and removed a small urn. I carried it to the stern, opened the container, and gently sifted Nick's ashes out upon the wind, where they floated into the warm gulf waters he had loved.

Good-bye, Nicky, rest well. Your dying wasn't in vain, I cried silently.

I tried to be brave and unselfish, but deep inside I wished for my brother back, even if it meant the Gideons had not been apprehended.

Mitch stood silent beside me. When I tossed the empty urn into the waters, he handed me a spray of bright yellow chrysanthemums, day lilies, and tiny orchids. The color of sunshine had been Nick's favorite, and I dropped the yellow flowers one by one into the shining water.

Later that day, we sat on the deck outside the cottage, sipping wine as the sun sank beneath the horizon.

"The Gideons are finished, thanks to Nick and you," Mitch said.

I sighed. "The Gideons, yes, but the conditions that produced them still exist. Unless something changes those conditions, it's only a matter of time until the Gideons, with a new name, are back again."

"You're tired." His hand massaged the back of my neck, smoothing the tension away. "When you've had a good rest, things won't seem so bleak."

I yielded gratefully to his presence and his touch.

"It was hard," I said, "saying good-bye to Nick. Today was the first time I've really faced the fact that he's gone forever."

"Remember the Eliot you read at Moira's mass?"

I nodded. "Making an end is making a beginning?"

"Maybe it would help to think of today that way."

The last sliver of sun slipped beneath the teal blue waters, marking the close of day. For me, it marked the end of the Gideons and the end of being a twin as well. I studied the handsome face of the man beside me.

"To the end." I raised my wineglass.

He touched his glass to mine. "To the beginning."

Author's Notes

I am indebted to several sources, which detail the prevalence of the white supremacist movement in the United States today: Mary H. Cooper's "The Growing Danger of Hate Groups" in *Editorial Research Reports,* James Ridgeway's *Blood in the Face: The Ku Klux Klan, Aryan Nations, Nazi Skinheads, and the Rise of A New White Culture,* and *A Season for Justice* by Morris Dees with Steve Fiffer.

**NOWHERE TO RUN . . . NOWHERE TO HIDE . . .
ZEBRA'S SUSPENSE WILL *GET* YOU—
AND WILL MAKE YOU BEG FOR MORE!**

NOWHERE TO HIDE (4035, $4.50)
by Joan Hall Hovey

After Ellen Morgan's younger sister has been brutally murdered, the highly respected psychologist appears on the evening news and dares the killer to come after her. After a flood of leads that go nowhere, it happens. A note slipped under her windshield states, "YOU'RE IT." Ellen has woken the hunter from its lair . . . and she is his prey!

SHADOW VENGEANCE (4097, $4.50)
by Wendy Haley

Recently widowed Maris learns that she was adopted. Desperate to find her birth parents, she places "personals" in all the Texas newspapers. She receives a horrible response: "You weren't wanted then, and you aren't wanted now." Not to be daunted, her search for her birth mother—and her only chance to save her dangerously ill child—brings her closer and closer to the truth . . . and to death!

RUN FOR YOUR LIFE (4193, $4.50)
by Ann Brahms

Annik Miller is being stalked by Gibson Spencer, a man she once loved. When Annik inherits a wilderness cabin in Maine, she finally feels free from his constant threats. But then, a note under her windshield wiper, and shadowy form, and a horrific nighttime attack tell Annik that she is still the object of this lovesick madman's obsession . . .

EDGE OF TERROR (4224, $4.50)
by Michael Hammonds

Jessie thought that moving to the peaceful Blue Ridge Mountains would help her recover from her bitter divorce. But instead of providing the tranquility she desires, they cast a shadow of terror. There is a madman out there—and he knows where Jessie lives—and what she has seen . . .

NOWHERE TO RUN (4132, $4.50)
by Pat Warren

Socialite Carly Weston leads a charmed life. Then her father, a celebrated prosecutor, is murdered at the hands of a vengeance-seeking killer. Now he is after Carly . . . watching and waiting and planning. And Carly is running for her life from a crazed murderer who's become judge, jury—and executioner!

Available wherever paperbacks are sold, or order direct from the Publisher. Send cover price plus 50¢ per copy for mailing and handling to Penguin USA, P.O. Box 999, c/o Dept. 17109, Bergenfield, NJ 07621. Residents of New York and Tennessee must include sales tax. DO NOT SEND CASH.

HER LIFE HAD BEEN THREATENED . . .

"You're a detective. Tell me what you think."

"The call was probably a nuisance one," Mitch said. "People who make those calls often pick a page in the phone book at random, then go down the list until they find someone at home, or better yet, someone who reacts in a way that plays to the caller's sense of power."

I shuddered. "You mean they feed on fear?"

"Fear, outrage, any intense emotion. Indifference is what they can't stand."

I shook my head before he finished. "But he didn't give me a chance to talk. He hung up before I could ask any questions."

"If this was my investigation, I'd have to say there's no real evidence of a crime, no apparent reason for anyone to harm or threaten you."

I sighed, frustrated by his logic. "So you'd drop the whole thing?"

Mitch grinned. "I didn't say that. I'd watch and wait to see if any hard evidence turned up."

"Great. If this man kills me, you'll have hard evidence of a murder. That's reassuring."

A strange expression, like a spasm of pain, crossed his face, and he rose abruptly and paced to the water's edge. He shoved his hands in his back pockets and stood looking out to the sea.

I followed him. "I'm sorry. I shouldn't have bothered you with my problems."

He turned and took my hand and together we walked up the beach in the bright moonlight.

"You haven't done anything that needs forgiving. You've only reminded me that I haven't always been able to look out for those I loved . . ."

Turn the page to see what the critics have said about this fabulous author's previous works . . .

Raves for Jacaranda Bend:

"The twisted passions and smoldering secrets at Jacaranda Bend keep Rowena's life and heart at risk and make the book good reading."
—*Tampa Tribune*

"Deftly describes the harsh and sandy beauty of Florida and merges this with a well-crafted mystery."
—*Romantic Times*

"A cleverly written plot that kept me guessing until the very end. . . . A fast and enjoyable read."
—*Affaire de Coeur*

"Many will enjoy *Jacaranda Bend* for the respectful homage it pays to 'the memory of Florida forever lost' and the distinctive historical context . . ."
—*Gothic Journal*

"Douglas fans will be delighted!"
—*St. Petersburg Times*

Raves for Darkness at Fair Winds:

"Captured me from the first page and didn't let me go!"
—*St. Petersburg Times*

"Blends historical fact and gripping fiction with smooth, seamless skill."
—*Tampa Tribune*

"Shows real feeling for intriguing characters and settings."
—*Ft. Lauderdale Sun-Sentinel*